MW01134481

When Things Go
Left

When Things Go Left
Copyright © 2017 Tanisha Stewart

All rights reserved.

When Things Go Left
is a work of fiction. Any resemblance to actual events, locations, or persons living or dead is coincidental. No part of this book may be reproduced in any written, electronic, recording, or photocopying form without written permission of the author, Tanisha Stewart.

Books may be purchased in quantity and/or special sales by contacting the publisher, Tanisha Stewart, by email at tanishastewart.author@gmail.com.

Editing and Interior Design: Janet Angelo
www.indiegopublishing.com

Cover Design: Tyora Moody
www.tywebbincreations.com

First Edition

Published in the United States of America
by Tanisha Stewart

Dedication & Acknowledgments

First and foremost, I dedicate this book to God and my Lord and Savior Jesus Christ. Without Him, I would not be here today.

Secondly, I would like to dedicate this novel to my family and friends. To my mother, Alice Jenkins, my beloved "Alice Jean," who has been the driving force behind most of my life's accomplishments. You have been there through thick and thin, through good and bad, through the struggle, and now through the triumph! Words cannot express how thankful and grateful I am for you. To my little sister, my "favorite girl" Goleana Grant, thank you for always supporting me. I am your biggest fan!

To my brothers James Auston, Thomas Stewart, Arthur Caldwell, and James Stewart, I love you all, and I thank you for supporting me in my endeavors. To my grandmother, Sue Stewart, thank you for your wisdom and your sense of humor, and for always encouraging me. To my father, James Stewart Jr., I love you, and I thank you for your constant encouragement and inspiration. To all of my extended family and my friends, God bless you all. I dedicate this to you!

To my editor, Janet Angelo, thank you for answering my questions and providing constant encouragement, information, and support. Your thoughtful editing really helped bring the story more to life! Also, thank you to my cover designer, Tyora Moody of Ty Webbin Creations, for your excellent work.

Next, I would like to dedicate this book to all of my college students past, present, and future. You guys wake me up every morning and keep me on my feet throughout the day. I love you all, and you each inspire me in your own way.

Last, but certainly not least, I dedicate this book to you, the reader. Without you, no one would hear the stories being told. I pray that this book will bless you, and that God will be glorified in and through your life, in Jesus's name, Amen.

him away with it.

Twon coughed.

"See, that's why I told you to stay in your room! You wouldn't be coughing if you had done what I told you to do."

"Why couldn't I have a party?"

"Look, I'm not going to sit here explaining myself to you. You couldn't have a party because I said so. Now get out of my room. You're making me miss my show."

She turned up her TV and took a long drag from her cigarette. Twon stood there hoping that she would change her mind, but it was no use. Her eyes were glued to the screen, and she didn't seem to notice that he was still there.

Tears formed in Twon's eyes as he watched his mother laugh at the show, but he refused to let them fall. Instead, he turned around and went back to his room where he kicked his toy truck into the other corner and slumped on his bed to cry.

* * *

Hype and his cousin Quaid walked into their kindergarten class after their grandmother, G-Ma, dropped them off. Today was their first day of school. They were nervous but excited. They were happy to learn that they were in the same class. Hype's other cousin, Charles, was also at the same school, but Charles was in another kindergarten class.

When they got there, the teacher welcomed them warmly and led them to their seats. Hype was seated next to a boy named Twon, and Quaid was seated at a different table.

"What's up, homie? My name is Hype." Hype gave Twon some dap.

"Hey. I'm Twon."

Hype looked at Twon's attire, a simple uniform and some no-name sneakers that he probably got at Payless. He busted out laughing. "Damn, nigga, you broke or something? Where your shoes at?" Hype extended his foot to show his fresh pair of Jordans.

Twon sank in his seat and looked embarrassed. This made Hype feel kind of bad.

"Hey, I was just playing."

Twon's expression lightened. "Oh, okay," he said with a smile.

"What kind of name is Hype?" said a girl at the table behind them. Her name was Ashley.

Hype turned around in his seat with a quickness that made the girl flinch. "Shut up, bitch! That's why your breath stink!"

Ashley's eyes widened then filled with tears. Suddenly, she began screaming hysterically and ran to the teacher, who was in the middle of a conversation with a parent.

"What in the world?" said the teacher, looking around then down at Ashley. "What's wrong, honey?"

"He called me the B word!" Ashley pointed to Hype.

Hype sat in his seat with his hands folded on his desk like a little angel.

"Excuse me for a moment," the teacher said to the parent, who turned to leave when her child was settled. Her expression stern, the teacher said, "Did you say a bad word?"

Hype shook his head. "No, Ma'am," he said in his most convincing voice.

"Hey!" said G-Ma, standing between them. "Both of y'all need to calm down. This is about the kids, remember?"

Both of them were silent as Rose put a bandaid on his cut and Shameka sat back down in her seat.

"Hype, you heard what I said, right?" said G-Ma, her voice stern.

Hype nodded in response.

"Good boy. Now go play with your friends."

Hype ran back to the bouncehouse.

* * *

Twon was having so much fun with Hype, Charles, and Quaid that the time flew by. He barely noticed that the entire weekend had passed, and he hadn't heard from his mother.

"Twon, honey," said Rose on Sunday night. "Do you have another phone number for your mother? I've been trying to call her all day, but I think her phone is off. It keeps going to voicemail."

Twon shook his head. "No Ma'am." He looked up at her with big eyes, wondering what was coming next.

"Okay." She sighed. "I will try her again." She dialed the number one more time, and she finally got through. "Hey, it's Rose, Hype's mother. I was just calling to see what time you're picking Twon up."

Twon heard his mother's loud voice through the phone. "Oh, girrrl, I completely forgot. I been so caught up in work that the time just slipped right by me. Could you possibly keep him for just one more day?"

Rose's eyes popped open in shock. She couldn't believe this woman was asking her to do this. "One more day? You know tomorrow is Monday, right? The boys have school."

"I know, girl, but I'm just so caught up in this work, and I have to get it done. I'll pay you an extra twenty dollars if you'll just keep him 'til tomorrow afternoon. I am so sorry to spring this on you, girl. You understand, right?"

Rose started to roll her eyes, but then she noticed that Twon was watching and listening intently to their conversation. "Okay," she said finally. "No problem, girl. I'll keep him 'til tomorrow, but please make sure you pick him up before five because I have to go to work myself."

"I sure will!" said Charlene, so loud and boisterous that Rose had to hold the phone away from her ear.

"Okay, see you tomorrow."

"Bye bye!" said Charlene.

Rose looked at Twon. "So, I guess we're all going to spend one more day together, Twon!" She smiled to reassure him. "How does that sound to you?"

"Yay!" said Twon, and he ran off to play with Hype and the other boys.

Rose went back into the kitchen where the women sat at the table talking.

"What she say, girl?" said Quaid's mother, Gina.

"Tell me why she pushed him off on me again!" said Rose.

"*Whaaaat?*" said Shameka.

"Yes, girl. She talking about she so caught up in work that time just slipped her by. You know I wanted to say, 'What kind of work is that?' but I kept my mouth shut."

"So she just gonna leave her son with total strangers for an entire weekend and not even try to call or check up on him at all?" said Gina.

"That's what I'm saying!" said Rose. "She doesn't even know me! Literally, the first time I ever saw this woman was when she dropped Twon off at my front door Saturday morning. She looked like she didn't even want to be bothered with him. She was halfway to the car when the child was trying to say goodbye."

"You all should let me talk to her," said G-Ma.

"No, Ma. You be blowing things all out of proportion."

"Well, clearly she is not doing right by that boy, and I don't like it." G-Ma glanced around at everyone. "Somebody need to straighten her out."

"Ma, it's really none of our business though," said Rose.

"Well, she's making it our business by leaving her boy here like she doesn't even care about him."

"How about we just keep an eye out for him and watch over him instead?"

"That's all fine and dandy, but you never know what's going on behind closed doors at that boy's house!"

"Ma! It's none of our —"

"Mommy! Mommy!" Quaid came running into the kitchen. "Hype keeps saying bad words!"

"Oh, Quaid, hush," said Rose, before Gina, Quaid's mother, could speak. "He's not hurting you, is he?"

"Girl, I keep telling you—" G-Ma started, but Rose cut her off.

"Ma, Hype is *my* son, okay! I'm raising him how I see fit. Plus, you be cussing too."

"Don't talk back to her like that," said Shameka.

"Okay, but this conversation is between *me* and *my* mother, okay. You need to mind your own damn business. And besides, don't try to sit here and act like Charles is a little saint!"

"Who you think you talking to like that?" Shameka jumped up from her seat. "And what did I tell you about bringing my son into your shit?"

"Both of y'all stop!" said G-Ma. "Quaid, go back and play." Quaid ran back with the boys. "Now for you two...." She pointed back and forth between the two women. "I keep telling y'all that you can't keep letting these boys get away with everything. You need to tighten up on them now, or somebody else will later on down the line."

Rose sucked her teeth. "It's not even that serious."

"Yes, it is that serious."

"Why you always wishing bad on my son?"

"Nobody is wishing bad on your son. I'm trying to tell you something that will keep bad from coming down on him, that's what! And it's for your good too."

"Yeah, whatever, Ma. Can we get back to Twon's situation now?"

* * *

After school on Monday, Twon was on the way to Hype's house in the backseat of G-Ma's car along with Hype, Charles, and Quaid. In just a short time, the boys had become inseparable. Even though Charles was in a separate classroom from Hype, Twon, and Quaid, they all had played so much with each other over the weekend that it didn't matter.

"What did you boys learn in school today?" said G-Ma, quickly glancing at them in the rearview before returning her attention to the road.

"We learned about animals," said Hype.

"That's good. Charles, did you learn about animals in your class too?"

"Yes."

"Oh, G-Ma, guess what!" said Hype. He was bouncing in his seat, he was so excited. "Our teacher had a contest to see who could name the most animals, and it got down to Quaid and Twon!"

"Oh really?" said G-Ma. "And who won?"

"Twon did!" said Hype. G-Ma looked at Twon, and he gave her a big happy grin. Quaid just looked out the window in embarrassment. G-Ma noticed Quaid's discomfort. He had always tried to be the best at everything, even at home, and she knew Twon's situation with his mother, so she knew she had to tread lightly so that both boys would be encouraged.

"Quaid, you did good too. You and Twon named the most animals! All of you boys are so smart! How about a treat?"

"What kind of treat?" Hype was already excited.

"Oh, I don't know … how about we go get some ice cream before we drop Twon off at home?"

Hype's head whipped up toward G-Ma. "I thought Twon was staying with us again."

"No, his mother wanted him to go home. You will see him tomorrow in school. Now, how about we get some ice cream first?"

"YES!" the boys shouted.

G-Ma chuckled. "That cheered you up pretty quickly." She pulled into the parking lot of Harvey's, a popular restaurant that specialized in ice cream along with food.

The boys ate their ice cream, then G-Ma dropped Twon off at home before bringing Hype, Charles, and Quaid to Rose's house.

* * *

"Mommy, can you go with me this week?" said Tierra, looking at her mother as she stood at the door waiting for the church bus to come pick her up, as it did every Sunday.

"Oh, honey, not this week...." Her mother busied herself in the kitchen.

"But you never go with me!"

"I know, honey, and I'm sorry."

"So why don't you go with me?"

"I will have to explain it to you when you get older."

"Why can't I know now?"

"Because I said so, okay!"

Tierra's eyes filled with tears.

Her mother's expression softened. "I'm sorry, Tierra. I didn't mean to yell at you. But there are some things you just wouldn't understand. You're a child."

"Okay, Mommy," said Tierra, sniffing back her tears.

"Make sure you behave at church, and make sure you listen to what the preacher says, okay?"

"Okay."

Just then, the church bus pulled up.

"Okay, here they are." Tierra's mother took her by the hand and led her out the door to the church bus. She helped her get in and buckled her seatbelt for her. "You be good now, okay? And I *will* be quizzing you on your Sunday School lesson when you get home, so you make sure you listen."

"Okay, Mommy. I love you!"

"I love you too, baby," she said, and kissed her on the forehead.

Tierra's mother watched the bus until it was out of sight.

* * *

"SHANEECE!"

Shaneece jumped at the sound of her father's voice.

"Yes, Daddy!"

"COME DOWNSTAIRS!"

She quickly jumped up off her bed and ran downstairs to her father. He was standing in the kitchen with a grim expression on his face. He held a white sheet of paper in his hands.

"What is this, Shaneece?" he said, leaning down to her level and showing her the paper. It was a list of spelling words that she had been working on with her older sister, Shanelle. Shaneece was just entering kindergarten, and Shanelle was in fifth grade.

"What is what, Daddy?"

"There are *three* misspelled words on this paper, Shaneece. You know better than this. Do you want to fail out of school? Huh?" His face was very close to hers, and she could see the anger in his eyes. She stepped back in fear.

"I'm sorry, Daddy. I tried."

"Sorry doesn't make up for it. You will not go outside after school today until you get ALL of these words correct. You hear me?"

Shaneece's eyes filled with tears. "But Daddy—"

"No buts about it! No child of mine is going to fail. Shanelle is getting straight As in all of her classes. You are going to do the same."

With those words, he told her to go upstairs so she could put on the outfit her mother picked out for her to wear to school that day.

Ten Years Later…
High School, Sophomore Year

Twon, Quaid, and Charles were exhausted after playing five rounds of three on three against some other guys from the neighborhood. They were a few weeks into their sophomore year of high school. Hype could not play with them because he had to stay after school for detention. He had gotten into an argument with another student, and wouldn't stop talking when the teacher told him to.

"Damn, my nigga Hype *stay* in lockup!" said Charles.

"I know you aren't talking, Charles," said Quaid. "If it wasn't him, it would be you."

Twon chuckled. "I know that's right. Y'all niggas stay in trouble."

"Man, fuck that school shit," said Charles. "Those teachers don't care about us. I'm just staying in 'til I can drop out."

"Drop out and do what?" said Quaid, looking concerned.

"Well, I damn sure ain't about to join the choir like you, Church Boy!" said Charles. The other guys often made fun of Quaid because he was the "goody good" of the group. He went to church because he wanted to, not because his parents made him go. He obeyed everything his mother and G-Ma told him to do, and he refused to sneak out and go to parties and drink with the other guys.

"I'm not in the choir, Charles," said Quaid with exasperation and impatience from having to explain this yet again. "I just go to church. I like it."

"Whatever." Charles shook his head. "This school shit just ain't for me. I'm trying to make some *real* money."

"Doing what?" said Quaid.

"Get out my business," Charles retorted. "I'm not telling you just so you can go snitch to your mom or G-Ma."

"I'm not a snitch!" said Quaid, clearly offended. "I…." His voice trailed off as he stared at something in the distance.

"Cat got your tongue?" Charles smirked.

"No, *that* got his tongue," said Twon, pointing toward a girl who was walking by the basketball court. "Yeah, boy!

"She's in my homeroom," said Quaid, blushing.

"Have you tried to talk to her?" said Charles.

"No. Well … not really."

"Well, why don't you try to get her number?"

"No!" he exclaimed. "I mean … I'll do it later."

"Pussy!" said Charles.

Twon was already jogging over to the girl.

"What is he doing?" said Quaid.

"Nigga, what you think?" said Charles. "He's doing what your ass is too scared to do."

Quaid's heart dropped as he watched Twon talking to the girl of his dreams, obviously making her happy that he had singled her out for his attention. Tierra was her name. Quaid had been crushing on her from the moment he first saw her. She was the most beautiful girl he had ever seen in his life. He had made small talk with her each day during homeroom, but he was too afraid to make a move and ask her for her number. It seemed like she might have feelings for him too, but he couldn't really tell.

Quaid's heart sank even further as he saw how Twon finessed Tierra with ease. She was giggling and looking up at him as if he was the only boy in the world.

"Oh well," said Charles. "Guess you gotta find somebody else.

Present Day…
High School, Senior Year

Twon

I walked into the house after work exhausted. I work twelve-hour shifts at a factory every Saturday and Sunday. My boss is always riding me, trying to get me to do extra stuff because I'm a good worker. I can't wait 'til I go to college so I can finally quit this job.

Oh yeah, my name is Twon. I should have started with that. I'm a senior in high school. I like to play basketball, and when I'm not with my girl Tierra, I'm hanging with my boys Hype, Charles, and Quaid. All of them are cousins, but I see them as my brothers, especially Hype.

Shit, they are more than brothers to me; they are basically the only family I know. I never met my father, and my mother doesn't seem to want anything to do with me.

I don't know why she treats me like she despises me. It's always been that way. I have spent my entire life bending over backward trying to please her, but it seems like nothing works. I get almost straight As in school, I work a job, I saved up to buy my own car, and I've never been in trouble with the law. But my mother doesn't seem to care about any of that. The only thing she seems to care about is—

"TWON! I KNOW YOU HEAR ME CALLING YOU!"

I shook my head to clear my thoughts as I walked into the living room where my mother was laying across the couch, propped up on one elbow watching TV while smoking a cigarette. This was her favorite pasttime.

"Yeah, Ma?" I said, rubbing my tired eyes.

"I need you to go to the store to get me a pack of cigarettes. I just ran out."

"Ma, I don't think you should keep smoking like that."

"I don't give a damn what you think, Twon. Just hurry up and go to the store." She waved me off dismissively and turned up the TV volume.

I stared at her for a few moments then sighed as I went to the front door to go to the store.

* * *

All of us were hanging out at Quaid's house after school. Quaid and I sat in the middle of the living room playing chess while Tierra and Hype sat watching us. Charles was out doing Lord knows what.

"Checkmate," said Quaid, with a smirk on his face.

For some reason, ever since we first met in kindergarten, me and Quaid have always been in competition with each other. I don't know why; it just happens. Both of us work, both of us got a car, both of us do good in school, and both of us stay out of trouble. The only real difference between us is that Quaid is a Christian and goes to church faithfully, while I'm not. So I guess he got a one-up on me. But then again, I got a girl and Quaid don't.

"Damn, you suck, nigga," said Hype. He took a sip of his juice.

"Fuck you," I said, heated that I had lost.

"I'm just sayin, nigga. What was that, like four, five games you lost? *Damn*, you *suck*!"

"Hey!" Tierra said. "Don't be talking about my man like that."

I turned toward her and smiled. "Thank you, baby."

Quaid fidgeted in his seat. "So, you want to play another game?" He looked kind of eager, probably hoping to beat me one more time.

Hype looked at Tierra. "Girl, this is grown man's business. If your man sucks, he sucks. I'm-a tell him like it is."

"Let's see you play!" I said.

"I don't play chess."

"That's cuz yo ass too stupid to figure shit out."

"No, it's cuz there aint no *point* to it."

"No point to *chess*, nigga? *Get* the fuck outta here."

"What's really the point of takin' three and a half hours pushing pieces around a board just so you can say checkmate? If you ask me, that shit is wack, nigga."

"But ain't nobody ask you. That's *my* fucking point."

"Whatever, nigga. There ain't no point in chess, and that's it."

I'd heard enough. Hype was like a brother to me, and I loved him to death, but that nigga got mouth for days. And he *never* knows when to shut the fuck up.

"*Damn*, Hype! I swear you talk too much shit! Can't you shut up for ten seconds? Damn!"

"What, you on your period or something?" He chuckled.

"Fuck you, Hype."

"Pussy ass nigga."

"So see me then." I stood up. Hype stared at me for a second then laughed.

"Man, *sit* yo ass down." He pushed me.

"What? What you gonna do?" I pushed him back, and we started wrestling.

"Guys, stop fighting!" Tierra said, jumping up.

"And here we go," said Quaid, rolling his eyes as he got up from his seat. "See how immature your 'man' is?" he said to Tierra.

For some reason, I felt some type of way about that statement, but I was kind of in the middle of wrestling Hype, so I couldn't really respond. Me and Quaid would have to get up later.

"Come on guys. Break it up."Quaid somehow got in the middle of us to push us apart. We all stood there panting for a moment, then we burst out laughing.

"So, are you ready for another game, Twon?" said Quaid. Everything was silent for a little bit cuz everybody was watching us play. Then Hype, of course, had to open his mouth again.

"Fuckin pointless ass game."

"Nigga, shut the fuck up! You just mad cuz I was whoopin' yo ass."

"No, you wasn't, nigga. I had you in the nastiest headlock."

"Bullshit." Hype jumped up.

"So I ain't have you in a headlock? Say I ain't have you, nigga."

"You ain't have shit."

"So let's go again then."

"A'ight, nigga."

"Oh, gosh," said Quaid, rolling his eyes at Tierra. He repeated his statement from before: "You see how immature your 'man' can be?"

"Boys," she said, rolling her eyes in agreement.

Hype

I slowly made my way home from school after detention. I seem to have a habit of always getting in trouble in school, especially during the first couple of weeks. Every year of high school, I have spent at least one day during the first week in detention. Niggas be trying to roast me about it sometimes, calling detention my second homeroom.

Oh yeah, by the way, my name is Hype. I'm a tall, caramel-colored brotha with good hair and green eyes. You tryina holla? Just joking, but anyway, I'm mostly a good kid, but I do have a ruthless side.

I have two cousins, Quaid and Charles, and one best friend, Twon, but we all grew up together, so we see each other as brothers. Even though Quaid and Charles are my actual family, I'm closest to Twon out of all of them.

I honestly feel like each of them brings out a different side of me. Twon is my right hand, and he's also real smart, so he brings out my rational side. Quaid's smart too, but he's kind of soft and compassionate, so he brings out my good side.

Charles, on the other hand, is another story. Charles is kind of reckless, but both of our mothers basically raised us the same way, so I could say that he definitely brings out that reckless side in me.

But anyway, enough of this story shit. I'm 'bout to go play some ball.

Me, Quaid, and Charles was playing basketball against this corny ass nigga Shawn and his cousin Spike, along with another kid from around the corner named Jamil. Twon was at work, so he wasn't with us. Of course me, Quaid, and Charles was waxing they asses, so them niggas was mad heated.

"That was a foul! I don't give a fuck!" said Shawn. He looked like he had had enough. I smirked.

"Mah dude. Chill. Stop bein' a sore ass loser."

"What, nigga? Who the fuck you think you talking to?" Shawn stepped to my face with a fierce look in his eye.

"Yo, nigga. *Back* da fuck up." I pushed him back off of me.

"Hype. Shawn. Chill," said Quaid.

"Nah, fuck that nigga, Quaid!" said Shawn. "He just fouled the fuck out me, then had the nerve to put his hands on me? Fuck that shit!"

I could damn near see the veins popping out of Shawn's forehead, he was so heated. Spike didn't look much better. Jamil stayed out of it, probably because he and Charles had just got into it a couple of weeks ago, and it did not end well for him.

"Eyo, nigga," I said. "First of all, I ain't foul you, and second of all, you shouldn't be yelling all up in my face wit yo stankin' ass breath. You lucky all I did was push you. I shoulda fucked you up."

"Yo, this nigga talk way too much shit for his own good! I'm-a fuck this nigga up! I swear! I don't give a fuck!"

"Yo, shut yo corny punk pussy ass up. You ain't gonna do shit, nigga."

"I ain't gonna do shit? That's what you said?"

"Yeah, you heard right. You ain't gon do shit cuz you ain't nothing but a bitch." I turned to walk away when I heard Quaid yell "Hype!" — his voice full of fear.

I turned and saw a fucking gun pointed in my face. Aw, hell no.

"What?" I said, cool as fuck.

"Yo, Shawn, chill son," said Spike, looking scared too. Jamil had mysteriously disappeared.

"Yeah, who's the bitch now, nigga?" said Shawn, feeling himself. I guess he thought his gun was gonna scare me, but he was about to get a rude awakening.

"Um, obviously you are," I said. "You the one with the gun in your hand, nigga."

"What, nigga, are you crazy?" Shawn looked back and forth between the gun and me. "I will fuckin end you right now!"

"You ain't gon do shit. I can see the bitch in your eye. You ain't got the heart to pull that trigger." Everybody was silent as hell watching, waiting to see what Shawn would do. But I already knew. The funniest shit about the whole thing was that I was the only one who wasn't scared, except maybe Charles, and I was the nigga wit the gun pointed in my face. Just like I knew he would do, he lowered the gun.

"Man, whatever, nigga." He tried to walk away.

"Nah, fuck that shit, nigga. Where you think you going? You 'bout to get this work!" Anger and adrenaline rose up in me as it finally clicked that this nigga had really just put a gun to my head.

"What?"

"You was talkin' all that shit. Let's see you do something." I was on ten now. "You man enough to put a gun in my face, then you man enough to fight. So let's go." I squared off.

Quaid said, "Hype, chill. Let's just go!"

"Nah, Quaid, I wanna see what this nigga got."

"For real, y'all, that's enough," said Spike. "It never should have even got to that level."

"It's just a basketball game," said Quaid.

Everything they said just made me angrier.

"Nah, nigga. He fucked up when he pulled the gun out," said Charles, finally speaking. He had a smirk on his face during the entire interaction because he knew, like I knew, that Shawn's bitch ass wasn't 'bout to pull no trigger.

"Nigga shouldn't have pulled a gun on me." I quickly punched Shawn in the face. He did nothing. "Whatchu got, pussy?" I said, taunting him. "Where you at now?" I hit him again, then again. He did nothing in response.

"CHILL, HYPE! LET'S GO, MAN!" Quaid was about to go crazy for real. There were tears in his eyes and everything. I calmed down a little.

"A'ight nigga, calm down. This nigga clearly ain't about to do shit, so I'm done."

Shawn just stood there breathing all heavy.

"Let's *go*, Hype."

"A'ight."

Me, Charles, and Quaid ain't say shit to each other on the way to his house. When we got there, Quaid turned on the TV and we watched videos for a little bit. He finally spoke up.

"Hype, you need to chill sometimes."

"What are you talking 'bout?"

"You are living really reckless nowadays. It's like you don't care what you do or say."

"I don't."

Charles busted out laughing, watching the interaction between me and Quaid. "Man, shut your soft ass up, Quaid."

"Come on, Hype," said Quaid, ignoring Charles. "You could have got shot out there."

"I don't give a fuck, Quaid. I ain't gon let no nigga punk me. I ain't no bitch. I'd rather die like a man than run like a coward."

"I know that's right," said Charles, dapping me up. See, that's why I need that nigga in my corner. When shit like this goes down, Charles always comes through.

"I understand that," said Quaid, clearly not finished stating his case. "I really, really do. But there's a difference between being a punk and being stupid. We all know Shawn is a punk, but you never know what a scared person will do to you. Those are the guys you have to watch out for. He could have just as easily shot you if you got him scared enough."

"Man, whatever, nigga," said Charles, not at all convinced by Quaid's words. I actually thought Quaid was right, but I wasn't trying to hear that right now.

"Hype—"

"I'm not feeling this conversation. Let's talk about something else."

He shook his head. "Okay, Hype." His shoulders slumped in defeat.

I felt bad for basically telling Quaid to shut up, but I was on my Charles shit right now. I told you that both of them bring out a different side of me. Quaid was definitely right, and I will end up telling him so later, but my temper is crazy, so I'm sticking with Charles for now.

Tierra

The first thing I thought when I saw him was, *Damn, he is fine!* That's the only thing I *could* think when looking at him. Even after we exchanged words and then numbers, even after that first day became a week, then week became a month, a month became three, then five, then six, and then a year, and finally, a year and a half, I'm still in awe of how fine he is!

Antwon Davis, Twon for short.

Six-five, well built, light skinned with golden-brown eyes ... heck, yeah, my man is fine! He keeps his hair in the flyest braids. His hair is long, too. He got the crazy hang time. What's even better, he thinks I'm fine too, caramel colored, with shoulder-length brown hair, regular brown eyes, and skinny with a B-cup and a nice booty. I'm the type of girl that's not the best looking thing around or the smartest, but I'm definitely not the worst either. Most guys give me about a high seven, low eight. In school, I make Bs and Cs. Twon gets mostly As. He is incredibly smart.

We are in our senior year of high school, and I am so glad. It's been a long time coming. I'm so excited about the future! Anyway, I was just reminiscing about the first time Twon and I kissed. It was during the last couple of months of our sophomore year. We were at his house chilling on the couch, *supposedly* watching a movie....

"Why you sitting all the way over there, girl?" He was staring at me sideways with those beautiful eyes of his.

12

"Um, I don't know," I said, shyly.

"Why don't you come sit over here?" He patted his lap.

"Okay." I went over and sat on his lap. He put one arm around my back and the other one across the back of the couch. "Am I heavy?" I whispered nervously.

"Nah, girl, I bench press your weight. Whatchu weigh, about one twenty, one thirty tops?"

I nodded. "One twenty-two."

He licked those juicy lips and smirked.

I tried to focus on the movie, but after a while, I noticed he was staring at me. I looked at him. He licked his lips again and smiled.

"What?" I said innocently.

"Whatchu mean, what?"

"Why you staring at me like that?"

"Cuz you pretty."

"You think so?" I blushed.

"I know so."

I could feel my face growing hot. I hoped he couldn't tell how nervous I was.

"Baby," he said softly.

"What?"

"You got some sexy lips."

"I do?" I giggled.

"Yeah. Can I get a taste?"

"Okay."

He leaned in slowly. I closed my eyes. I felt our lips touch and like, this crazy, crazy feeling came over me. You know, like how they say it is in movies and books. It felt like that but better. That's when I knew I was going to end up in love with Twon. And I did. And almost two years later, I still am. It's like, I feel so happy. I don't even remember what life was like without Twon. I mean, sure, we had a couple of differences over time, but that's how it is with everybody. We never broke up though. That's one thing about us. We've stuck together through it all.

* * *

I had nothing to do with my life on a Saturday, so I decided to go to the basketball court to watch Twon and the boys play. It was fun to watch them because they were always so intent on beating each other.

"Come on, nigga! Stick that D! Stick that D!"

"I am, nigga! Get off my balls!"

"Eyo! I'm open! I'm open!" *BONG!*

"Damn!"

"Shit!"

"That's eighteen, nigga! That's eighteen!"

"Damn, y'all suck! I got next!"

That's Twon and his boys, Quaid, Hype, and Charles, playing basketball. They're all good-looking. Quaid is about six-two, dark skinned with his hair cut short. He's got some nice waves and regular brown eyes, but he has crazy long lashes. He's so sweet and mature, and he's really an all around nice guy.

I actually met him first before I met Twon, Hype, and Charles. I had moved here from Florida at the beginning of my sophomore year of high school, and Quaid was in my homeroom. I originally had sort of a crush on him, and he seemed to like me, but he never said anything. Then, of course, I ended up with Twon.

Sometimes I wonder what would have happened if Quaid had asked for my number, but he never did. I guess it doesn't matter because Twon's my man now anyway.

Hype is fine too, like Quaid, except he's shorter. He's about five eleven. He's caramel colored with these crazy green eyes. You would swear he stole them from a white person or a Puerto Rican, and they're so, so pretty. But nope, they're his. Hype and I are the closest out of all of Twon's friends, although I am kind of close with Quaid too. Hype's the type of guy who's cool and funny, but you get sick of him if you hang out with him too long because of his attitude. He's very sarcastic. I remember one time when all of us were ordering popcorn at the movies — well, *they* were ordering popcorn. Twon and I were too busy kissing. Anyway, Hype came up and pushed us apart.

"Whatchu *doin'*, nigga?" said Twon.

"Can y'all spend one second apart? Damn!" said Hype.

"Shut the fuck up, nigga. You just hating cuz you ain't got nobody to kiss."

"Fuck you, man. And anyway, what's the point of letting somebody push their spit around in your mouth? If you ask me, that shit is nasty."

That's Hype for you. Anyway, moving on to Charles, he's about six-three, skinny, but he's nice looking. He's caramel skinned with regular brown eyes. He's got long lashes too, but not like Quaid's.

Charles is cool, but I don't really talk to him that much. He's also very rude and sarcastic at times, so maybe that's why he and I never really hit it off.

You're probably wondering by now, *Girl, don't you have any girl friends?* Trust me, I know. I have actually been looking for a good girl friend to hang out with since I got to this place, but I haven't been successful. I'm really close with my mother, and I mainly tell her everything, but some things I just don't feel like I can share, like the situation that me and Twon are currently going through.

I haven't told anyone this actually, but lately, all Twon wants from me is sex. I know this might sound strange with today's society and all, but I'm a virgin, and I don't feel like I'm ready to give it up. Unfortunately, Twon doesn't seem to understand that. He's not a virgin, so naturally he wants to do it.

I often feel like I don't know what to do. I mean, I love Twon, and I know he loves me, but I honestly feel like this might be the one hurdle that we may not be able to get over. That thought devastates me because I'm so torn between just giving him what he wants and sticking to my own convictions.

I'm hoping the situation will work itself out, but at this point, I just don't know....

Shaneece

I grabbed the last box from my bedroom as I prepared to leave the house for good. My parents (mainly my father) decided to up and move me from my hometown to a whole other state in my senior year of high school. The semester already started like two weeks ago, which means I'll already be behind in my coursework, but my father, of course, will expect me to hit the ground running and get straight As on every assignment. I am so sick of his shit.

Wait, let me back up. I never introduced myself. My name is Shaneece. I'm eighteen. I'm a senior in high school, as you know. I'm light skinned, and I have long hair that flows down my back, so boys always flocked to me — which of course, led my father to stay on me like a freaking shadow, monitoring my every move, and immediately shutting down every relationship I have tried to forge with a boy.

Little does he know that I have had a boyfriend right under his nose for two years. I had to break up with him because my father is moving our family three hours away, but at least it was fun while it lasted.

I honestly wish that I could just meet someone to take me away from all of this, expecially from *him*. I have asked my parents a few times if I could move in with my older sister Shanelle to finish out my high school years, but my father refused. Shanelle, his golden child, could be trusted, he said, but not me. Little did he know, once again, the main reason Shanelle left home after college was because of his overbearing and crazy ways.

"SHANEECE!" I jumped at the sound of my father's booming voice from the living room. I turned around, almost dropping the box I'd been packing when I saw him standing at my bedroom door. How did he get there so fast? I secretly prayed that I hadn't said any of my thoughts out loud, because I was terrified of what the results would be if I had.

"Yes, Daddy?"

"I have been calling you for the last five minutes. You need to stop slothing around and get your ass in the car. We're already running late because of you and your absolute refusal to let any of your silly things be thrown away. Hurry up and let's go."

He snatched the box from me, which caused me to slightly lose my balance, and then he made his way out of my room and to the front door. I stared at his back, swallowing a lump in my throat. I looked back at my room one last time before walking outside to join my parents in the car.

* * *

I nervously made my way to my first class of the day.

"*Damn*, who dat?" I heard as soon as I walked into the room. The teacher was standing up front, and all of the students were seated at their desks already. I tried not to blush as I handed the teacher my class schedule and a letter from my guidance counselor stating that I was a new student.

After I finished introducing myself to the teacher, my eyes searched the room for a seat. One was open at the back of the room between a friendly looking girl and the guy who had made the statement about me when I first walked in. I knew this because he smiled at me when I glanced between him and the girl. I made my way to the back and sat in the open seat feeling like all eyes were on me.

"Wassup, lil mama?" He licked his lips. "Whas yo name?"

Wow. He didn't even let me fully sit down before he started in on me.

"Shaneece," I said in a quiet voice, trying not to call too much attention to myself. "What's yours?"

"I'm that nigga Hype you prolly heard about. My reputation precedes me." He said this with a proud grin. "Where you come from, sweet thang?"

"Connecticut. Is Hype your real name?"

"Nah, baby. It's short for Hyphen."

"Oh. That's … nice. You have really pretty eyes. Are they yours?"

"Oh, for sure, girl. It's all authentic, baby."

This guy Hype was so wack. I felt like laughing, but I didn't want to ruin his silly little flow. I turned to the girl.

"Hi, I'm Shaneece. New girl." I made a face of mock embarrassment, and she smiled.

"Hi, I'm Tierra."

I smiled. "That's a pretty name. Is this class hard?"

"Well, it's only been a couple of weeks, but the teacher seems like he's okay. He gives a lot of peer review type papers, from what I hear."

"Oh, really? Well, I hope the papers aren't on crazy hard or boring subjects."

"Girl, me too. At this point, I am just so ready for graduation."

"Oh my gosh, same here!" I smiled. Tierra smiled back. It was a good thing the teacher didn't seem to notice us because we were definitely talking up a storm. I propped my elbows on my desk and scrunched my face against my shoulder, leaning closer to Tierra so Hype wouldn't hear what I said next. "So, are there a lot of fine ass guys at this school?"

"Yeah, a couple. Not too many, but enough to go around."

"Enough of what?" Hype said with a grin.

"Boy, you mind your own business!" Tierra said with a mock scolding look, and we all laughed.

Tierra seemed pretty cool. We sat there talking the entire class period. We barely paid attention to anything the teacher said. By the time the period was over, I felt like we had been friends for years. We clicked that smoothly.

I went to my Physics class next, and once again, I had to hand my schedule and the note from my guidance counselor to the teacher. When I turned around to find a seat, my heart literally dropped to the ground.

Sitting in the second row of desks was the most drop dead gorgeous guy I had ever seen. He was staring intently at the problems he was working on, so I got a chance to get a full view of him as I made my way over to the seat behind him. He was beautiful, with muscular arms and fine long legs stretched into the aisle, his sensual looking eyelashes contrasted against his face as he peered at his paper then looked up at me and made my own eyelids flutter, with juicy lips that he just happened to lick as I walked past him, and braids so fresh that I wanted to run my fingers through them.

I don't know what came over me, but I have literally never been this taken by a guy's looks before. I wanted — no, I *needed* to speak to this guy. There was just something about him that immediately drew me to him.

He must have felt me staring at him because he turned around in his seat. "Hey, you new here?"

"Yes." I blushed shyly. "My name is Shaneece. What's yours?"

He flashed a smile at me before he answered, and his dimples made my heart drop again. "I'm Twon. Nice to meet you, Shaneece."

Hype

I was at Quaid's house chilling with my boys Charles and Twon, watching smack battles and talking about music. When the subject of rapper 50 Cent came up, Twon and Charles got into a heated discussion. Twon was not budging on his opinon.

"Nah, nigga, fuck that. That nigga was wack as hell, point blank."

"No he wasn't," said Charles. "I'm tellin' you."

"So you tellin' me that nigga spit hot bars?"

"Yeah. Everybody listened to him."

"That's cuz he was commercial as hell, nigga. That nigga never spit no hot shit!"

"What?" I sat up in my seat, not believing my ears. In my opinion, 50 definitely had bars, among other things. I was definitely jumping into this conversation.

"Yo, on some real shit, 50 was the truth." Twon and Quaid looked at me like I was crazy. "50 was the truth, and I'm-a tell you why."

"Why?" said Quaid.

"Yeah, I gotta hear this shit." Twon crossed his arms and sat back on the couch.

"50's one of the only niggas that had a plan in the game, and followed it."

"Bullshit." Twon stood up, trying to end the discussion.

"I'm serious. 50 said from jump that he was here to make money. And where's he at right now? What's he doing? Making money. He's one of the richest dudes out there. That nigga got music, sneakers, clothes, fuckin movies, a video game, a TV series, and water. This nigga got WATER! Tell me he ain't nice!"

"Damn," said Twon. He sat down on the arm of the couch.

"That's true," said Quaid.

"Told y'all niggas," said Charles.

"You can't never win an argument with my nigga Hype, yo," said Twon. He looked at me. "You argue better than a bitch."

"Fuck you, nigga." I pushed him and caught him off guard, and he flipped over the couch. Everybody busted out laughing except Twon. He jumped up off the floor and charged at me. I had him in the mean headlock, but then I slipped on some magazines scattered on the floor. Seeing his advantage, he scooped me up and slammed the shit out of me.

"You lucky as hell, nigga," I said, panting for breath as I got up.

"Whatever nigga. I fucked you up."

"Nigga, you can't beat me. I slipped on the fuckin magazines!"

"Bullshit, nigga!"

"So what you wanna do?" We squared off.

"Here we go again," said Quaid.

* * *

I just had the craziest ass day. Tell me why that nigga Shawn and his cousin Spike and some other nigga tried to jump me! They waited 'til I was by myself then tried to come at me on some sneaky shit. The next day, I met up with my boys at school to tell them the story.

"So after I fucked Twon's ass up, I left and shit, and—"

"Nigga, you did not whoop my ass," said Twon.

"Yes I did, nigga!"

"No, the fuck you—"

"Just get on with the story," said Charles.

"So anyway, I left Quaid's house, and I was like two blocks from my house when them niggas came out of nowhere. I was barely even paying attention cuz I had just seen this shorty wit a fat ass, and I was tryin'-a holla. So I'm going toward shorty, and these niggas spring up out the bushes on some ninja shit. I'm like *what the fuck?* And it's that nigga Shawn and them."

"Shawn and who else?" said Twon.

"Spike and some other nigga. So all three of them niggas is comin' at me talking crazy shit about how they was gonna fuck me up. So you know I ain't no bitch. I was saying some shit back to Shawn, and I guess I struck a nerve or something, cuz this nigga started comin' at me, and the other ones were close behind. I ain't have shit on me but my blade, so I took that shit out and started wiling. Them niggas was still coming at me, though, until 5-0 showed up and everybody scattered. And after that I just went the fuck home, nigga."

"Man, them niggas is *pussy*." Charles shook his head. "They lucky I wasn't there. We would have set shit OFF!"

"I heard them niggas be up at Four Square Park," I said. "What you wanna do?"

"They be mad deep?" said Twon.

"I don't know. I think so."

"A'ight, so you call some niggas, and we gonna call some niggas, and let's meet up at the park and get shit popping."

Quaid chimed in. "I don't think that's a good idea, especially since Shawn pulled that gun on you at the basketball court."

"Man, stop being so scary, Quaid!" I wrinkled up my nose at him. Quaid was a Christian, so he was always on some peacemaker shit, but I wasn't trying to hear that today. Besides, me, Twon, and Charles already had this plan down.

"I already got some niggas in mind," I said to Twon and Charles. "We gonna leave Quaid's ass at home, and I'm gonna call some more people."

"A'ight." Twon got out his phone and made his calls while Charles and I made ours. Quaid kept protesting, and Twon started to change his mind for a minute too because of the whole gun thing, but then he made up his mind when he thought about how those niggas tried to jump me. Quaid stood his ground. He just isn't built for this street shit, and I respect that.

By the time we finished making our phone calls, we had about forty niggas ready to bang, maybe even more. We rolled up to the park deep as hell with more niggas coming. We saw Shawn, Spike, and Marc up at the courts. We ran up on them niggas.

"You was gonna jump my brother, nigga?" said Twon, immediately squaring off.

"Nah, Twon, I got this." I went and snuffed the shit out of that nigga. He stumbled back then fell to the ground covering his nose to stop the bleeding. He stared at me in disbelief, all shaking and shit, then he got up and looked at his boys. None of them was stupid enough to do anything. He threw me a sorry ass swing. I easily blocked it, cocked back, and knocked the shit out of that nigga. Fucked his whole shit up. He was on the ground, and I ran up on him and stomped that nigga out. Twon and Charles got bored or something, so they came up and started stomping that nigga too. Spike and Marc just stood there shook as fuck. We straight disrespected them niggas and left on some movie shit. After that, we went to my house and chilled for the rest of the day, then Twon left to go be with his girl, and me and Charles invited some girls over and shit.

* * *

That new chick Shaneece is a baddie. I am definitely trying to holla at her sexy ass. After our English class, I stopped Tierra before she could leave the room. Shaneece was already gone. "Eyo, Tierra." She turned around.

"What?"

"I have an assignment for you."

"Aw, shit," said Charles. He knew what was coming next. "I'm finna go. Bye Tierra."

"See you." She stared at me, waiting to hear what I wanted. "What is it?"

"Hook a nigga up."

"What do you mean, 'hook a nigga up'?"

"I'm saying, I see you and Shorty are gettin y'all friendship on and shit, so hook a nigga up. I wanna get with her."

"No you don't, Hype. You just want to have sex with her."

"So?"

"I'm not turning her into a jump-off for you. You need to stop messing around with all these girls anyway before you catch something."

"And you need to stop telling me what I need to do."

"Look, Hype, why don't you just find a nice girl and settle down?"

"Cuz I ain't a nice guy. And plus, you know my motto: Find em, fuck em, and forget about em. Fuck all that commitment shit. That's how niggas get hurt around here."

"How you know?"

"From damn near every nigga I've seen!"

"Well, I'd rather be committed with somebody than get AIDS."

"I use protection."

"So? That doesn't protect you all the time."

"It protects me."

"What *ever*, Hype. I'm done with you. You need to get tested before you hook up with even one more girl, and besides, I respect Shaneece too much to let her be ruined by you."

"Here you go again, tellin' a nigga what he need to do. So what? Can I get some pussy or what? Is you gonna hook a nigga up?"

"Hype, she seems like a really nice girl. I don't want to mess up her life by affiliating her with you."

"I aint gonna do shit to her! Damn, you act like I'm-a kill the bitch."

"I don't know, Hype."

"Fine. I'll do it myself." I started to leave.

"Come on, Hype. Don't be mad at me."

"Why not? You fucked up."

"How am I fucked up?"

"You aint tryin'-a help a nigga out."

"Oh, my gosh! Okay, Hype. I'll hook you up, but you better be a good boy with her." My frown slipped into a smile.

"Thank you! I promise I'll be good." I grabbed her and picked her up in a bear hug.

"Stop it, Hype," she said, laughing. "Put me down!"

"Okay, but thank you, for real." I put her down and gave her a rough kiss on the cheek before I zipped out of the classroom. I don't know why I was so excited about it. I could have any girl I wanted. Shaneece was just another girl, but there was just something about her….

* * *

The next day after school, I went over Tierra's house to start working on scholarship applications. I know, I know, I'm a complicated nigga.

"Yeah, so what's the GPA requirement for this shit?" I looked at the paper. It was talkin' 'bout a ten thousand dollar scholarship for two years.

"It's two point five. The scholarship is mostly need based, though, so you need a copy of your Student Aid Report to send in with it."

"Oh, word? That's cool. I'm definitely fucking with it then." I looked at it more closely. "Wait. Hold the fuck up."

"What?"

"It's talkin' 'bout I gotta write a thousand-word essay on somebody who influenced me in life and shit. I can't do that."

"Hype, yes you can. All you have to do is work on it. Just think of it this way: It's *one* thousand words for *ten* thousand dollars."

"But I ain't even a good writer! What if I don't get the scholarship after all that work? I probably won't. That'll be a waste of time."

"Come on, Hype. Where's your self confidence?"

"I got confidence, Tierra. Just not with writing."

"You can get people to help you with the essay. I'm a pretty good writer. I'll help."

"But I'm saying, though, I don't wanna waste your time and shit."

"Hype, stop it. If you want these scholarships, you have to put in the work."

"I know, but—"

"Have you applied to any colleges yet?"

"Yeah, a couple."

"Which ones?"

"Like, three of the ones we looked at last time. Fuckin State, the community college, and some school in Florida."

"Well, you had to write essays for all of those, right?"

"Yeah, but they wasn't all that hard."

"The point is that you were still able to do them, so don't sit there and tell me that you can't do this." I was silent at first, but then I gave in.

"A'ight, a'ight. You got me."

"Okay then." There was more silence.

"Yo, Tierra. On some real shit, can I ask you something?"

"Yeah. What is it?"

"Like, do you really believe that a nigga like me could get into college and shit? Like succeed and shit?"

"Yes, Hype, I really do. In fact, I know you can. If you believe in yourself, you can do anything you set your mind to."

"People always say that, but I think it's bullshit."

"How is that bullshit?"

"Cuz I'm black."

"Oh, that's original." She smiled and gave a playful nudge against my shoulder.

"It's the truth, though. On some real shit, a black man has such limited opportunities that it's not even funny, yo. All they gotta do is look at my name and they already got a judgement about my ass. Wherever I wanna go in life, I ain't gonna get too far because of the color of my skin. I love my mother and all, but I think it's kind of fucked up that she gave me a black ass name."

"What are you talking about?"

"As fucked up as it sounds, black people can't really name their kids black names no more, not if they want them to go somewhere in life." She looked at me like I was crazy, but I wasn't stopping now. "Listen, yo. If you some white corporate muthafucka looking at an application to see who gets the job, who you gonna pick, Raequon Davis or Philip Simmons?"

She busted out laughing, but that only added fuel to my fire.

"Nah, nah I'm serious! For real though, on some true shit. Even though they did the same shit, and Raequon may have done more work than the other dude, you gonna pick Philip. Why? Because you know he's *white*, and stereotypically speaking, when you think of somebody in a corporate office, who pops into your head? A white ass scholarly looking muthafucka named Phillip or Timothy with a three-piece suit and a tie, that's who. It ain't Raequon, no matter how hard he busted his ass to get there."

She stared at me.

I waited for her to say something, but she didn't. "You understand what I'm saying?" I finally said.

"Yeah, but what about the black men who *do* get professional jobs, like President Obama, for one? Hello!"

"Yeah, they get the job alright, but it's still a fucked up situation. You gotta deal wit all kinds of racism and discrimination. You gotta work twice, maybe three times as hard than the white employees cuz you gotta prove that your black ass got the right to be there. And no matter what you do, you *still* the first one to get fired."

She was completely silent, staring at me very intently. Finally, she said, "Damn. That's true."

"I know."

"But you still have to rise yourself above all of that. You can't be a quitter. I *know* you're not a quitter, Hype. I mean, come on."

"I know, but knowing the truth kind of fucks it up cuz it's discouraging as hell. Most of the time I wonder what the fuck I'm doing here if there's a better than fifty percent chance that I'm wasting my time."

"Damn. I don't even know what to say to that."

"There ain't shit *to* say."

"Well, my mom always instilled in me that your mind is a powerful weapon. Regardless of what life throws at you, you can rise above it, even as a black man."

"But where are all the black men at, though? Dead or in jail, or out in these streets!"

"Hype, not all black men are like that."

"I understand that, but I'm talking about my situation. I got two male cousins, plus Twon's like my brother. None of us grew up with our father. You think that shit don't have an effect?"

"I understand, but that's a different subject."

"It's related though! Where's your father at, Tierra?"

She paused again, trying to take in my words. It looked like she was getting kind of discouraged. Sometimes I could get too deep with my thoughts and my words. I tried to catch myself sometimes, but other times, I couldn't help it.

"Anyway," I said, trying to change the subject, "you should be good though. Tierra is a pretty safe name."

"Shut up, Hype!" Her expression softened, and she pushed my arm.

I chuckled. "I'm just trying to encourage you like you always doin' to me!" She laughed with me.

"But hey, why did your mother name you Hyphen anyway?"

"She had an undying love for punctuation marks. When she was a child, she vowed that at least one of her kids would be named after the hyphen cuz it was her favorite symbol."

"Wow. Really?"

I couldn't take it anymore. I busted out laughing. "You mean to tell me you actually believed that shit? *Damn*, you gullible." I was rolling on the sofa, laughing so hard. She pushed me again.

"Shut up, boy. But really, why did she name you that?"

I shrugged my shoulders. "Shit, I don't know. The fuck your momma name you Tierra for?"

"Because she thought it was a pretty name."

I raised my eyebrows. She punched my arm.

"Fuck you, Hype." She started laughing.

"Hey, you started this shit."

"*What* ever."

"Anyways," I said. "On another subject: I did what you told me to do."

"What are you talkin' about?"

"You don't remember we was talking, and you told me I should get tested and shit?"

"Oh, for HIV?"

"Yeah. I should get my results in a couple of weeks."

"That's good. Are you nervous?"

"Not really," I said, playing it off. Deep down, I was shook as fuck after that conversation when I had time to sit and think about it. That's the real reason I went to get tested. I knew I was living a reckless life, fighting, sleeping with different girls, and talking crazy, but I'm not all bad. I do have some good qualities. It's just that sometimes I feel like I honestly don't know who I'm supposed to be, like, which one should I pick, the good me or the hood me? Both of them are part of my personality, but I know that eventually I'm going to have to decide which one I really am. Damn, I'm on some Quaid shit right now.

Tierra

I walked out of my science class hungry as hell. Good thing it was lunchtime. I went to my locker and dropped off my books, then made my way to the cafeteria.

"Tierra!"

Shaneece was making her way over to me. I slowed down until she caught up. "You're going to lunch, right?" she asked.

"Yeah."

"Do you mind if I sit with you? I don't mean to bother you, because you don't really know me that well, but I am so sick of eating my lunch in the bathroom, and you're the friendliest person I've met so far."

I looked at her like she was crazy. "You've been eating your lunch in the bathroom?"

"Yes." She looked embarrassed, but then she relaxed when I said, "That must have been interesting!" I made a face.

"Yeah, there were definitely some occasions when I regretted that decision...." She wrinkled her nose, and we burst out laughing together. "I probably should have asked you before now, since we talk like every day in class, but I didn't want to impose on you."

"Girl, you are definitely not imposing on me. I think you're cool, and I would love to eat lunch with you. Plus, I can introduce you to some of my friends." I had been meaning to talk to her about Hype anyway, so this was perfect.

"Okay, thank you." She gave me a quick hug.

"Yeah, sure." I smiled. We went into the cafeteria, got our food, and found an empty table. "So, aside from eating lunch in the bathroom, how do you like the school so far?"

"It's pretty good. I like the teachers and the classes, and I've seen a couple of cute guys so far. But there's this one guy who's extra fine."

"Word? What does he look like?"

"He's tall and light skinned with braids."

"Oh, for real?" I had to restrain myself from blurting *His name isn't Twon, is it? Cus that sounds a lot like my man.'* I definitely had to sell her on the idea of being with Hype.

"Yeah. He's in my Physics class."

"Oh, okay." I made an effort to sound casual. Twon took Physics too. "So is there anyone else besides him who you like?"

"Not really. Why?"

"Well, you remember Hype from English class, right?"

"Yeah, why?"

"He's interested in you."

"I'm definitely not interested in him. He seems like a straight-up hoe. Not my type at all."

"For real?"

"Yeah."

"Damn."

"Why? Did he ask you to hook us up?"

"Yeah."

"Wow. Oh, shit. There he is!" She nodded in the direction of the door.

"Who, Hype?" I turned around.

"No. The fine ass guy I was telling you about!" I stared in shock. My suspicious were true! The guy she was talking about was Twon.

"Oh."

"Do you know him?"

"Yeah, I know him alright."

"Who is he? Do you know his name?"

"That's my man."

"Oh, I'm sorry." She looked embarrassed.

"It's okay."

"But damn, girl, get it. He is fine!"

"Yeah, he sure is."

Twon spotted us and walked over.

"Hey baby." He leaned down and gave me a kiss.

"Hey, boo, how's it going?" I smiled at him.

"Nothing much. Hey ... Shaneece, right?"

"Yeah."

"YO, NIGGA! TWON!"

We turned in the direction of the lunch line. Hype and Quaid were standing near the front. Charles was probably skipping school, normal for him. Hype was gesturing for Twon to hurry up — they were trying to save a place for him in the line.

"HURRY UP, NIGGA!"

"Be right back," said Twon, and he raced to the line with his friends.

"Wow. They're all cool with each other?" said Shaneece.

"Yeah. Quaid and Hype are cousins, and they have another cousin named Charles, who sits on the other side of me in our English class. Twon and all of them have known each other their whole lives practically. I met them in the beginning of tenth grade when I moved here from Florida."

"Oh, really? That's cool. So how long have you and Twon been going out?"

"Almost two years."

"Are you guys in love?"

"Oh yes, most definitely." I wanted to make sure this point stuck with her. I mean, Shaneece was a nice girl and all, but still.

"Aww, that's so sweet!" She smiled.

The boys came to our table. Twon sat across from me, Hype sat next to Shaneece, and Quaid sat across from Hype.

"I'm just sayin, nigga. If them niggas was really down for us, then why the fuck it take so long for them to help out the victims? Iss cuz they was *black*, nigga!" said Hype.

"Some white people were there too," said Quaid.

"How many? Get the fuck outta here. There wasn't no fuckin white people up in Nawlins."

"Yes there were!"

I had to interject. "Wait, you guys are arguing about Hurricane Katrina?"

"Yes we are, as a matter of fact." Hype looked at me like *you got a problem with that?*

"That's mad old!"

"It's still relevant," said Hype, not missing a beat. "Ain't shit changed since then for black people in America. But anyway, back to you, Quaid, where'd you see that, some photoshopped YouTube video or something? Only white muthafucka I saw was one of the soldiers that was supposedly helping niggas get out and shit. And that's the *only* white person I seen. There's no fuckin arguing 'bout that, nigga. The government don't give a fuck about black people. When the tsunami hit somewhere in Asia, the government was on they ass like that..." he snapped his fingers "...but the minute some shit happens to us in our own fuckin *country*, Niggas take damn near a week and shit. And why? Cuz they ain't makin' no money off of it. They aint makin no fucking money, and they don't give a fuck about us. Simple as that."

I couldn't take anymore of Hype's foolishness. "How do you even remember all of this stuff? That was like, elementary school!"

"I stay relevant," said Hype.

"Okay, but relevant would be having a discussion about something that happened this year, not twelve years ago."

"But that's not the point though. The point is that this country didn't care about us then, and it damn sure don't care about us now."

I just stared at him. Hype is always talking about the disadvantages black people had in America. I don't know where he gets it. I mean, of course I care about the struggle too, but Hype was deep with it.

"Yeah, I'm-a have to agree with Hype on that one," said Twon.

"Alright, I understand how they don't care about us," said Quaid. "But you're saying that they didn't make any money off of Katrina. So what, they made money off the tsunami?"

"Nigga, you stupid." Hype sighed and thumped the table with his hand. "Wake the fuck up. Hell yeah, they made money off the fuckin tsunami. What, you think they ain't get their cut of the donations? Ain't no way in hell all that money made it to the people." Hype sat back, arms folded, pleased with himself.

Quaid leaned forward to give Hype some dap. "Yeah, I feel you on that. You're right. You got that."

"Thank you."

"Yo, Hype, you smart when you wanna be," said Twon.

"What the fuck is that supposed to mean?"

"Nah, for real. Sometimes you be saying some real ass shit."

"This is true. I learn a lot from you," Quaid said, surprising us all.

Hype looked around in amazement. "Aw, stop it, guys. You're making me blush." We all stared at him for a second, then everybody busted out laughing.

"You my nigga, Hype," said Twon.

"Always," said Hype. They gave each other dap.

* * *

I giggled. "*Stop*, Twon. You're going to get us caught!"

"Girl, as of right now, I don't care! Now give me some of that good stuff!" He attacked me again, kissing on my neck, lips, just about anywhere he could. There was a knock on his door. "Damn," he whispered, and got off me. I sat up in his bed. He went to open his door, but before he did, he turned back to me. "One of these days," he said, and gave me a wink.

"No time soon."

"Very soon."

"Whatever."

He opened the door, and Quaid walked in.

"What's up, my brother?" said Quaid. They gave each other dap.

"Nothing. What's up with you?"

Just then, Twon's mother, Charlene called from downstairs. She sure could yell loud enough when she wanted to.

"TWON!"

"What?"

"COME HERE!"

To Quaid, Twon said, "Hold on, nigga." He went to see what his mother wanted.

"So, how are you, Tierra?" Quaid said.

"I'm good."

"You ready for school on Monday?"

"Yes and no."

"Why, may I ask?"

"Math is just too hard sometimes."

"Have you tried getting a tutor?"

"Yeah, I did last year, but Twon made me stop."

"Why is that?"

"He said the boy who was helping me was getting a little too close for comfort."

"So you just stopped?"

"Yeah. I didn't feel like messing up our relationship."

"Tierra, you shouldn't allow anyone to hinder you in trying to better yourself, especially in school. If you want, I could tutor you. And I can handle Twon if he gets crazy jealous for no reason."

"For real?"

"Would you want that?"

"Would she want what?" Twon said, catching the last bit of conversation.

"Me to tutor her."

"Yeah, that's cool. But yo, I'm about to go to the store to get my mom a pack of cigarettes. I'll be back." Before either of us could say anything, he left.

"That boy is a trip," I said.

"He sure is. But anyways, what do you say? Do you want my help?"

I had barely been paying attention to our conversation, but something about the way he said that made me look at him. Quaid was so intense. A lot of times it seemed like he was more of an outsider, and not really a part of us.

"Um, yeah. That'd be great."

"Alright. I'd be happy to assist you in any way you need me to." There it was again, his funny little way of talking so proper sometimes. "We can work out the details of when and where later."

"Sounds good," I said, not sure what else to say.

Quaid nodded intently. "So, how's your relationship with Antwon going?"

"It's alright."

"Just alright?"

"Yeah. I mean, we're cool and everything, but—"

Quaid waited.

"Sometimes I'm not sure about him."

"What do you mean?"

I had been dying to tell somebody, anybody about how Twon had been acting lately, but I didn't know who to trust. For some reason, I felt completely safe with Quaid, and this seemed like the right moment to just get it out.

"He wants me to have sex with him, but I'm not ready." I turned away. "This is so embarrassing."

"Tierra." He put his hands on my shoulders and gently turned me toward him.

"What?"

He stared into my eyes. "You shouldn't let anyone pressure you into giving up your temple."

"My ... *temple?*"

"Your body. Your virginity. Your innocence."

"Oh."

"Your virginity is a very sacred thing. It should be treated as such. You should never give it up unless you are truly ready and you're sure you truly love and trust the recipient."

"That's what I was thinking, but—"

"But what?"

"Twon really wants to do it, and I don't want to disappoint him." There. I said it.

"But, Tierra, Antwon has to understand that you should both be ready before you make that leap. You don't want to go rushing into something like that, especially if you're not ready. That would just take away from the whole meaning of it. Sex is supposed to be a special thing that happens in a relationship. Don't just give in. You don't have to do it. Just talk to Antwon about this. I'm sure he'll understand." Something about the way he said *I'm sure he'll understand* made me think he didn't really believe it.

"Quaid, we both know Twon. When he wants something, he usually gets it."

"Yes, I know that all too well." He stared at me. "But just remember, you don't have to give it up, and I'm always here if you need me."

"What do you mean by that?" I was starting to feel uncomfortable.

"Exactly what I said. You can trust me." His eyes bore into mine.

"Um, Quaid? What do you mean—?"

Twon burst into the room. "Yo, baby, let's go. I gotta take you home."

"Why? What's wrong?"

"Cuz my mom is trippin'. Come on." He gently took my arm. "Quaid, you gotta leave too, she said."

"What's up with your mom?" said Quaid.

"You know how she get sometimes. She in one of her bitchy ass moods. Now she gonna start messing with me all day. I really don't wanna deal wit that headache, but I gotta stay here cuz the computer guy is on his way."

Quaid looked perplexed. "Oh. Okay."

"So for now I'm finna take Tierra home then come back here to deal wit this shit."

"I was going to my grandmother's after here anyway."

"A'ight. Tell G-Ma I said hi."

"I'll be sure to." Quaid left, then Twon and I got in his car and he drove me home.

"I'm sorry about my mom, and I'm-a call you later tonight, okay?"

"Okay."

"Gimme kiss." I kissed his lips.

"Bye baby."

Twon

"So what you wanna do this weekend?" I stared at her, but she seemed to be in a daze. Tierra's been like that a lot lately. It was really starting to bother me. "Baby?" I reached across the table and gently touched her shoulder. She jumped and bounced back to reality.

"Huh? What?"

"I said what you wanna do this weekend?"

"Oh. My bad. Whatever you want to do."

"Baby?"

"Huh?"

"What's wrong with you?"

"What do you mean?"

"I mean, what's going on with you? You been real distant lately, like something's on your mind."

"Oh, nothing's wrong. I'm fine." Her voice and actions didn't convince me.

"You sure?"

"Yeah. I just been worried about applying to colleges and wondering if I'll get in. Talking to Hype makes me wonder if I'll ever make it out of here." I chuckled.

"You don't need to be listening to Hype, girl. Now, that's my nigga, but he's mad pessimistic about the world, and especially about blacks in society."

"I know, but the stuff he be saying is true though."

"I know, but you can't take it completely to heart. You'll be fine, Tierra. You're smart, and you got a good head on your shoulders. You don't need to worry. Just keep on going how you been going, and you'll succeed."

"I can try, but—"

"But what?"

"My grades … they're not as good as they could be."

"So? You been working real hard this semester. Quaid's been tutoring you, and you've been passing all your tests and all of that. I wouldn't be surprised if you raised your GPA significantly. Wait till we get our first report cards. I know you gonna be happy. And your mom's gonna be proud of you too."

"You really think so?"

"I know so, baby girl. You got that, ma." She smiled. That's what I wanted to see. Tierra had such a beautiful smile. Damn, she was fine. Sometimes I just step back and admire her. I love the shit out of that girl. "So, is anything else bothering you?"

"Um … no."

Alright, that was *definitely* a lie. "Baby, what is it?"

"Nothing."

"You can talk to me."

"I know, but … it's complicated."

"Well, go 'head, girl. Let it out. I'm listening."

"I … I really can't put it into words."

I could see that she wasn't gonna tell me what was going on, at least not tonight.

"A'ight." I sighed. "But whenever you wanna talk about it, you know I'm here."

She smiled again. "I know. Thanks."

"You ain't gotta thank me. It's what I'm here for."

"Well...."

"What's up?"

"I kinda been wanting to go to church lately."

"WHAT?" I sat up straight and stared at her.

"As you know, I've been filling out scholarship applications at Hype's grandmother's house, and she be telling us all kinds of stuff while we're there. She talks a lot of trash back and forth with Hype, but she also tells about God and church. I used to go to church a lot when I was younger, but then a couple of years before I moved here, I stopped. I don't want to go to hell, Twon." She looked worried.

"Tierra, you're not going to hell."

"How do you know?"

"Because you're a good person. Only bad people go to hell. You never killed nobody or hurt nobody before."

"But Hype's grandmother said—"

"You really going to listen to Hype's grandmother? G-Ma's cool, but she's not a preacher or anything."

"I know, but she knows what she's talking about."

"How do you know that she knows what she's talking about? Did she tell you that you were going to hell?"

"No, she didn't say that, but she said that everyone needs to be saved, and I'm not saved. I don't even go to church like that."

"You don't have to go to church to be saved."

"What do you have to do then?"

"I don't know."

"So then I should go!"

"Why are you so worried about this?" I could feel myself getting upset.

"I just told you. I don't want to go to hell!"

"And I just told you that you're a good person, so you have nothing to worry about."

"Well, how do you know? Are you a preacher?"

"No, but—"

"And you don't even know what I have to do to be saved. You just don't want me going to church."

"I never said I didn't want you going to church."

"Well, that's what you're acting like. As soon as I mentioned it, you got all defensive."

"I'm not the one getting defensive, you are. I'm just trying to help you."

"Well, you're not."

"Alright, fuck you then." I got up and started walking toward the door. She followed me.

"Where are you going?"

"I'm not needed here, so I'm out."

"Twon, you don't have to leave."

"I'll leave anywhere I'm not wanted."

"I never said I didn't want you! What makes you feel that way?"

I stared her up and down. "I think we both know the answer to that question."

"Twon, please don't make this about sex. Please, not today."

"Bye, Tierra."

I walked out the door and slammed it behind me.

* * *

I got home on Saturday after working twelve hours at my factory job. I was exhausted. Today had been tiring as hell. My boss was on my ass all day. All I wanted to do was take a shower and collapse.

After my shower, I was walking toward my bedroom when my mother called my name.

"Twon!"

"Huh?"

"Come here!"

"Damn!" I muttered. I was so close to my room, and my bed was screaming my name, but I went downstairs anyway.

"What do you want?" I said when I got to the living room, where my mother was sitting on the couch watching her soaps.

"Go to the store and get me some cigarettes."

"Ma, I am so tired."

"I ain't ask you that, boy. Now go get me some cigarettes."

"I thought you was quitting."

"Don't worry about that. Just go."

I stood there waiting. She looked at me like I was crazy. "Whatchu standing there for?"

"Don't you need to give me some money?"

"Uh … *you* paying."

"What?"

"Boy, don't get smart with me. You buying cuz I ain't got no change, and I don't feel like breaking a twenty."

I rolled my eyes.

"Fine."

"Don't you sass me."

It was a long ass walk to the store cuz I was tired as hell, and I was afraid that if I drove, I would fall asleep at the wheel. I figured that maybe the fresh air would help me stay awake. On my way back, a car rolled up beside me. The window rolled down. It was Shaneece.

"What's up, Twon? You need a ride?"

"Sure. I'm tired as hell." I hopped in the passenger seat.

"Where you coming from?"

"Damn, this seat is comfortable." I laid my head back against the headrest.

"Where you coming from?" she repeated.

"The store."

"Why you so tired? It couldn't have been that long of a walk."

"Oh nah, cuz I just worked twelve hours. All I wanted to do after my shower was fall the fuck out, but my moms got me before I went to my room and sent me to the store."

"Damn. That's crazy. Where do I go from here?" We had stopped at a light.

"Just turn left and keep going straight. I'll tell you when we get to the house."

"Okay." We drove a little then stopped at another light. I noticed her sneaking glances at me.

"Hey, do you work out?" she said.

"Huh?"

"I said, do you work out, cuz your arms are kind of big." She started feeling on my muscles. "Damn, boy. I can only imagine what your chest looks like." Her hand lingered on my arm. I shifted away from her.

"Um, the light's green."

"What? Oh, my bad!" She did a cute little flirty laugh. I was glad we got to my house soon because she was making me nervous in all kinds of ways.

"Thanks for the ride." I turned to get out, but she grabbed my arm.

"Wait."

"What?"

"Any time you need a ride, you can call me, okay?"

"Um, I have a car. I just felt like walking tonight."

She looked embarrassed. "Oh … sorry. I thought—"

"It's a'ight." I stared at her. She was still holding on to my arm. "Um … is there anything else you wanted to tell me?"

"Why?"

"My arm."

"Oh!" She quickly let go. "I'm sorry, Twon. I'm so silly. I don't know where my mind is at." She did that cute laugh again.

I smiled at her. "Maybe you need some sleep too."

"Yeah, maybe."

"Well, a'ight. Thanks again for the ride."

"Oh, any time — I mean, you're welcome!"

Shaneece

I've have only been at this school a short while, and I'm already caught up in a dilemma. For the record, I'll just say this: I feel like it's totally unfair that Twon makes me feel the way he does without even really knowing him, and he has a girlfriend.

And why did I have to meet Tierra first? I mean, not that I'm a homewrecker or anything, but I meet a really cool girl, we hit it off instantly, then I meet the man of my dreams, all in the same day, only to later find out that this fine man and my cool new friend are in a relationship. Life is so unfair.

Why did my father have to move us to this stupid place? I mean, I like the school, and the people seem to be cool, but I have these crazy feelings for Twon, and I don't know what to do about it. I sit behind him every day in our Physics class, and most of the time, I have to stop myself from staring at him or finding excuses to talk to him. I fake like I don't know the answers to the questions sometimes just so he can explain them to me.

I know, I know, it's pathetic, and I really should just let him go, expecially since Tierra and I are becoming such good friends, but I don't know if I can.

My phone rang, causing me to jump out of my stupor. I looked at the caller ID before answering. It was my sister, Shanelle. I quickly answered before she hung up. I loved my sister to death. I often feel like she is the only person in this world who truly understands me. I tell her everything, and she has firsthand experience with our father, even though she is his "golden child," so she gets me.

"Hey," I said, scooting up in my bed.

"Shaneece! How is the new school?"

"It's great so far, but of course, you know that Dad is always on my back about making straight As."

"You can do it, Shaneece."

"No, I can't. I'm not you." My heart panged at my last statement. All my life, Shanelle had always been better than me at school. She never made even an A minus on an assignment. She was so smart, and my father never let me forget it.

"You don't have to be me. You can be yourself. You are incredibly intelligent, and you can do this."

"But that's the thing, Shanelle, I can't. I've made mostly As and Bs my whole life, and I've always been on Honor Roll, but Dad never seems to recognize it. I push myself as hard as I can, but I just can't do it. I don't have a brain like yours. I'm just not smart enough."

"Shaneece, please don't beat yourself up about not being perfect. Nobody is — not even me. We both know all of the things I did behind Dad's back when I was living in that house. I know exactly what you are going through. That's why I had to get away. Besides, the college admissions offices will accept a few Bs. You are an outstanding student. Your essays will rock them out. Don't let Dad's craziness push you over the edge."

I swallowed a lump in my throat as I took in all of her words. I knew she was right. My father was way too hard on us when we grew up, expecting nothing short of perfection. But despite the fact that I know Shanelle is being sincere with her words, I can't shake my frustration at not being perfect. Most people would probably think I'm lame for being so worried about not making straight As, but they don't have my father. They haven't had to deal with years of being criticized and compared to their "perfect" older sister, all because she was a top-notch student and better at sneaking out to blow off some steam.

"Shaneece? Are you still there?"

"Yeah." I sighed. "What were you saying?"

"I was saying just to think of it like this: This is your senior year. By the time summer hits, you will be off to college and won't have to live under Dad's roof. Let that be your motivation."

"You're right. Thanks for the encouragement."

"Anytime. Well, I love you, but I have to get back to my shift." Shanelle is a nurse at a big hospital in my hometown. She is always busy with work.

"Okay, I love you too. Don't work too hard."

"Hey, here's in idea. I'll try to convince Dad to let you come visit me soon. A trip out of town would do you good. We'll have a shopping day, a beach day, and a salon day!"

I smiled. Shanelle's the best big sister on the planet. "Yes, please do."

"Okay, girl, let's do this. Talk to you later."

"Bye."

* * *

I sat with Tierra again the next day at lunch. Sometimes Twon and the guys sat with us, but other times they sat with some other guys holding rap battles and talking sports. I definitely enjoyed spending my lunches with Tierra because she was so cool, but I often had to force myself not to sneak glances at whatever table Twon was at when he and the guys weren't sitting with us.

"Girl, why is it that no school cafeteria can cook?" I poked my plastic fork into what was supposed to be lasagna, but looked more like red and yellow slop.

She burst out laughing. "Girl-l-l-l-l, you are crazy!"

I laughed. "Seriously, who cooked this?"

"I have no idea, girl. I wouldn't touch that stuff if I were you!"

"I wish they made all of the cooks audition before they were allowed to even enter our schools. Or maybe the person who creates the recipes needs to be fired. Or shot."

We shared another laugh.

"So how are you adjusting to all of your classes and everything?" said Tierra, biting into an apple.

"I'm doing okay," I said, grabbing my own apple from my lunch tray. There was no way I was eating that lasagna. "The teachers seem like they do a pretty good job, and I feel like I understand the material."

"That's great," she said with a smile. "My only problem is my math class."

"Oh really?" I jumped slightly when Hype set his tray down next to me. Quaid and Twon sat across from me.

Hype wasted no time launching in. "Man, them niggas is bugging. Twon definitely won that battle."

"What battle?" said Tierra. She looked at Twon.

"I just finished battling this dude named Mar over at another table. Steve and Trey were the judges, and both of them had the nerve to say that Mar was the winner."

"Well, Mar did have a few more bars than you, in my opinion," said Quaid, looking back and forth between Twon and Tierra.

"Nigga, *what?*" Hype and Twon said at the same time.

"Mar's whole flow is trash. That nigga can't even stay on beat!" said Hype, jumping in to defend Twon.

"I know," said Twon. "Matter of fact, you go sit over *there,*" he said jokingly, pointing to an empty table near one of the walls. "You need a time out for that."

"My opinion is the same," Quaid said smoothly.

"Anyway," said Hype, turning to me. "How is your day going?"

"Um, pretty good," I said, suddenly interested in my lunch. I even took a bite of the lasagna. It tasted horrible. I almost spit it out, but I didn't want Twon to think I was gross.

"That's good," he said, taking a bite of his pizza. "I see you not feeling that lasagna — you want half of this?" He quickly cut his pizza down the middle, put it on a napkin without touching it, and slid it over to me.

"Awww," said Tierra. "That is so sweet!"

I felt totally awkward and embarrassed. I didn't know what to do because Twon was sitting right there, but at the same time, I didn't want to seem rude. I reluctantly took the pizza, shooting Hype a smile.

"Thank you," I said.

"Oh, no problem," he said, smiling. "Anytime."

I shot a quick glance in Twon's direction to see his reaction, and I could have sworn that he looked a little disappointed at Hype offering me the pizza, but I couldn't tell for sure because I had to quickly glance away so that I wouldn't get caught.

Wow. I really have it bad for this guy.

Hype

I was at my crib with this girl named Shena, but I was secretly dardreaming about Shaneece. I don't know why I just won't ask her out. I've never been afraid to approach a girl before, but there's something different about Shaneece. She seems like a real good girl, and that is hard to find these days. But then, I honestly don't know if a good girl wants a guy like me.

"Hype, I wanchu." Shena pressed herself up against me. She whispered in my ear. "I think you are *so* fine. We should be together. I can make it worth your while."

"Oh, word? How you gon do that?"

She let her eyes travel down to my pants then back up to my eyes. She licked her lips and smiled. "Let me worry about that."

"Well, shit. Do what you gotta do then."

She pushed me back onto my bed and did her thing.

After she was done, she went to the bathroom. When she came back, she said, "So how was that? Was it good?"

My ass was on cloud nine. "That was *great*."

"So, did it make you think about what I said?"

"What you mean?"

"About us being together."

My high instantly wore off. Damn, she always had to bring this shit up.

"Shena, you know how I feel about that. I'm-a free agent, ma."

She sucked her teeth. "So you just gonna let me do *that* to you and not give me nothing in return?"

I looked at her like she was crazy. "Shit, I ain't put a gun to your head and *make* you do it."

"You are so fucked up, Hype. I'm through with you."

I shrugged my shoulders. "Okay."

She left with both of us knowing that she would be back before next week.

* * *

"Yo, that bitch was *wiling*, son. Straight up. But her head game is outta control though."

Quaid just looked at me and shook his head. "Why do you constantly give these girls false hope? Why do you treat women that way?"

"Nigga, Shena ain't no woman. She a fucking hoe."

"She *is* a woman, and you still shouldn't treat her that way. You're using her. You shouldn't treat anyone that way."

"You think I'm-a take advice from *you*? When was the last time you got some pussy?"

Quaid gave me a dark ass look.

"That was a low blow, Hype," said Twon.

"My sex life doesn't matter," said Quaid. "That's not what this is about. This is about the disgusting way you treat girls. You need to stop living the way you do. You're going to get caught up in something you can't handle, or you'll catch a disease. And that's the truth."

"Man, stop acting like you my bitch or somethin'. Nobody wanna hear all that shit." Once again, I knew that Quaid was spitting nothing but truth, but I wasn't willing to let that show just yet.

"You're my cousin, Hype. I'm just—"

"Then be my cousin. Get off my dick. I ain't ask you for no advice. I don't need nobody tellin' me how the fuck to live my life. I do what I do. I ain't dead yet, so I must be doin' something right."

Quaid persisted. "Did you get your results back?"

This nigga was really working my nerves.

"Why do you need to know, Quaid?"

"Did you?"

"No, I ain't got the results yet. But when I do, I will march my black ass over to your house and gladly show you that you don't know what the fuck you're talking about."

"Hype, listen—"

"No, I'm tired of talkin' about this shit. What I do ain't got nothing to do wit you, so leave it alone. Mind your business. Let's talk about something else."

"Eyo, y'all seen the game last night?" said Twon.

"Hell yeah, nigga! Ninety-eight to forty!" I said.

Later on, we went to my grandmother G-Ma's house and opened the door. She was sitting on the couch watching *General Hospital*.

"Hello, Grandma," said Quaid.

"Hey, baby," said G-Ma.

"Hi, G-Ma," said Twon.

"How you doin', Twon?"

"I'm good, and you?"

"Shit, I *know* you good." She felt his arm muscles. "Damn, you gettin' big, boy!" Twon chuckled. "You been workin' out?"

"Yes ma'am!"

"Wassup, G-*Nanny*!" I rushed over and gave G-Ma dap and a hug.

"What's up, Hype?" She returned the love. "And what you been up to, huh? Lookin' all sexy with your green contacts and three-sixty waves."

"I'm tellin' you, these ain't contacts, G-Ma."

"Whatever, boy. Ain't no grandchild of mine but you got them eyes."

"I can't help it if I look good." I smirked.

"Whatever, boy. Get your ass in the back somewhere. You know Charles is here, right?"

"Oh, word?"

"Yeah, he's in the back with that XBox, or whatever that thang is called nowadays."

"Oh, for real?"

"Yeah. Get on back there."

"A'ight." Before I could go, G-Ma grabbed my arm.

"Hype. Let me holla at you for a minute." She had this serious look on her face.

"Yeah?"

"Keep your focus."

"What you mean?"

"I know you got a lot going on in your life, but stay on your grind."

"Oh, for sure, G-Ma. You know I got dat."

"No, I'm serious, Hype. Keep your head in them books and bring your black ass to college."

"I'll try."

"No, no. Forget that trying shit. *Do* it. You hear me?"

"Yeah, I hear you."

"*Do* it." She released my arm and went back to watching her stories. I stood there reflecting on her words. Yo, on the real, my grandmother is beyond fuckin cool, nigga. We can joke around and everything, but when she be saying shit like she just told me, it's like her whole persona changes. You can see the wisdom in her eyes. It's crazy.

* * *

"Hype," a soft voice called my name. I turned around.

"Damn girl." I licked my lips. "What's your name?"

"Oh, you don't remember me?"

"Nah," I said, trying to recall where I had met this girl.

"You don't remember, from the party...?"

I was barely paying attention to her words cuz I was too focused on her body. Momma was shaped like a cola bottle, no lie, son. I couldn't believe that I ain't remember her.

"So, would you like to try it again?"

I jerked back to attention.

"Huh?"

"I said do you want to try it again?" She licked her lips.

"Oh, sure, sure."

She smiled then slowly made her way over to me. I leaned my head down to kiss her, and she tilted her face up to me. We started kissing, with her as the aggressor.

"Damn, ma, slow down."

"No," she said, and she kissed me hungrily. "You don't know how long I've been wanting this."

"Huh?" I said, but that was all I got out. I could barely speak. She unbuckled my pants and pushed me backward. We were out in the open, straight up in the middle of the park. But it was nighttime and wasn't nobody around anyway. She was practically devouring me, and at first I was gonna try to slow her down, but then it started turning me on, so I just let it go. Before I knew it, she was on top of me putting in some serious work. As soon as I reached a climax, I remembered that I didn't have a condom on.

"Oh, shit!" My head was swimming as I pushed her off of me. "Yo, we just had sex without a condom."

"I know," she said, and something in her voice made me turn to her. She looked mad evil, all devilish and shit. All of a sudden she wasn't looking as good as she did before. She was actually looking kind of scary the way she was smiling at me and shit. I felt queasy.

"Why you say it like that?"

"Payback is a bitch," she said under her breath.

"Huh?"

She stood up and glared down at me. "I said, payback is a bitch!"

"What the hell are you talking about?"

"You really don't remember me, do you?"

"No," I said irritably. This bitch was really scaring me now.

"You fucking played me, Hype. You told me that you wasn't messing with no one else but me, and it was a lie. You broke my heart. I really cared for you. You thought that shit was real fucking cute, didn't you?"

"What are you—?"

"Nigga, don't act like you don't know what I'm talkin' about! You fucking played me, and now you're gonna get yours!"

I jumped up. "Yo, what the fuck are you—?"

"Welcome to AIDS, MUTHAFUCKA!" she screamed.

I woke up, sweating and shaking like crazy. I ran to the bathroom and threw up for like twenty minutes. Shit was crazy. I looked at the clock. It was three in the morning. No matter how many times I tried to go back to sleep, I couldn't. Whenever I closed my eyes, I saw her face. And I swear, her face got scarier and scarier every time. And all I could hear were those words, "WELCOME TO AIDS, MUTHAFUCKA!"

When I told Twon, Quaid, Charles, and my white homeboy Rick, they all howled with laughter except Quaid.

"Yo nigga, you fuckin stupid!" said Twon.

Quaid looked serious as hell. "That's not funny," he said.

"I know," I said.

Charles smirked at me. "Yo, Hype, nigga. Why you taking this shit to heart, dog? It was just a dream, mah dude."

"I know, but that shit felt real as hell. It made me wanna...." I stopped and looked at Quaid.

"Made you wanna what?" said Quaid.

"Nothing."

"Yo, man. That shit was crazy as hell, dog," said Rick.

"I know."

"Do you think it means something?"

"Yes," Quaid cut in. Everyone stared at him.

"No, it doesn't," said Charles, flipping his hand at Quaid. "Don't even get started. You 'bout to have this nigga shook for no reason."

"Some dreams DO have meaning, Charles," said Quaid.

"But how you know his do?" said Charles.

"Because I can see it."

"Aw, shit. He on that spooky shit now." Charles sucked his teeth. "Okay, what does the dream mean, Mr. Witch Doctor?"

"I'm not a witch doctor, Charles. But that dream means something important."

"What does it mean?" I said, feeling panic rising in my stomach.

"It was a warning. You need to stop messing with all of these girls, or something bad is going to happen to you."

"Something like what?" I said, dreading the answer.

"I don't know. But from the content of the dream, it sounds pretty dangerous."

"Man, why you always trying to scare somebody?" said Twon. "Everybody ain't a perfect little choir boy like you."

"I'm not perfect, and I'm not a choir boy. Hype is family, so I'm just trying to tell him like it is."

"Man, I don't know, man," I said. "But that shit ... yo, I can't get that bitch out my head. I am tired as hell though." I rubbed my eyes.

"Well, that's understandable," said Quaid. You were up all night."

"I don't know what the fuck I'm-a do tonight if I have that dream again."

"You better pop some pills or suttin, nigga," said Charles.

"I wouldn't even worry about it," said Twon.

"I'm trying not to, but that shit was wild, though."

"It was just a dream, nigga," said Charles. "Watch, by tonight, you gonna forget about that shit. Stop reading into this shit and just drop it."

"I can't just do that."

"Ey, did you ever fuck a girl without a condom?" said Charles.

"No."

"But that's not all it could mean," said Quaid, trying to jump in again. "It could—"

Charles held his hand up. "Then you ain't got shit to worry about."

* * *

"Hype!" I stopped walking and turned around. Two very angry looking girls were making their way over to me.

"What?" I said, holding out my arms like *Look at me, I'm innocent.*

"I thought you told me you wasn't fuckin this bitch!" said Shena, gesturing toward the other girl, this chick named Wanita.

"Ey, ey—"

"Who you callin a bitch, *bitch*?" said Wanita, pushing Shena aside and standing in front of me.

"You, bitch!" Shena pushed her back.

"Ladies, ladies." I broke them apart before they started fighting. "Chill. Both of you need to calm down."

"No, Hype. I need to know, are you fucking her?" said Shena.

"Yes, he is," said Wanita. "And?" she added, with more than enough attitude.

"He better not be cuz he is *my* man, okay?"

"Waaaaaaaaaaaait. Wait up." I turned to Shena. "I ain't nobody's man, girl. I told you before like I'm-a tell you right now. I'm a free agent, and it ain't none of your business who I'm fuckin or not."

"But—"

"But nothing. You need to chill like I told you before. If you don't like the situation, you can bounce."

"Hype...." Desperation was written all over her face.

"What?" My anger was rising now. Shena looked at Wanita, who stood there with her hands on her hips, her face full of attitude. Then she broke down. Out of nowhere, she broke down.

"I-I can't take this anymore," she whimpered, her voice cracking.

"What the hell is wrong with you, yo?" I was confused as hell, and my confusion added to my anger.

"Why you gotta treat me like this?" She had this hurt expression on her face.

"What the *fuck* are you talking about?"

"You! Me! This whole thing we got going! I give up other niggas for you. I stop messing with other dudes for you. I give you my heart and soul, and you treat me like this? I give myself to you on the regular, and you treat me this way? I want to be with you, Hype. Why can't you understand that?"

"I told you from jump what the deal was."

"So? Does that mean it couldn't have changed by now? We been messing around for six months, Hype! Doesn't that mean anything to you?"

"Not really."

She stopped cold. Her mouth dropped open.

"Oh. So that's how you gonna do me, huh? When I'm standing here pouring my heart out to you, you just gonna be all cold and evil? Do you care about my feelings at all? I love you, Hype!"

"No you don't."

"Yes I do!"

"WELL I AIN'T ASK FOR THAT SHIT!" My temper was raging out of control. "What is it with y'all hoes nowadays? I told your ass from jump I wasn't in this for no relationship. I don't do that love shit, and I don't do commitment. It ain't my fuckin fault that you ain't pay attention to what I told you. I ain't ask for your heart. I ain't ask for no feelings. This was a no-strings-attached deal. You knew I was fucking other bitches from the beginning. And now you wanna make me out to be the bad guy. If you wasn't down for this, then why you go through with it? You know what? I'm-a do you a favor. Don't talk to me no more. Don't call me, don't say hi to me, don't do shit. Don't even look at me no more." I erased her number from my phone right in front of her just to let her know I wasn't bullshitting.

"Hype—"

"No. I don't wanna hear it. If you couldn't stand the heat, you shoulda got the *fuck* out the kitchen." I turned my back on her and stormed off.

Now, I know that mighta seemed kinda fucked up what I did right there, but Shena had that shit comin' to her, word up. How you gonna come to me as a hoe and expect me to wife you up just cuz we been fuckin for a while? I ain't never told that girl nothing about having no relationship. I made it very clear from the start that she wasn't nothing but a booty call. If she ain't like it, she coulda left. Now, I admit, that was kinda rude what I said to her, but she irritated the hell outta me. And plus I was tired as a mutha. I ain't been to sleep for the past two days. I can't stand this shit. I feel like a madman, and it's all because of that stupid bitch in my nightmares.

* * *

I was laying in my bed staring at the ceiling when I came to the realization that my life is fucked up. I have no idea how I got this way, and I have no idea how I'm-a fix it.

I know I sound like I'm on some bullshit, but hey, cut me some slack. This is my third day without sleep. I'm having hallucinations, and they're scaring the shit out of me. I'm thinking about going to a doctor or something to rid me of this insomnia. This shit ain't no joke, for real.

Yo, I ain't all bad. I can be a good dude sometimes. Just not with girls. I don't know why I'm like that toward these chicks out here. Maybe I just haven't found the right one yet or something. I'm kind of taken by that new chick, Shaneece, but I don't know if she would be feeling me like that. She seems like a good girl. Plus, she's probably heard about my reputation with women, so she probably wouldn't even want to talk to me like that. I can't front, though. I have a major crush on her. But I'm hesitant to step to her, because if I was a girl, I damn sure wouldn't want me. Besides, I would probably end up being a grimy ass boyfriend. I'm a good friend, though. I'm a down ass nigga. I ride or die for my homies yo, word up. Can't nobody say I won't. What the fuck is wrong with me? I really have no idea.

"WELCOME TO AIDS, MUTHAFUCKA!"

"OH, SHIT!" I sat up in bed sweating like crazy. My head was pounding like a mutha. So was my heart. I could feel the fear rushing through me. I was shaking. My thoughts were swarming. I couldn't grab hold of none of them.

"Yo, Hype, nigga, you a'ight?" My cousins Charles and Quaid were standing over my bed. I tried to look at them, but I couldn't. I was seeing double. My breathing increased, and then I was hyperventilating. I started to panic.

"Yo, get this nigga a paper bag!" I heard Charles say, and then I blacked out.

I woke up in a bed I ain't recognize in a room I ain't recognize either. G-Ma and my mother were sitting next to me.

"Ma? G-Ma? What the heck is goin' on?" My voice was hoarse, and my lips were chapped as a mutha. I knew my breath had to be rough as hell. My mother spoke up.

"You had an anxiety attack, baby. Then your body shut down because you were so exhausted from not getting no sleep. You been sleeping now for about twenty-four hours."

"Twenty four hours??? Word? You *serious*?"

"Yup. But the doctor said you would be alright after you woke up. He said most of your anxiety probably came from not getting any sleep. Is he right?"

"Um ... yeah, I guess."

"You sure?"

"Yeah."

"Cuz if there's anything you need to talk about, baby, I'm here."

"I know, Ma." My mother was a real sweet woman, but I wasn't finna lay there and tell her my life troubles.

"Okay. Now baby, I got to use the bathroom, and then I'm gonna get us some coffee. You want anything?"

"Nah. Probably just some water."

"Okay. I'll be back."

"A'ight." Soon after she was gone, G-Ma turned to me. Her face said things were 'bout to get real.

"What's goin' on?"

"Nothing."

"Don't you play with me, boy. I know there's something wrong with you. Now it ain't no sense in lying to me cuz I'm-a get the truth out of you one way or another. So you can pick which way you want it, easy or hard."

"Okay." I chuckled. My G-Ma can get anything out of anybody. I told her everything that was goin' on wit me, about tryin'-a get into college, and applying for scholarships, and how I ain't think I was gonna make it. Then I told her about how it was for me in the streets, tryin'-a uphold my level of respect out there while struggling to keep my head in the right direction. Then I told her about the situation wit Shena and how I be treating girls. And finally, I told her about this whole AIDS situation, how I got tested, and about that nightmare I been having.

"Damn, boy. You going through a lot."

"Yeah."

"But I'm-a tell you something else though: it ain't nothing you can't handle. Now I know it ain't gonna be easy, but you can change how you doing things. You keep up with your schooling and applying for colleges and all that. Don't let nothing stray you from that. There's plenty of people your age who graduate and move on with their lives, and I expect you to do the same. Just don't consider failure as an option, and you'll succeed.

"About that street respect thing, boy, I don't know how many times I got to tell you to let go of all that. Now, I know you ain't no punk, and you know you ain't no punk, so it don't even matter what them other fools think of you. I know you're presented with situations that you sometimes can't get out of, but you got to think of how you got into those situations in the first place. You got to ask yourself, could I have avoided this? And if you could, then you need to take that and apply it to your life for the next time. This is a crazy world, Hype. You can't walk around with your eyes closed, cuz one day you might not have the chance to open them up and see.

"And them girls — boy, I know good and well, just like you do, that you ain't gonna leave girls alone. But since that's true, how about you try to change the way you treat them? You ain't gotta be all evil. You ain't gotta be no player. And you definitely don't gotta be messing with all of these hoes, cuz that can get you into more than one type of trouble. Now the AIDS situation, I can't really help you out with that. All I can say is that you should pray that those results don't come back positive, and to wrap it up every time if you don't already do that. But you really are messing up right now, Hype. And you know I ain't telling you nothing you don't already know. I just hope you take these words to heart, not as a meaningless bunch of rambling, but as words of wisdom that you can take with you and use in your life."

"Thanks, G-Ma."

"I don't need no thank you. I just need you to take action. Move. Separate yourself from all that bullshit that surrounds you, cuz you the one that's gonna suffer from it if you don't."

"Alright."

"And one more thing: Start coming to church. God has all the answers."

I reflected over G-Ma's words for the rest of my stay at the hospital.

* * *

"Yo, y'all niggas is crazy!" I said, laughing with my boys Twon and Quaid as we left the basketball court. Charles was out doing who knows what. We had just got finished playing three on three wit some other niggas from the block.

"Nah, *you* the one that's fuckin crazy, nigga,"said Twon. "I still can't believe all that shit you was talking. Every point you made you got cockier and cockier. That nigga Rashad looked like he wanted to bust your ass."

"It's all part of the *game*, my brother. You got to get into the *mind* of your opponent. You got to shake em up, because it's then and only then when you have total control." I kept my serious face for about five seconds then I busted out laughing along wit Twon and Quaid.

"Nigga, shut da fuck up wit yo Malcolm X ass," said Twon.

"Man, fuck you." I started laughing again. We were just about to go our separate ways when two cop cars rolled up on us and three cops jumped out running toward us.

"Freeze!" yelled one of them.

"What the *fuck*?" said Twon.

"Yo, what we do, son?" I said.

"I am not your son," yelled the other cop. "Get against the wall!"

"Why?" I said.

"Just get against the fucking wall!" The cop pushed me against the wall.

"Yo, what the fuck?" I looked at Quaid and Twon. Two officers had them against the wall already.

"Turn around and spread 'em!"

"What's going on?"

"Just do what I said!"

I reluctantly turned around.

"Spread your legs!" he barked. I did. He searched me slowly, fuckin feeling on me and shit.

"Yo, son, hurry up and do what you gotta do," I said.

"Didn't I tell you not to call me son?"

I turned to look at him. His face was red with anger.

"Face the fucking wall!"

I turned back around. "Fuckin breath stink anyway," I mumbled.

"What did you say?"

"Hype," said Twon.

"Shut the fuck up!" the cop yelled to Twon, then he put his face close to mine and said, "What the fuck did you say?"

"Nothing."

"That's what I thought, fucking wise ass. Now, we got a call a little while ago that you and your buddies here robbed a convenience store about a mile back."

"What?" said Twon.

"We just came from the basketball court!" said Quaid.

"Yeah, bullshit you did. Now, none of you have anything on you, so where'd you stash the guns?"

I was really getting' heated now. "We ain't got no guns, man!"

"Cut the bullshit! I know all about you gangbangers, and believe me, I will be glad as soon as I have you down at the station so you can get the fuck out of my face!"

"Yo, we ain't do nothing," I said.

"Oh, yeah? Well, you fit the description of the criminals the lady at the store described. She said there were three black males, and what do we have here?"

"Well, we ain't got nothing on us, so it don't look like you got shit to me," I said evenly.

"Oh, you got a lot of mouth, don't you?" He stepped to my face and put his gun to my head. "You're not so bad now, are you?"

"You can't do that!" said Twon.

"Shut your fucking mouth!"

"Get that gun away from my cousin!" said Quaid.

"I said shut it!"

"Hey, guys, we gotta go," said one of the officers. "The suspects were spotted over on Main Avenue."

"Are you sure?"

"Yeah, it just came in."

The officer lowered his gun. "Guess I'll have to catch up with you later, huh, punk?" He stared at me with a smirk then sauntered to the patrol car. The others followed, and they drove away. We stood there dazed, taking in what had just occurred.

"Man, I hate fucking cops, yo," said Twon.

When I got home, I took a shower and ate some food. I even watched TV, but I couldn't shake what had happened. Fucking cops are crazy. They can do whatever the hell they want, and you have no control. They just rolled up on us, searched us, one of them put a fucking gun to my head, then they left like nothing happened.

I was so edgy that when my phone rang, I nearly jumped outta my skin.

"Hello?"

"Is this Hype?" a male voice boomed.

"Yeah, who dis?"

"Don't worry bout that, nigga. Just know that when I see you, I'm-a fuck you up!"

"Man, cut the bullshit. Who is this?"

"You fucked around with my cousin Shena. She came to me all crying and shit, and she told me what you did to her."

"So the fuck what?" My temper was flaring up again.

"So I'm-a fuck you up. When I see your ass, it's over."

"Well, don't talk about it, be about it, nigga. You so bad, come see me right now."

"I'll see you when I see you." *CLICK*. I checked my phone to call back, but it was a private number, so I couldn't. Just my fuckin luck.

First the cops wanna fuck wit me, and now I gotta watch my back cuz some nigga after me. I sat back and thought about how my life was becoming more and more messed up by the day.

"I gotta change something, yo," I said to myself.

I briefly considered going to church regularly, as G-Ma suggested, but I decided against it.

"Nah, I got this on my own."

* * *

I slammed my locker door in frustration. It was only third period and I was having a fucked up day already. I had a test in my math class that I completely forgot to study for, and I left my essay at home for English, which meant the teacher would mark it down a grade just for being late. Shaneece kind of smiled at me, though. That made things a little better. But with the way this day was going so far, who knew what the next class would bring? I sighed and walked toward the stairwell.

"There go that bitch ass nigga right there!" I heard a voice say from behind. I turned around and saw four niggas comin' at me. I stood my ground. I knew all of them. One of them I had fought before, this dude named Ty. The other two, Rasheen and Shamel, were in my gym class. And the last nigga, Leevad, was somebody I never liked from jump. It was no surprise that he was the one doing the talking. "I told you I would catch up to your bitch ass, nigga!" He got in my face.

"Step off, B."

"What you say?"

"I said step off, B."

"The fuck you gonna do if I don't?"

"Ask your boy." I gestured toward Ty. He shrank back.

"Oh, you a tough guy now, huh?" Leevad stepped even closer. These niggas had me surrounded. "Let's see how that changes when I get through wit you." He swung at me, but I blocked it and pushed him off of me. Then I squared off. I was paying attention to all sides in case one of them other niggas tried anything.

"What's going on here?" Two school cops approached us.

"I'm 'bout to fuck this nigga up!" shouted Leevad.

"Yeah, let's see you do that, nigga," I said.

"None of that's going down," said one of the cops. They took us to mediation where they asked us questions that neither of us answered. Leevad tried to jump across the table at me, and one of the cops held him down. We both got suspended, me for a day and him for a week. My life is fucking crazy, yo. Something's gotta give.

Tierra

My mom was at work, and Twon and I were in my bedroom doing things we had no business doing. I knew if my mom came home and caught us, we would be in deep trouble. We were mostly just kissing and laying around, but I knew my mother definitely would not approve. At first, everything was cool, but then Twon tried to take things further. Whenever this happened, I got nervous, because I knew what was coming: He was going to start pressuring me for sex again, and I was going to have to let him down.

"Come on, baby. Why not?"

"Because I'm not ready."

"We gotta do it some day. Why not now?"

"Because…."

"Cuz what?"

"I just can't."

He sucked his teeth. "Man, you fucked up." He rolled over and got off of me.

"Twon, please…." My eyes filled with tears.

"*What*, Tierra? What?" Frustration was written all over his face. "What the fuck do I got to do to prove to you that it's gonna be a'ight? Ain't nothing bad gonna happen. What the fuck are you so scared of?"

"Stop yelling at me."

"IM NOT FUCKIN YELLING AT YOU!"

I jumped at his words. "Twon, yes you are."

"A'ight, a'ight, I'm sorry. But baby, what's goin' on? What are you so scared of?"

"I'm not scared of anything, Twon. I'm just not ready. I don't want to have sex yet."

"Well, when you gonna be ready?"

"I don't know. I just know that I'm not ready now."

"Man, you selfish. I'm leaving." He turned to go.

"Why? Why you always gotta leave, Twon? This is all you want lately. All you want is sex. Why can't we be like we used to be?"

"Cuz I'm a *man*, girl! Nigga's got needs!"

"Why can't you just wait?"

"Wait for what? And for how long? Why the fuck should I have to wait? You know I love you. You know I ain't goin' nowhere. So what the fuck?"

"Stop swearing at me."

"I'm not, Tierra. You keep skipping the subject." He sat down. "Baby, let's talk about this. Don't I make you feel secure? Don't you know I'm there for you?"

"It's not that ... it's just—"

"Then what is it?"

"I just feel like this isn't the right time. If we do it now, I feel like we would be rushing it."

"Tierra, we been together for a year — more than a year. How is us having sex right now rushing it? You know how many couples have sex after just two weeks? Two days, even. We been together a year and a half, and you talking about we rushing it."

"Twon, I can't even talk about this to you."

"Why not?"

"Because all you do is shoot me down. Every time I say something, you act like it don't mean anything. You make me feel so small, like what I say doesn't mean anything. I'm just not ready to give up my virginity to you. Why can't you accept that?"

He stared at me. Then he sighed and got up.

"A'ight. I gotchu. You aint ready for me." He put on his coat and started for the door.

"Are you mad at me?"

He just looked at me then walked out of my room, closing the door behind him.

* * *

Twon has been giving me the silent treatment all day. He barely even looks at me. I know I haven't done anything wrong, but I still feel bad. It was all I could think about in school, and then when I went to Quaid's house for our tutoring session, it was still heavy on my mind.

"What's wrong, Tierra?" said Quaid.

"Twon," I said.

"Ah, trouble in paradise. What's wrong with you two?"

"The same stuff I told you before." I told him what happened.

"Wow...." His voice trailed off like he didn't know what else to say.

"What do you think I should do?"

"I think you two should discuss this."

"But he's not talking to me!"

"Try to pull him aside. Get him alone. He'll listen."

"I don't know ... you sure?"

"Of course. He's just a little upset."

So the next day, I got Twon alone finally, during lunch. I caught him right before he went into the cafeteria.

"Twon!" He slowly turned around.

"What?"

"Can we talk? Please?" He made his way over to me.

"*Now* you act like you wanna talk."

"Twon, please. Can we do this without attitude?" He put his head down.

"A'ight." We went over to an empty stairwell and sat down. "So what you got to say?"

"I just want to talk about what's been going on with us. I know that we've been having problems lately, and I just wanna find a way to resolve it."

"Sometimes I don't think there is a way we can resolve this, Tierra."

"Why not?"

"Because no matter how much we talk about this, it always ends up the same way. I wanna have sex, and you don't. I'm ready, and you're not."

"So what can we do about it?"

"There ain't nothing we can do."

"So what does that mean?"

"It means what I said: there ain't nothing we can do."

"Twon?" My voice quivered. *Is he saying what I think he's saying?*

"Yeah?"

"Do you still love me?"

He stared at me strangely. "What do you mean?"

"I mean do you still love me like before, or is us not having sex making you love me less?"

He sighed. "I'm always gonna love you, Tierra. You know that, girl. We got history together."

"Okay."

"So don't think that just because you don't wanna do it I'm gonna feel any differently about you. You my heart, girl. I love the shit outta you."

My eyes welled up with tears. "For real?"

"Yeah, girl." He stood up. "Come on, baby. You ain't gotta cry. Come here, girl." He held out his arms. "What's the matter? What you crying for?"

Tears were rolling down my cheeks. I stood up, and he enveloped me in his arms.

"I can't help it. Sometimes I feel like I'm letting you down."

"Nah, baby, chill. It's not like that." He rocked me back and forth. "I get mad sometimes, but that's on me. Don't feel bad, girl."

"I love you."

He kissed my forehead. "I love you too, baby."

* * *

I was laying on my bed attempting to study for my math exam when my phone rang.

"Hello," I said, my droll tone betraying how bored I felt.

"Tierra?"

"Oh, hi Quaid!" I sat up and stretched. "How you doing?"

"I'm okay. What about you? How are things with Antwon?"

"We're cool. We made up the other day."

"Oh. That's nice." He sound like he didn't really mean it, like he was being polite.

"Yeah. He told me that he loves me and that us not having sex ain't gonna change how he feels for me."

"That's good."

"Yeah."

"So, what are you doing now?"

"I'm up here trying to study for this math test, but I just can't seem to understand it."

"Do you need help?"

"Yes."

"Well, you know you can come over again tonight for tutoring. When is your test?"

"Tomorrow."

"Tierra! Why didn't you tell me last time we met?"

"Um … I don't know."

"Come by my house, okay?"

"Right now?"

"Yes. You have to pass that test."

"Okay, I'm on my way."

I went to Quaid's house. He went over the problems with me and explained how to do them. His way was a heck of a lot easier to understand than the teacher's. He made it so simple for me. By the time we were done studying, I was damn near ready to teach the class myself.

"Quaid, you are so smart!"

"It's not a matter of intellect. It's just a matter of how you learn. You didn't understand it the way Ms. Andrews taught it because her way isn't the best way to do it. That doesn't mean you are any less intelligent. It just means she could probably teach it better."

"You're right about that! Well, thanks anyways for the help. Now I know I'm going to pass this test."

"You definitely are."

"Yeah." We sat there staring at each other for an awkward moment. Breaking the silence, I stood up and reached for my coat. "Well, I gotta go," I said, all brisk and efficient. "I'll see you later."

"No, wait." He grabbed my arm. "Why don't you stay for dinner? I'm about to cook."

I laughed. "You can't cook, Quaid!"

"Yes I can. I'll show you. Just stay for dinner."

"Okay, I guess so. I gotta see this."

He smiled. "Dinner will be ready soon. Wait here." I watched music videos for about half an hour as the house filled with the delicious aroma of food being cooked. He returned carrying two plates. He handed them to me while he got two TV table trays for our plates. He went into the kitchen then came back with two glasses filled with soda. He handed one to me and sat down beside me.

"So, what have you cooked for me? It looks and smells divine," I said.

"It's something I made up. I like to throw down in the kitchen, a bit of this and that, chicken, onions, rice. Taste it." He watched me as I took a bite.

"Damn, Quaid! You got skills!" I practically dove in. I hadn't noticed how hungry I was. I finished mine before he finished his. "I gotta come over here more often! You can cook, boy."

"Feel free," he said, chuckling. "I'm glad you enjoyed it."

"You sure you made this yourself?" I teased. "Or did your mom make it, and you just warmed it up?"

"Yes, I made it. I created the recipe for it."

"Wow. What made you think of doing something like this?"

"Well, I love to cook, and you know, we're not the richest of all families, so one day I was looking through the cabinets for something to eat and naturally, there wasn't much. So then I saw the chicken, the onions, the rice, and the wheels started turning. I put some seasoning on it, and I was done. It came out tasting pretty good."

"It sure did."

He finished his meal and stood up. "Let me get your plate."

I handed it to him along with my glass and followed him into the kitchen. He filled the sink with soapy water to wash the dishes.

"Let me do that. You shouldn't have to clean since you cooked."

"No, it's okay."

"No, I'll do it. Just let me go to the bathroom, and I'll be right back." I went to the bathroom, and when I came back, Quaid was placing the last dish in the rack. "Quaid! I said I was going to wash the dishes."

"Too late!" He smirked, waited a beat, and flicked soapy water at me.

"Oh, no you didn't." I rushed over to the sink and flung some at him. This sparked an all-out water fight. By the time we were done, we were soaked. "Boy, you are crazy," I said wiping the soap bubbles from my face.

"And you are beautiful."

I froze at those words.

Deflecting, I said, "Uh ... where's the mop at?" He pointed his thumb toward the little alcove next to the kitchen but didn't move to get it.

"Okay," I said with a grin. "I guess I'll have to get it!" I was making my way past him when I slipped on some soap on the floor and flipped backward. Quaid reached out to grab me, but I was falling so hard that he stumbled, and we ended up with my legs between his as we lay in a tangled heap on the floor. He lifted me up with ease, and we stood there staring at each other.

"I think we should clean up this mess before your mom comes home."

"Yeah." We cleaned in silence.

"Thanks for dinner, Quaid, and also for helping me study."

"Any time."

"See you later."

"Peace."

I walked home. When I got in the door, my mother was sitting on the couch watching *Law and Order, SVU.*

"Where you been at, girl?"

"Quaid's. He helped me study."

"Oh, that's cool. So you think you straight for that test?"

"Heck yeah. He taught me better than the teacher does."

"Damn. Sound like we need some Quaid around here!"

"Ma, you crazy." I laughed as I took off my coat.

"Why you all wet?"

"We got into a water fight." I told her what happened.

"Girl, you crazy. You gonna mess around and catch you some pneumonia out here."

"I know. We were acting like some straight-up fools."

"Sure was. But yeah, you better get in the shower and get to bed. You know how you don't like to wake up early in the morning."

"Alright, Ma."

"Good night, Tierra."

"Good night, Ma."

I made my way to my room and got ready for bed. After my shower, I hit the sheets. I tried to fall asleep, but I couldn't stop thinking about Quaid.

Why does he keep acting all strange whenever we're alone? Everything is just fine, and then he starts acting weird. I don't know what's up with that.

Twon

I was at Charles's house with Tierra watching *The 40-Year-Old Virgin*. Quaid was there too. We were at the part in the beginning where they all find out that Andy is a virgin. We all busted out laughing.

"Yo, this shit is funny as hell, nigga!" said Charles. This was his first time seeing the movie.

"I told you!" I said. Suddenly, the doorbell rang. Charles hopped up.

"Y'all mind if I pause it?"

"Go head, nigga."

He went and opened the door, and Hype walked in with this crazy ass look on his face.

"Wassup with you?" said Charles.

"Yo, I love you, man," said Hype. He hugged him. Charles patted his back a couple of times.

"I love you too, but what the hell is goin' on?"

"Matta fact, I love all y'all muthafuckas!" said Hype. "On some real shit, I do."

I stared at Hype. "Yo, nigga. What the hell is goin' on wit you?"

"I got my results back."

I immediately tensed up. "Yo, do *not* tell me that you got that shit." Yo, if Hype had that shit, I didn't know what I would do.

"Nah, nigga. I ain't got it, but I thought I did though, on some real," said Hype. "There was mad niggas there gettin' results for different things. There was a couple of girls too. They called everybody in, one by one. I was one of the last niggas to go. Yo, y'all shoulda seen how many people had that shit. You could tell who had it and who didn't just from how they acted when they walked out that room. At first, it ain't look too good, cuz niggas was comin' out one by one looking like they lost their lives. Then there was like two people who came out happy, so you know they ain't have nothing, but those other people ... man, that shit was crazy."

Hype looked more serious than I had ever seen him.

"Wow," I said. It was all I could think to say.

"Once I got my results and they was negative, nigga, I felt like crying. My life was that close to being basically over."

"Hell yeah."

"It felt like a blessing from God, yo, word up."

"I know."

"Yo, I'm-a change my life around, yo. Straight up. Cuz this shit ... I can't fuck wit no AIDS, yo. Ain't no pussy worth that shit."

"For real."

Charles looked horrified. "What you saying, Hype? You gon stop fuckin?"

"Man, hell naw!" said Hype. "I just meant I was gonna slow down. Maybe try to find one chick to mess with. Stick with her and shit. Make sure she ain't got that shit either, though."

"True," said Charles. "Maybe I'll think about settling down myself."

"I'm happy for you, Hype," I said.

"Me too."

The rest of the night went pretty good. When we finished watching *The 40-Year-Old Virgin*, we started *House Party Three*, but I fell asleep during that. When I woke up, Hype and Quaid were gone, Charles was passed out on the couch, and Tierra was leaning on me asleep. I watched her sleeping cuz she looked like a little angel, but then I had to wake her up.

"Baby." I shook her gently. "Baby."

"Hmmm?"

"You gotta get up. We got school in the morning." I helped her out the door and to the car. She fell asleep again on the way to her house. When we got there, I ain't feel like waking her up again, so I carried her to the door. Her moms answered it, and at first she was kind of mad because she had called both of our phones multiple times to see where we were, and because our phones were on silent, we had missed all of her calls, but then I explained to her that we had all fallen asleep watching some movies, and she understood. I carried Tierra to her bedroom and laid her on the bed. I tucked her in and kissed her on the forehead.

"Good night, my sweet angel." I went home and fell out.

* * *

"Checkmate." Quaid looked pleased with yet another win.

"Damn, nigga! That's the third game in a row! How you be winning like that?"

"You have to keep your focus," he said.

"I do, but it's mad hard to beat you, yo. You the only person I can't beat."

"That's because I am the man," he said.

"Nigga, shut the hell up." I laughed. "One day I'm-a get you."

"In your dreams."

"Whatever. Ey, what you get on that Physics exam?"

"B minus."

"I got a A plus. You not fuckin wit me!"

"I was tired."

"Whatever. What was you tired from?"

"Well, first of all, I was up until midnight helping Tierra study for her math test, then I hardly got any sleep because I had to study for the Physics exam, then I still couldn't sleep because Charles got arrested again, and his mother came over all hysterical because her 'baby' was going to have to spend a night in a cell. So I had to pay for Charles to get out, and that was some of our rent money."

"Damn. What's wrong with Charles? Why he always in some shit?"

"I don't know. I try constantly to tell him that there are better things out there than girls, drugs, and money, but he doesn't listen. He doesn't respect anybody. I don't see why Hype is always trying to protect him."

"Charles *is* his cousin."

"He's my cousin too, but I'm not getting myself caught up in any trouble with the police or all these thugs out here for him. Hype actually has a good chance of getting out of here. I don't see why he's jeopardizing that for Charles. That boy doesn't care about anything."

"I feel you, but that's family, man."

"I understand that, but it just frustrates me. And then my aunt is another story. I love her to death, but she doesn't ever push him in any area. She doesn't make him go to school, get a job, or nothing. And then, when Charles does something crazy, me and my mom, or Hype's mom, or G-Ma always have to bail him out."

"Yeah, that is crazy."

Quaid's cell rang. I could hear a female voice in the background.

"I'm sorry," Quaid said. "Yes, I'm busy. I'll talk to you later."

"Who was that?" I asked.

"This girl named Rasheeka. She calls me every day."

"You fuckin her?"

"Antwon. Calm down. I don't fuck anybody. If I was with a girl, I would make love to her."

"Whatever, nigga. So what's goin' on with you and Shorty?"

"Nothing much. She just calls me all the time. I think she likes me."

"Is she cute?"

"Yeah, she's pretty."

"So … are y'all talkin?"

"We talk from time to time. But I'm not interested in her."

"Why not?"

"She's not my type."

"What you mean?"

"She's too ghetto."

"So what? You don't like black girls or something?" He looked at me like I was out of my mind.

"Of course I like black women!"

"So what's wrong with Rasheeka?"

"She's *too* ghetto. I mean, I can deal with a girl who uses slang and does all the eye and neck rolling, but Rasheeka does it too much. There's nothing sweet about her. Nothing womanly. Besides, I like a woman of mystery. Rasheeka puts herself out there too quickly. She feels like she should have sex with me just to keep me, and I'm not that type of guy. I like a girl with enough self-esteem to stand up for herself and not mold herself around my wants. It has to be a mutual thing."

"Damn. That's deep."

"You should know what I'm talking about. Isn't Tierra like that?"

He caught me off guard with that one. I thought about it. "Yeah. Actually she is."

"You have a good thing with her, Antwon. If I were you, I'd stick with it."

"I am, but—"

"But what?"

"It's just ... yo, nigga, I'm-a tell you this, and you can't tell nobody."

"I'm listening."

"It's like ... I love Tierra. I really, really do. But she ain't givin it up."

"And?"

"And I'm a man, nigga! I need some pussy! I ain't fucked in so long."

"You have to be patient."

"I have been patient, but I don't know how much longer I can wait, yo. Sometimes I feel like I'm goin' crazy cuz I ain't had none in so long."

"Well, you know there are two sides to every relationship. Did you ever try to understand her side of things?"

"Yeah, sort of. She be saying that she just ain't ready and shit, but I feel like it's more than that. Maybe she just don't wanna lose it to me. Maybe she don't think I'm right for her. She been acting real weird lately too. I think she might be falling out of love wit me."

Damn. That would be the worst shit in the world if Tierra broke up wit me. I don't know where I would be.

"I don't think that's it," said Quaid. "I think maybe she's just scared, or maybe she's just really not ready to give it up. Losing your virginity, for a girl, is considered to be one of the most sacred things that can happen in life."

"I know, but damn. What's the worst that could happen?"

Quaid didn't respond. I could tell he felt like he'd said his piece. I don't know what's going on wit Tierra, but I hope she tells me soon.

* * *

I walked into my Physics class and sat in the back. I was the only one in the room. I always got there first cuz the class I got before it is right across the hall. I sat in my usual seat as the other students filed in talking and laughing with each other.

A dude walked in a couple of minutes after everyone was there and wrote his name on the board: Mr. Slevinski. So we had a sub.

He turned around to face the class. "Excuse me!" he said, and he waited for silence.

A couple of people turned around to listen to him. "I am your substitute for today. Mr. Richards had an emergency so he had to leave this morning. He didn't leave any work for you. He just said to begin reading the next chapter. If you need help with anything, I'll be right up here." With that, he went to Mr. Richards' computer, put on some headphones, and focused on the screen. So to me that basically meant that he ain't give a fuck what we did. Just then, Shaneece walked into the room and saw the sub. She looked around for a seat. When she saw me, she smiled and walked over.

"What's up?" she said. She turned the desk and chair around so that when she sat down, she was facing me.

"Nothing much. What up wichu?"

"I'm just chilling. I'm kind of happy Mr. Richards isn't here because I wasn't prepared. I didn't get to do much work last night because I got into a fight with my parents and I was too mad after that to do anything."

"Oh word? What you fight about?"

"The usual. They don't appreciate anything I do. They constantly compare me to my older sister. They want me to be like her because she's a registered nurse, but I'm not into the medical field at all. I'm just not that type of person. But they don't understand that. They're always complaining about everything I do, including my grades."

"Your grades? Don't you do good in school?"

"Yeah, I do. I get all As and Bs, but they want me to get all As. I'm not that smart. I can't do that."

"Damn, girl. That's crazy."

"I know."

"But you doing good, so I don't see what the problem is."

"Me either." She sighed.

"My mom is kind of like your parents, but different. She knows how I do in school, but she don't care. I could walk in the door wit straight As every marking period, and she wouldn't give a damn. Sometimes I think she only wants me around to help her pay the bills, and to order me around and run get her cigarettes for her, like that night you saw me walking home and you gave me a ride."

"Damn, that's messed up."

"I know, but I love her though. That's still my mom, regardless."

"Yeah, that's true. But you're a really good guy. One day she'll see what a blessing she has in you."

"Thanks for saying that."

"Any time."

"So what else been goin' on wichu?"

"Nothin' much really. Right now I'm looking for a man."

She took me by surprise with that one. I mean, she came straight out with it. I played it cool. "Oh word? For what?"

She gave me a sly little smile. "What do you think?"

For some reason, I had this funny feeling in the pit of my stomach.

"Girl, you crazy." I felt more nervous than I acted.

"I ain't crazy. Shoot, I ain't had none in a long time, not since I broke up with my ex, and that was before I moved here."

"Damn."

"I know, right? I'm just trying to find somebody out here who's a good guy and who I can connect with."

"Damn. You ain't found nobody yet?"

"Not really. Well ... sort of." She crossed her legs and leaned forward to show off her cleavage and her curvy hips. It took some serious effort on my part not to look.

"Oh word? Who is it?"

"I can't tell you who."

"Why not? Maybe I could hook y'all up."

"He has a girl."

"Oh. Damn. Are they serious?"

"Yeah. That's the worst part."

"Damn. That's fucked up. Well, maybe one day they'll break up."

"That's what I was hoping for, but I don't think it'll happen."

"How can you be so sure?"

"I don't know, actually. That's just my guess."

"Well, I'm sure you'll find another guy if this one don't work out."

"I know, but I really like this guy. Like, I'm really feeling him. Damn, he just doesn't know…." She got this dreamy look on her face. "The things I would do to him…." She swung her leg and smiled as the tip of her shoe touched my leg for a brief second.

I shifted in my seat and laughed nervously. "Girl, you wilin'."

"I know, but I can't help it…."

* * *

When I opened the door to let Tierra in, I just had to appreciate the view. "Damn, girl." I stared her up and down. "You lookin' good." She was wearing my favorite outfit: a pink crop top that showed her belly button and these tight ass jeans that showed off her curves.

"Boy, stop." She giggled. "I've worn this outfit plenty of times."

"I know, but you know what it does to me."

"Whatever." She stepped into the house. I watched her walk into the living room before I closed the door. I slid my arms around her waist from behind and rested my chin on her shoulder.

"So whatchu wanna do today?"

"I don't care. We could just chill if you want."

"How 'bout we chill here for a while, then we hit up the movies or something?"

"That would be cool. I want to see that new Tyrese movie."

"Yeah, me too."

"He is so fine."

"He don't look better than *me* though. Right?" She turned in my arms to face me.

"Right?" I repeated.

"I don't know about all that."

"What?" I tickled her. "Whatchu say?" She laughed and tried to break out of my grasp.

"Okay, okay," she gasped. "I was just playing." I tickled her a little more before I released her.

"That's what I thought," I said.

"Cheater."

"I ain't cheat. I just know how to win."

"Whatever. Bye." She pushed past me and started for the door. I spun her around.

"Where you think you're going?"

"I'm leaving."

"No you're not."

"Yes I am."

"Girl, what I just tell you?" I gently pushed her.

"Don't push me."

I pushed her again.

"I said stop!" She reached out to push me back, but I grabbed her arms and pulled them around my neck. I covered her lips with mine and kissed her slowly and sensually. She responded by tightening her arms around my neck, pulling me closer to her. I gently walked her backward until she was against the wall. Our kisses grew hungrier, more passionate. I lifted her up by her butt and she wrapped her legs around my waist. I carried her to the living room couch, slowly placing her down with me on top. I started caressing her body the way she liked it. Then I started sucking and kissing on her neck. She moaned with increasing passion as I grew more persistent.

I kissed her lower and lower, and then I lifted her top and kissed around her belly button. I started sucking on it, and she moaned more deeply. My hand crept up her leg and past her thigh to the space between her legs. I put a bit of gentle pressure on the spot, and she shivered at my touch. She always did that when I touched her there. It turned me on. I moved my kisses back up higher and higher while gently caressing that spot. Her moans were getting deeper and deeper, and I could feel her heating up. My hand moved to the button of her jeans, and I unfastened it. I pulled down the zipper then I slid my hand down there and pushed her panties aside. My finger was just beginning to explore her wetness when I heard a sharp intake of breath. She pulled my hand away. I looked at her face. She looked terrified.

"What's wrong?" I asked.

"I can't do it."

"You scared?"

She nodded slightly. "Yes."

"It's gonna be a'ight, baby. I won't hurt you."

"I know, but...."

"But what?"

"I … I just can't do it."

I stared at her for a couple of moments, and at first my anger started to build, then it subsided when I thought about how it must feel for her.

"I'm sorry, baby." I got off of her. She zipped her jeans and buttoned them.

"It's okay. I don't mean for you to think I'm tryin'-a pressure you. It's just that I can't help it sometimes."

"I know. Sometimes I can't help it either. I want you so bad, but … I can't explain it. Maybe we should go out and not be alone in the house together."

"Okay, let's get out of here."

She looked relieved and gave me her sweet smile. "Okay."

* * *

I had just got home Sunday night from working a twelve-hour shift. I was extremely tired, but before I drifted off to sleep, Tierra called and started talking my ear off. She went to Hype's grandmother's church that day, and she wanted to tell me all about the service.

"And you will never guess who I saw there today!"

"Who?"

"Hype *and* Charles."

"Bullshit."

"No, for real! They were sitting in the second row and listening to every word the pastor said. Then, when he called the prayer line, they were the first ones to get up. Isn't that crazy?"

"Hype and Charles in a prayer line at church." I couldn't believe it. "I never thought I would see the day. They must be really serious. Was Quaid there?"

"You know he was. He's there every Sunday. He's one of the most devoted people I know."

I reflected on her words. "Yeah, he is. Did your mom go with you?"

She paused. "No, she didn't go. I asked her, but she said she was tired. Why don't you come to church with me sometime?"

"I don't know. I thought about it, but I guess I'm just not ready."

"What do you mean?"

"I don't know. I just feel weird about it. Like, I know I should go, but—"

"Are you scared?"

"What? Girl, you crazy! I ain't scared." I laughed uneasily.

"You sure?"

"Yeah!"

"Then come with me next Sunday."

"Um...."

"Yeah, ummmmmmmmmm. Boy, you know you ain't right!"

"Whatever," I chuckled. "But listen. I gotta go though."

"Oh, for real? What you about to do?"

"My mother wanted me to do a couple of things for her. You wanna get together in like a couple of hours?"

"I can't. I have to study."

"Quaid helping you?"

"You know it."

"Tell him I said what up."

"I will."

"A'ight, I'll talk to you later then."

"Okay."

"Bye, baby. I love you."

"I love you too."

I was just finna jump in the shower when my phone rang.

"Hello? Twon?"

"Yeah, this me. Who's this?"

"Shaneece."

"Oh, hi, Shaneece."

"What's up?"

"Nothing. Just chillin'. I was 'bout to get in the shower cuz I gotta do some things for my mother."

"Oh, for real?"

"Yeah. Why? What's poppin' wichu?"

"Well, I was wondering if you wanted to chill with me."

"Doing what?"

"Nothing much. I was just so bored, and I wanted to walk around the mall or something. Maybe catch a movie."

"Oh, that sounds cool."

"So you're gonna come?"

"Yeah, sure."

"Okay, do you wanna meet up, or…?"

"I'll pick you up. I owe you one," I said with a smile, remembering the time she gave me a ride home.

"Oh, yeah, that's right!" She did that cute flirty little laugh she does around me.

"Yeah. So why don't you give me your address and I'll pick you up at like six."

"Okay. That's cool."

I wrote down her address and put the note on my dresser.

"A'ight, I'll see you later, Shaneece."

"Okay."

"Peace."

I contemplated calling Tierra to let her know where I was going, but decided against it. She knew that me and Shaneece were cool.

* * *

I was on my way to the store for my mom's cigarettes when I spotted Hype coming from one of the side streets.

"Eyo, Hype!" I yelled to get his attention. He turned around and grinned. I jogged up to him.

"Wassup, nigga?" I said, giving him dap.

"Nuttin much. I just got back from church a lil while ago."

"Yeah, I heard about that. So you and Charles is really serious, huh, about changing y'all lives around?"

"Yeah. Well, at least I am."

"What you mean by that?" We crossed the street.

"Charles walked into that church talkin' about how he was through wit dis playa shit, and he walked out with three girls' numbers."

"What?"

"Yeah! That nigga crazy. I was like, 'Charles, I thought you was slowin down, nigga.' He said that he was. I said 'How?' He said cuz if it was the old him, he woulda walked out wit six numbers." We both laughed at that one.

"Yeah, that nigga is crazy." I shook my head. "But what about you? You ain't see no fine ass shorties in there that you liked?"

"Well, there was a couple, but I wasn't there for that, nah mean?"

"Nah, not really."

"I mean, like ... this whole AIDS situation sorta opened my eyes. I ain't tryin'-a get that shit, yo. I'm tryin'-a be clean."

"Yeah, right nigga. You gon be clean 'til you see a fresh piece of pus—"

"Come on, nigga! Have some faith!" He pushed me.

"A'ight." I laughed. "A'ight. But I'm-a have to tell ya, judging from your past actions, I'm-a have to see this change before I believe it."

"Yeah, I know. It's gonna be hard."

"I know it is!"

"But there is this chick that I think I wouldn't mind settling down with for a while."

I glanced at him sideways. "Who?"

"That new chick Shaneece."

My ears could not believe what they just heard. My heart dropped. I kept my eyes averted. "Shaneece, huh?"

"Yeah." He noticed I wouldn't make eye contact with him. "What's up? She a THOT or something?"

"Nah, nah, I don't think so."

"So why you look all depressed all of a sudden?"

"I'm not depressed. It's just—"

"Just what?"

I shrugged my shoulders. "Nothing, man. Don't worry about it."

"You sure?"

"Yeah."

"A'ight."

I changed the subject. "So anyway, where was you 'boutta go?"

"To play ball. What about you?"

"I had to go do some shit for my moms, then I was goin' to chill at the mall with Shaneece."

"Shaneece? The same Shaneece I'm talking 'bout?" He stopped in his tracks and looked straight at me.

"Yeah."

"What you chillin' wit her for?"

I shrugged my shoulders. "She said she was bored, so she called and invited me."

"*Only* you?"

"Yeah. Why?"

"You and Tierra fightin' or suttin?"

"Nah, we cool."

"Do she know about this?"

"Nah, I ain't tell her."

"So ... what the fuck is goin' on?"

114

I stared at Hype. He was confusing me for real. "What you mean, what's goin' on?"

"I mean, why is you goin' to chill wit fine ass Shaneece *alone*, and your girl don't know about it?"

"What's wrong wit that? We're *friends*, Hype."

"Friends my ass. Me and you is friends."

"So is me and Shaneece."

He stared at me then sighed. "A'ight, Twon. Whatever. I ain't gon argue wichu. I'm just gonna tell you one thing: be careful." He turned toward the basketball court and started walking.

"Nigga, why is you ridin' me like this?"

He turned back. "Because of the smile on your face when I asked you what you was gonna be doin'." With that, he walked into the court.

"Whatever." Hype was just tripping.

* * *

I pulled up to Shaneece's house and honked the horn. She came out of the house looking fine. "You look nice," I said, trying to sound casual. She was wearing a red form fitting shirt with these tight ass black jeans and some red and black Jordans. She had her hair out and straightened.

"Thank you." She smiled. "Wow, this is a really nice car!"

It was my turn to smile. "Thanks. I saved up since I was twelve for some shit like this." I had a red Acura with tinted windows and red leather interior. My car was my baby. I kept it in top condition. I was currently saving up for some rims.

Shaneece got in the car and buckled her seat belt. "So, how's everything with you?" she said.

"It's cool."

"How's your mom?"

"She straight. What about you?"

"I've been alright mostly, but sometimes...." She trailed off.

I turned toward her. "What's going on?"

She faced the window then looked at me with puppy-dog eyes. "Sometimes I feel like I'm useless." Her bottom lip trembled, and the tears flowed from her eyes. It pained me to see her look so sad. Shaneece was a really sweet girl. I pulled into a nearby parking lot and stopped the car.

I squeezed her hand. "What's going on with you? You can tell me."

"It's just ... they make me feel like I'm nothing. They're always talking down to me."

"Who? Your parents?"

"Yeah." She sniffled. "They always compare me to my sister. They say I should be like her and make straight As. I should be a nurse. I should have gotten a full scholarship."

"What the hell?"

"My sister got a full scholarship to college. My mom and dad are beefing with me cuz I only got three quarters."

"What, they ain't got the money or something?"

"No, they have it, it's just that instead of getting a full scholarship, I got three quarters."

"I don't get it. You still covered, so what's the problem?"

"I don't know! They always find some reason, no matter what I do, to tell me I ain't shit. They're mad cuz I want to go to NYU instead of Harvard."

"NYU's a good school."

"Try explaining that to them."

"Damn, girl. You stressin'."

"I know." She wiped her eyes. "I'm really sorry for ruining your night, Twon."

"Nah, girl. Chill. You ain't ruining nothing. If anything, I feel closer to you now. Sometimes my mom be acting like that. Believe me, I know how you feel. My mom be acting like I ain't worth shit but the money I give her and the errands I run for her. No matter what I do to please her, it still ain't enough. And my dad? Don't even let me get started on *that* nigga. He washed his hands of me the day I was born, saying I was too damn light skinned to be a seed of his. Those were his exact words, according to my mom."

"What?"

"He accused my mom of cheating on him, then he left for good. He lives out in Las Vegas. I have never seen him in my life. He never writes, never calls, never even acknowledges my existence."

"Damn."

We sat in silence.

Finally, I said, "It's a fucked up life, but shit, you gotta rise above it."

"Yeah, I know."

Me and Shaneece had a pretty good night after that. We walked around the mall, ate dinner in the food court, then watched a movie. It was a very interesting night for me cuz I feel like me and Shaneece really connected. I could definitely see us becoming good friends.

* * *

Me and the boys were all playing Madden at Charles's house.

"So, Twon, how was your date?"

"For the last time Hype, me and Shaneece—"

"...is gettin too damn close to just be friends," he finished.

"Whatever, nigga."

Quaid looked interested. "What's going on between you and Shaneece?"

"Bangin' body Shaneece?" said Charles, and his grin said what he was thinking.

"Nothing's goin' on."

"Bullshit," said Hype.

"Yo, Hype. Why you keep pestering me about this shit, nigga? You act like you my girl or something. I told you wasn't nothin' going on. *Damn!*"

"You mean nothin' ain't going on *yet.*"

"No, I mean ain't nothin' going on at all. We just cool and that's it. We just friends."

"So why you be smilin' whenever somebody mentions her name?"

"Nigga, I don't be smil—"

"Yes, you do. Something's goin' on."

"Whatever, nigga. I ain't got time to argue about this shit."

"A'ight, I ain't gonna argue with you. I'm just gonna tell you to watch out."

"Watch out. Be careful. You're always giving me these warnings. What da fuck is that?"

"Just what I said." Hype leveled a steady gaze at me. I hadn't seen him look at me like that in a long time.

I sat back. "Whatever, nigga."

Charles busted out laughing. "Y'all niggas argue like a bunch of bitches!"

I glared at him, but I couldn't hold it back, and I laughed too. "Fuck you, Charles."

I was on my way home blasting "You Ain't Saying Nothing" by my man J. R. Writer when I noticed my phone ringing. I turned down the music and picked it up, but I had already missed the call. I looked to see who it was. Tierra. I called her.

"Hello?" she said.

"What up, ma?"

"Nothing. I was just wondering if you were still coming by today."

"Huh? Oh yeah! I forgot about that!" I quickly did a U-turn and headed toward her house.

"What you mean, you forgot? It was only this morning when you said you were coming!"

"I know, but I was at Charles's house wit the boys all day, and I forgot."

"I don't know what to do with you sometimes, Twon."

"I'm sorry, baby." I pulled up in her driveway. "I'm outside." I hung up and got out of my car. As I made my way up to her front door, she opened it. Her eyes brightened at the sight of me.

"Look at my man, looking all good." She wrapped her arms around my neck and kissed me on the lips. I wrapped my arms around her waist and squeezed her tight, lifting her off her feet.

"I missed you," I said softly.

"I missed you too." I put her down and released her, and we went into her house, closing the door behind us.

"So what you been up to all day?"

"Nothing. Just cleaning up a little."

"That's right, girl." I slapped her butt and watched it jiggle. "Clean it up real good for Daddy."

"Whatever, boy. It definitely wasn't for you."

"It *better* have been." I grabbed her by the waist and pulled her close, running my hands up and down her thighs.

"Well, it wasn't. What you gonna do about it?" She wrapped her arms around my neck and pulled me closer.

"This." I lowered my head down to hers and kissed her something fierce. Before long, we were all over each other. I lifted her up and had her against the wall with her legs around my waist. I kissed her hungrily, sucking on her lips. She ran her fingers up and down my braids, knocking my hat off. I stepped back and lost my balance. The back of my shoe caught the edge of an area rug and I tripped and fell on my back with Tierra on top of me. We didn't stop kissing. She slid her hands under my shirt and started feeling on my chest. I flipped her over and got on top. I grabbed her thighs and lifted her legs up. She wrapped them around me. I started kissing her all over her face. Then I kissed her chin and trailed down to her neck. I kissed the base of her throat, and she let out a deep moan.

"Twon," she breathed. "Stop." But I didn't. I kissed her, caressed her, and drove her crazy. I could tell she wanted it by the way her body responded, but then she went all stiff and said, "Stop," this time a little louder.

"Unh uh." I kept going. I lifted her top and caressed her stomach, moving my hands higher and higher. She released her legs from my waist. My fingers made their way to her back, and I unhooked her bra.

"Stop, Twon." She tried to push my hands away, but I persisted. I slid my hands over her breasts and stroked them. I felt her body stiffen. "For real, Twon. Stop it." She pushed me, and I got off of her. She re-hooked her bra and pulled her top down.

"You really get on my nerves sometimes, Twon."

"What you mean?"

She sucked her teeth. "You *always* trying to push up on me."

"What you talkin' 'bout?"

"You know what I'm talking about, Twon. You always try to go as far as you can."

"I can't help it."

"You can't or you won't?"

"I can't."

"Bullshit. You could control yourself if you wanted to, but you don't."

"Why are we arguing about this again?"

"Because I'm tired of your shit, that's why." She got up. I got up too.

"Tired of *my* shit? You ain't so fuckin innocent yourself, Tierra!"

"What?"

"You know what I'm talkin' 'bout. Don't try to front. You do just as much as me. You be leading me on like a mutha just to tell me to stop. But I don't never say shit to you about that, do I? Huh?" She was silent. "I'm tired of you always making me out to be the bad guy."

"Whatever." She crossed her arms.

"What you mean, whatever? Whatever nothing. You know I'm right, so admit it."

"Shut up, Twon."

"No. You wanted an argument, so now you got it."

"Get out."

"Oh, so it's like that? The minute you're wrong, I gotta get out?"

"I said get out, Twon."

"Whatever." I picked my hat up from the floor. "I ain't got time for this shit anyway." I went out the house and slammed the door behind me. I got in my car and drove away blasting "Writer's Block" again. Before long, my phone rang.

"What?" I said roughly.

"Twon?"

"Oh, wassup Shaneece."

"Are you okay?"

"Yeah, I'm a'ight."

"Oh, okay. Well, do you wanna chill today?"

I thought about it.

"Yeah, why not?" I needed something to take my mind off my troubles.

Shaneece

I was cheesing like crazy when I walked in the house after hanging out with Twon at the mall. We were there for hours, laughing, talking, window-shopping, and just having a good time together.

I kicked my shoes off and headed toward the stairs leading to my bedroom.

"SHANEECE!" I jumped at the booming sound of my father's voice.

"Yes?" I could feel the nervous tension rising within me.

"Come here, now!" His voice practically thundered through the house. As I walked to the kitchen, I had to clench my fists to keep my hands from shaking. When I entered the room, I saw my mother and father sitting at the table, and both looked livid. My father was holding a sheet of paper in his hand. "What did we tell you about this?"

"Tell me about what?"

"Don't play stupid, Shaneece. You know what we told you about your grades."

"What do you mean? I haven't brought any new grades home—"

"THIS!" He cut me off, flinging the paper toward me with disgust. The paper fluttered to the floor. I picked it up. "We found it in your room. What, did you think you could hide it from us?"

I looked at the paper then back at my father. "This isn't a real assignment. This is just a draft."

My mother spoke up. "What do you mean, it's just a draft?"

I looked at her. "We had to trade drafts of our papers for our English class. We had to give each other grades as if we were the teacher."

"And you're telling me that even your fellow classmates see that your writing is horrible? They gave you a B-minus? You know better than this!"

I looked back at my father. "Dad, it's just—"

"I DON'T CARE IF IT'S JUST A DRAFT!" He banged his fists on the table and stood up. I took a step back, my heart racing, fear in my eyes.

"Shanelle NEVER would have brought home any trash like this!"

"It's not a real grade, though," I said, my voice trembling. A tear slipped down my cheek.

"Stop crying. You're just making excuses. You better get these grades up immediately or we will take that car."

"Take my car?"

"Take OUR car," my mother corrected. "That car is in OUR names. We just let you drive it — for the time being, at least."

"Shaneece, I'm not playing with you." My dad glared at me. "You better bring home an A on this paper or the car is gone."

"When is the paper due?" said my mother.

"Friday."

"And when will your teacher return it?" asked my father.

"Monday."

"So on Monday, we better see an A, or you will be taking the bus to school. Now, take that to your room and start revising it now."

"But it's not due—"

"NOW!"

I went to my room feeling numb, and when I felt safe behind my locked door, I broke down and sobbed.

* * *

My parents barely spoke to me all weekend after seeing the draft of my English paper. But all of that was about to change. I pushed as hard as I could and got the grade they demanded.

"I'm so glad this is over," I said under my breath as I entered the house. I softly closed the door behind me and walked into the kitchen. My parents were sitting at the table in the same positions they were in when they saw the draft.

I decided to ease into the conversation. "Hi, Mom, Dad."

"Do you have the paper?" My dad barked at me.

"Yes." I handed it to him with confidence.

He quickly scanned through it, not reading it, but searching for the grade. He flipped it over to the back where the teacher had written some comments and my grade.

"The fuck is this?" he said, glaring at me before handing it to my mother.

She shook her head with disappointment.

"What do you mean?" I said.

"We TOLD you to get an A!" My father stood up.

"I got an A."

He banged his fist on the table. "Shaneece, don't FUCK with me. This is an A-minus!"

"Dad, it's—"

"Give me your keys."

"Why?"

"You didn't hold up your end of the bargain. Give me the keys. Now."

"No," I said boldly, in a voice so filled with confidence that I barely recognized it.

"What did you just say to me?" He stepped closer. I stepped back.

"I said no." My confidence waned as he moved even closer. I stepped back again, and now I was against the wall, cornered. I gulped. "I worked hard for that grade, and I earned an A. You can see it right on there. That letter is an A!"

"Who in the HELL do you THINK you're talking back to?"

My mother stood up from her seat. "Give him the keys, Shaneece. NOW." Her eyes narrowed as she dared me to defy her.

I reluctantly handed my car keys to my dad. "This isn't fair."

SMACK!

I landed on the floor holding the left side of my face. It was burning from the impact.

"DON'T YOU PUT YOUR HANDS ON HER LIKE THAT!" My mother screamed at my father as she pushed him. Silent tears streamed down my face as I watched them.

"She had no right to disrespect us in our house," my father said.

"I don't care. You hit her in her face. She's still our daughter." She turned to me. "Shaneece, go to your room."

I got up slowly and walked toward the stairs.

"I'm sorry," my father said in a sullen voice, but I knew he wasn't.

* * *

I put some makeup on to cover up the handprint my dad left on my face as I got ready to take the bus to the mall to find a job. If my parents refused to give my car back, I was just going to have to get a job, save up all my paychecks, and get my own car, like Twon did. I was sick of them controlling my life.

I put on a professional outfit and made my way downstairs. Without saying a word, I walked past my mother, who was sitting on the living room couch reading a magazine. I was about to open the front door when she said, "Where do you think you're going?"

"To the mall."

"How are you getting there?"

"The bus."

"Do you even know how to take the bus, Shaneece?"

"Yes, I printed out the schedule with all of the stops." I held it up to show her.

"How long are you going to be there? When are you coming home?"

"I don't know. Just a couple of hours."

"Wait. Let me see your face." She got up and walked toward me.

"It's fine, Mom. I covered it up." She flicked on the light and stared at my face, gently moving my chin from side to side with her hand.

"How does it feel?"

"I'll be okay." I swallowed.

"You know your father is sorry, right?"

"Yup."

"Shaneece, we just want the best for you."

"I understand."

She stared at me for a few moments. "Okay. I'll see you when you get back."

"Okay."

I walked out of the house and to the bus stop, blinking back tears the entire way there.

* * *

I got to the mall about an hour later. It took a lot longer than if I had driven there. I went to a couple of places to see if they were hiring, and two of them actually gave me paper applications to fill out. The other three said that all of their applications were online.

I sat in the food court filling out the applications. I was so engrossed in my work that I didn't notice someone standing right in front of me.

"Hey," said a male voice. I looked up. It was Hype.

"Hey," I said. I gave him a little smile.

"You looking really beautiful today."

"Thank you."

"What you doing? Mind if I sit down?" He grasped the top of the chair across from me.

"Um ... no ... I mean, sure, you can sit here."

"So what you doing?" He stared at my applications.

"Trying to find a job."

"Oh really? Well, my boy is a manager over at Sports Locker. I could tell him to hire you if you want."

"You would do that?" I raised my eyebrows at him. That was one of the stores that had given me a paper application to fill out.

"Sure. On one condition." He smirked.

"What?" I eyed him suspiciously.

"Let a nigga take you out." He sat back with his arms crossed over his chest.

"That sounds like a setup to me," I countered with a smile.

"Why it gotta be a setup? You single, I'm single. I think we would be a good match."

"Oh really? So just because we're both single, that automatically means we're meant for each other?"

"Only one way to find out."

I stared at him considering his words. He definitely wasn't bad looking. In fact, he was sexy as hell, and girls always fell all over him at school. But the only thing was, he had a horrible reputation of being a player. But from what I had heard, he was very skilled in the bedroom, and I hadn't had any in a very long time. I definitely still wanted Twon, but it didn't look like he and Tierra were breaking up any time soon. Maybe Hype could fulfill my needs for now, and then I would get with Twon later. By that time, Hype would probably be ready to move on to the next girl anyway....

"Okay. That's fine with me," I finally said.

"Cool." He smiled. He reached in his pocket and pulled out his phone, extending it toward me. "Put your number in my phone."

I took the phone. "Wait, what was your name again?"

He chuckled. "Oh, for real, ma?" He licked his lips. "You trying to play me like that?"

"No, I really don't remember your name."

"Whatever." He rolled his eyes. "My name is Hype. So what you like to eat?"

"What do *you* like to eat?" I stared at him with flirty eyes.

He held up his hands. "Whoa, wait. Hold up now. Don't talk to me like that if you ain't ready for this."

"Boy, bye. You just better make sure *you're* ready for *this*."

His eyes lit up with excitement. "Oh for real? It's like that?"

"Exactly like that."

"Okay, okay. Well, how about you finish your application, and then we walk it over to my boy Jamel. After that, we can head over to my crib and you can show me what you got."

"Sounds good to me, but you better have your game up because I've been known to give niggas a run for their money."

"You know what?" He said, his excitement apparent on his face. "I think you and me is going to get along just fine."

* * *

Hype definitely lived up to my expectations. I would even go so far as to say he exceeded them. The girls at school were not lying when they said he had SKILLS! I was on cloud nine the whole bus ride back home, and as I walked to my house, I was already contemplating the next time I would see him.

I was so lost in my thoughts that I bumped into my father as I made my way to the stairwell.

"Dad!" I exclaimed, jumping back.

"Who the FUCK is Twon?" he boomed.

"What?" My mind was racing. How did he know about Twon?

"You know what I'm talking about. I found *this* on your laptop." He threw some papers in my face. I blinked from the impact then reached down to pick them up. I looked them over nervously, then my nervousness turned to disgust mixed with anger. My father had printed out screenshots of every conversation me and Twon had on my social media messenger system. I must have left the app open when I went to the mall!

I could barely believe my eyes. "You *read* my messages?"

"You heard what I said, Shaneece. Who the fuck is Twon?"

"He's my friend, Dad. That's it."

He stepped closer. "Don't play with me, girl. Are you seeing him?"

"No. He's just my friend. Why did you read my messages?" I felt totally violated.

"This is MY house. I can read whatever the hell I want. If you say you're just friends, then why are you using all of these emojis?"

"Dad, I use those with everyone. We're just friends—"

"Prove it!"

"What? How?

"You know I don't allow boyfriends while you're still in high school, especially with those disastrous grades you've been bringing home. Prove it. Call him up right now in front of me, and put him on speaker phone."

"And say what?"

"Let me speak to him."

"No, Dad. He doesn't even know you!" My face was heating up with embarrassment.

"Okay, then you speak to him. Let's see if he says you're just friends. Prove it. Call him right now."

"Dad, this is ridicul—"

"CALL HIM NOW!"

Tears streamed down my face as I pulled my phone out of my back jeans pocket, dialed Twon, and put the phone on speaker.

He picked up the phone after the first ring.

"Hey girl, what's up?" he said, a smile in his voice.

"We're just friends, right?" I said coldly.

"Um … yeah. Why?"

"Nothing. I'll talk to you later."

I hung up the phone and stared at my father.

"See?" I said, totally humiliated.

"Good. You better stay just friends. I better not see anything even resembling a relationship between you two. You are to focus on your grades and nothing more. You hear that?"

"Yes."

"And you better not even think about creating another profile, or deleting messages, or doing any of the other stupid stuff you kids do to try to cover shit up. I know about it ALL, hear me?"

My dad was the director of IT at one of the local colleges, and he specialized in all things technology.

"Okay."

"I'm serious, Shaneece."

"I heard you."

"Now go upstairs and do your homework."

"Okay."

I walked upstairs to my room, wondering how I could possibly ever talk to Twon again.

Hype

Dang, that was easy as fuck! I never thought I would pull a girl as fine as Shaneece using that lame ass corny nigga game. But somehow it worked, and to make things even better, I already got her in my bed. I have to admit, I didn't think she would give it up that fast, but hey, I'm cool with it since she's the only girl I'm dealing with. This settling down shit might not be too bad after all.

My phone rang. I looked at the caller ID. It was Tierra.

"What's up?" I said.

"Are we still filling out scholarship applications tomorrow?"

"Dang, I can't even get a hello?"

"Shut up, Hype." She giggled. "Are we?"

"Yes."

"Okay, bye."

"Girl, if you hang up that phone—"

"You know I'm just playing, Hype. What you been up to?"

"Well … actually, I got myself a little thangy thang."

"*What?*"

"A new little girlfriend."

"A *girl*friend?"

"Yeah."

"I thought you didn't do relationships."

"Well, like I been telling everybody, I'm settling down and sticking to one girl from now on."

"Pssssht. I don't believe that for one second, Hype."

"Why nobody believe me?"

"Because you can't just change that quick."

"Why not?"

"Because … but anyway, let me ask you a question."

"A question about what?"

"What do you have to do to be saved?"

"Huh?" I raised my eyebrows.

"To be saved. What do you have to do? I want to make sure I go to heaven when I die."

This chick was buggin! "Uhhhh …Tierra?"

"What?"

"Is everything okay with you?"

"Yes, but I really want to know."

"I mean, you ain't trying to die tonight, are you?"

"No, silly. I just want to make sure I'm okay with God."

"I think you and God is cool. It's *me* and God that might have a problem."

"Whatever. So anyways, do you know what I have to do, or no?"

"No, I don't. That's really a question for Quaid or G-Ma."

"I'm kind of scared to ask G-Ma though."

"Why? She's cool."

"Yes, she is, but I don't know. It's like sometimes I feel like she can see right through me."

"Girl, go to bed! You been watching too many scary movies or something."

"I'm serious, Hype. I really want to know. Can you ask her for me?"

"Hell no!"

"Why not? I thought you said you were trying to change your life around," she said that last bit in a deep voice, play-mocking me.

"Don't try to turn this on me so I can do your dirty work."

"Come on, Hype!"

"A'ight, if you don't want to ask G-Ma, then ask Quaid. You ain't scared of him, are you?"

"No."

"A'ight then, problem solved. Quaid's your man."

"Boo, you are so wack. I can't stand you."

"You know you love me."

"Whatever."

"Or at least your mother does."

"Bye, Hype."

I burst out laughing. "Come on, you know I'm playing."

"Whatever. I'll see you tomorrow."

"A'ight. Tell Twon I said call me if you talk to him."

"Okay."

"Bet." We hung up.

I wonder why Tierra's all worried about being saved all of a sudden?

* * *

I walked into class on Monday feeling like a brand new man. Shaneece was badder than a mutha, and her bedroom skills was on point. Shorty might actually be a match for me, yo, word up. I never thought I would actually meet a chick that could possibly break me, but shit, this might be it. My eyes scanned the room looking for her. I saw Tierra sitting off to the side, looking like she was lost in thought. *Probably thinking about being saved and shit.*

I would have to talk to Quaid later and help her get her mind off all that. Shoot, I figure since she was helping me with scholarship applications, the least I could do was help her out with this situation. But for right now, my mind was pretty much set on seeing what was up with Shaneece. I continued to scan the room. I finally spotted her, but I hardly recognized her because what she had on was nothing like her usual stylish clothes. She was wearing black pants, a black hoodie, and a black snapback cap on her head, facing forwad. *The fuck? Is shorty trying to avoid me or something?*

Nah, I brushed that thought off real quick. There was no way she could be avoiding me, especially the way she was moaning and calling my name the other night after we left the mall. I made my way over to her.

"What's up, girl?" She looked up, a gloomy expression on her face.

"Oh, hey," she said dully.

"Fuck wrong with you?"

"Nothing. Just problems at home."

"What's going on at home?" I leaned closer to her so she could tell me what was up. I wasn't really used to having girls vent their frustrations to me as far as a relationship was concerned, but I'd had enough conversations with Tierra to know that females sometimes needed to vent, and they just needed somebody to hear them out while they did it. So I was going to be all ears, especially since I was planning on making shorty my girl.

"Nothing. Just my parents." She looked so depressed that I actually felt concerned. That was weird for me. I had never really got too concerned about any girl because I never cared about any of them. I was just in it to hit it and quit it, but there was something different about Shaneece. For some reason, I felt drawn to her, like I really wanted to help her instead of just being with her for sex. I might need to talk to Quaid about this shit or something, cuz I ain't used to having no soft ass feelings like this.

"What's up with your parents? Y'all had an argument or something?"

"I really don't want to talk about it right now. You want to skip last period and fuck?"

My eyes snapped at her words. "Huh?" Then I registered what she said. "Uh, yeah. That's okay with me. We could go to my crib. We could even talk about your home troubles if you want."

"I don't want to do any talking." She shot me a seductive look. My stomach filled with butterflies. At first, I thought she was on some emotional shit, but I guess not. Shorty seemed like she had a different mindset than these other chicks, but I could get down with it. Don't get me wrong, I was willing to listen to her vent out her emotions and all that, but if she just wanted to cut to the chase, that was fine with me too.

* * *

Me and Shaneece had just finished our third round together after school. We had been skipping random classes and lunch together for weeks, meeting up to have sex. We couldn't get enough of each other. She had so many tricks in the bedroom, I could feel myself definitely getting used to this whole 'settle down with one chick' shit.

"Where you going, ma?" I said as she jumped up from the bed, putting her clothes on in a hurry.

"I gotta go to work. Damn, I'm gonna be late!" She groaned.

"Well, you been working every day. Can't you take a day off or something?"

She looked at me. "No, I'm trying to save up for a car."

"What happened to the car you had?"

"My parents took it from me."

"Oh, damn. That's fucked up, ma. I wish I had some wheels. I would definitely drop you off."

"Thanks. Do you see my other shoe anywhere?"

I got up from the bed and helped her find her shoe. "Here you go," I said, handing it to her.

"Thanks."

"Matter of fact," I said, reaching for my phone. "Let me call this nigga Twon. He got a whip. I'm not sure if he's working today, but if he's not, I'm sure he wouldn't mind giving you a ride."

"NO!" she said.

She kind of startled me with how aggressively she said that. "Why not? I'm trying to help you out."

"I can't risk my parents finding out about our relationship. They're already riding me like crazy. I can't take it if they find out about this too."

I looked at her sideways. "And how exactly is Twon giving you a ride to work gonna alert your parents to our relationship?"

"Like I told you, my dad pops up on me everywhere. He actually comes to my job to make sure I'm working. He watches me way too closely for me to be caught in a car with a boy."

"So, even if Twon is just giving you a ride to work, your dad would still trip?"

"Yes."

This situation was unbelievable. I had heard of controlling, abusive fathers, but I had never actually seen it with my own eyes. I felt really bad for Shaneece. I wished there was something I could do for her.

She looked at her phone. "I gotta get to the bus stop."

"You want me to walk you?"

"No. I already told you, I can't risk anyone finding out about us."

Me and Shaneece had been keeping our relationship a total secret. Absolutely no one knew about us except us. I hadn't told my boys, Tierra, G-Ma, nobody. They all knew I had a girlfriend, but whenever they asked who she was, I just told them I would let them know when it was time. So me and Shaneece had to be strategic about our shit. We never walked together anywhere, we barely talked in class, we didn't eat lunch alone together at school, nothing. Shit's crazy.

Usually, I'm hiding who I'm messing around with because I don't want all of my women finding out about each other, but now I had finally settled down, and I couldn't tell anybody about it. Shit was frustrating. I was getting tired of it, but at the same time, I been catching mad feelings for Shaneece. That was something totally new for me, so I wasn't really sure how to handle it. I tried to be there for her the best I could, but she didn't really seem like she wanted to open up to me like that. Maybe it would just take time.

"After our last class tomorrow?" Shaneece waited for me to respond.

"Huh?" I had been so lost in my thoughts that I hadn't even realized she was talking.

"I said, do you want to skip and meet after our last class tomorrow?"

"Oh, for sure. No doubt."

"Okay. See you tomorrow then."

"A'ight." We hugged and kissed, and then she left. I had to find a way to help her out with her situation.

* * *

I walked into Quaid's house after school on Friday. Shaneece had to work directly after school, so we didn't get a chance to meet up. I wanted to talk to Quaid about the whole Tierra situation, so I decided to stop there early before everybody met up to play basketball.

"Hey, Auntie," I said, giving Quaid's mom a hug and a kiss on the cheek. Quaid was on his laptop staring intently at the screen.

"Eyo, Quaid. Let me holla at you for a second."

He held his hand up. "Hold on a second. I'm almost finished submitting this application."

"Where you applying to?"

"UCLA."

"Word? Doing big things, cuz!" I said, cheesing.

"I just wish Charles would stay in school and do good like you two," said Quaid's mom.

"You mean like Quaid does," I said. "My grades is not really up to par like that."

"But you're not failing or anything are you?"

"No, but I don't make straight As and Bs like Quaid either. I'm mostly a C student."

"Hype, all you have to do is apply yourself more. You can get As easy."

"I'm not really into the whole school thing like that."

"Why not?"

"To be honest, I don't really see the point in it."

"Oh, don't start talking like that, boy. Now you sounding like Charles."

"Charles isn't all bad, Auntie."

"I know he's not, but he's not into school like you guys, he doesn't work, he doesn't do anything. It's sad to say, but the road he's taking, it's only a matter of time…." Her voice trailed off.

"Don't think like that, Auntie. Charles will get better. We'll talk to him."

"Yeah, well, y'all do that, please."

"We will."

"Alright, well I'm about to go to the store right quick. I'll be back."

"Okay, Auntie. Love you."

"Love you too, Hype. See you later, Quaid."

"See you, Mom."

I turned to Quaid. "You done yet, nigga?"

He closed his laptop and turned around to face me. "Yup. What's up?"

"What you know about being saved and shit?"

"Being saved?" He said this slowly as if trying to wrap his mind around this subject. He looked shocked that I was asking him. "You want to be saved? You want to learn about salvation?" He looked eager. I held my hand up before he started shouting hallelujah or something.

"Hold your horses there, boy. It's not for me. It's for Tierra."

His shoulders slumped slightly. "Oh." He perked up a little. "Why is she asking about it? Does she want to be saved?"

"I think so. She was asking me about it the other day, but I ain't know, so I told her to ask either you or G-Ma."

He stared at me intently. "And what did she say then?"

"She was scared to ask G-Ma, so I told her to ask you. She never brought it up?"

"No, not yet, but we had to cancel our last tutoring session because she got into an argument with Twon."

Something about the way he said that sounded a little off, but I didn't say anything. It was probably nothing.

"Oh, for real? Well, can you explain it to her or something, cuz shorty is buggin'."

"Bugging how?"

"She's worried about going to hell and shit."

"Well, it sounds like she might be in the right frame of mind then."

I stared at Quaid, confused. "Huh? What you mean?"

"If she's worried about going to hell, then she's probably ready to be saved."

"So, you're saying that if a person isn't saved, they go to hell when they die?" I looked at Quaid as if he was speaking a different language or some shit. This shit just got real.

"Yes. Anyone who doesn't accept Jesus Christ as their Lord and Savior, who doesn't believe that He was raised from the dead to save them from their sins, will not be saved. You also have to confess this out of your mouth, but you have to believe it first before you confess it."

"You serious, nigga?" I never heard no shit like this before! Tierra's ass might be on to something.

"Yes. What did you think being saved meant?"

"I don't know." I shrugged. "I guess I thought it meant being a good person so you could go to heaven."

"Being a good person is a part of salvation, but it doesn't lead to salvation."

"So even if you're a good person, you can still go to hell?"

"Yes."

"But why would God send a good person to hell?"

"It's not that God sends good people to hell. God doesn't want any of us to go to hell. That's why He sent Jesus to die for us. We were sentenced to hell from pretty much the beginning of time. You remember the story of Adam and Eve?"

"Yeah. That was when Adam and Eve ate the apple and shit, right?"

"Yes. Before that, sin didn't exist in the world. But once they did that, it brought sin on all of us, because every child that was born after that came from them, all the way down to us. And because of that, we all are born sinners. We can't help it. God recognizes that we can't help ourselves, and that's why He sent Jesus to come down to earth and be born as a baby, live a human life, and die for us, so He could take the punishment for our sins. He died in our place, so now, the only thing we have to do to be saved is believe that He is the Son of God, and we have to confess, which means we have say openly in front of others that He is our Lord and Savior. Does that make sense?"

"Yeah, that makes a lot of sense, actually. So God was looking out for us when He sent Jesus."

"Right."

"And Jesus just straight died, no fight or nothing? He just gave up His life, just like that?"

"Yes. He was nailed to a cross while He was still alive. It's called crucifixion, and it was the most horrible form of punishment the Romans used against criminals at the time, but Jesus was the innocent Son of God. He gave up His Spirit and died on the cross for us, but He rose from the dead after three days then ascended into heaven."

"Damn. I never really heard it like that before." I sat back in my seat, deep in thought. Quaid had just dropped some serious knowledge on me. Before this conversation, I never even knew what it meant to be saved, or that there was something I had to do to get it. I figured as long as I lived a good life, I would be good with God. I guess not. It sounds like I got some serious thinking to do cuz I ain't on that hell shit either.

"So what do you think?" said Quaid. "Do you want to be saved?" He paused and waited. I was busy thinking. "I know you asked for Tierra, but we all need to be saved, Hype."

"That's true, but I ain't ready to be all perfect and shit."

"You don't have to be perfect. In fact, none of us are, or even can be. That's one of the reasons Jesus died for us, because He knew we could never live up to God's standards by ourselves."

"That makes sense, but a nigga ain't really ready for all that right now."

"Why not?"

Before I had a chance to answer, the doorbell rang. Saved by the bell! "That must be Twon and them."

"Yeah. I'll be right back." Quaid got up to get the door.

"What y'all niggas doing?" said Twon as he and Charles came in, dapping us up.

"Nothing, getting ready to bust y'all ass in some two on two."

Twon chuckled. "Yeah, a'ight nigga. We'll see about that."

We grabbed some water bottles from the fridge and headed out the door.

* * *

I been thinking about that conversation that me and Quaid had for a couple days now. That shit was deep as fuck. On some real, it was kind of bothering me that I wasn't saved. It wasn't haunting me day and night like when I was having those AIDS nightmares, but the shit was still on my mind heavy. I understood where Tierra was coming from. I mean, sure, G-Ma had been trying to get me into the church pretty much all my life, and I did go sometimes, and even when I went, I listened, but I guess it never really clicked with me that I was supposed to actually apply it to my life. Shit's crazy.

On another note, me and Shaneece haven't really been hanging out that much lately because she been working so much and shit. We was spending so much time in my bedroom for that first month that I had already caught feelings for her though. I was trying to give her space so she could get her whip and shit, but this whole shit about not seeing each other then never being able to tell anyone about our relationship was getting old. So I decided to do the forbidden. I decided to call her phone after 10:00 p.m.

"Stop!" she said to someone else, laughing as she answered the phone. "Hello?"

"Who you saying stop to?" I said, heated all of a sudden.

"Hold on." A couple of moments passed, and then she came back to the phone. "Hype, I just realized this was you calling me. Why are you calling me after ten?" She sounded like she was mad, but I was already heated, so fuck it.

"Who was you saying stop to, Shaneece? And where the fuck you at?"

"I'm at work! I told you I don't get off 'til eleven!"

"It don't sound like you at work to me! Sound like you got a nigga somewhere, if you really wanna know what I think."

"Well, nobody asked what you think. If you ask what I think, you sound like a female right now."

"Bitch, what?" I hopped off my bed full of rage. "Say I won't come to that job and beat the fuck out of whatever nigga you wit right now."

"You would really come to my job and get me fired? That is so childish!"

"You know what? Bitch, fuck you with your uppity ass attitude. This bullshit is over. Fuck it." I didn't bother to wait for a response. I hung up the phone and deleted her number. This relationship shit just wasn't for me.

The next day, I found myself looking through my call history and adding her number back in. Fuck it. I guess I really did have feelings for Shaneece, even though she was acting like a bitch. I decided that she really had no reason to lie to me about being with some nigga at her job. Besides, she said her dad be pulling up on her and shit, so she probably wouldn't risk that shit anyway. So I decided to give her the benefit of the doubt.

I decided to call her at one of our acceptable times.

"Hey," she said, answering the phone.

"Hey. Ey, my bad about what I said last night. I just had a lotta shit on my mind."

"That's fine."

"We good?"

"Yeah, we're fine."

"So, when's the next time you want to link up?"

"How about during lunch period tomorrow? We could meet in the locker room again."

"Cool. I can't wait."

"Me either."

"Alright, I'll talk to you later."

"Okay." We hung up. Our phone conversations never lasted more than a few minutes because Shaneece didn't want her father getting suspicious. She said he checked her phone records daily, and if he saw any phone conversation over ten minutes, he automatically assumed it was a boy, no matter what name the number was saved under. Shaneece had me saved under some random female name. At first I thought that shit was weird as fuck, but once I learned more about her situation, I realized she had to do what she had to do.

* * *

Me, Twon, and Charles were riding home from watching *Straight Outta Compton*. Quaid was at church. We was turned the fuck up, especially with all the hot music they was playing. Charles had already bought the soundtrack before we went to see the movie, so we were bumping it in the car on the way home.

"Yo, nigga, you see that?" Charles whipped his head around to get a second look.

"Yeah, nigga. Shorty got a fatty." We stared at the girl as she walked down the street, all of our eyes focused on her behind.

"Eyo, bay-bee!" Charles yelled out the window. The girl looked at us as we passed but kept walking. "Y'all see that?" He sat back with a big smile on his face. "I definitely could have pulled that, especially since y'all niggas is all wifed up and shit."

"Hype, when you gonna let us know who your girl is?" said Twon.

"I'll tell y'all when it's time."

"Whatever, nigga, wit your mysterious ass."

We saw some blue lights flashing at a standstill in the distance. Just as we were approaching them, the song "Fuck the Police" began to play.

"Eyo, nigga, turn that shit up!" I said, looking at Charles with mischief in my eyes.

"Nigga, you crazy," said Twon.

"Come on, nigga! Hurry up, before we pass them!"

"Fuck it." Charles blasted the music, bass and everything. He rolled the windows down as we passed the cop car.

"Yo, y'all niggas is crazy!" Twon said, full of excitement as he looked back at the cops.

"That shit was classic, nigga!" I said.

"Oh, shit!" Charles said, looking back again. The blue lights were flashing directly behind us.

"FUCK!" said Charles, turning the music down. "I knew I shouldn't have done that shit."

I felt a little nervous as we pulled over to the side of the road. Charles stopped the car and killed the ignition, then put his hands on the steering wheel.

Two cops approached the car, bellowing at us. "GET THE FUCK OUT, ALL OF YOU, WITH YOUR HANDS UP!"

We all got out of the car slowly with our hands up.

"AGAINST THE FENCE! NOW!"

"A'ight, nigga. No need to scream at us," I said, making my way to the fence.

"What did you say, nigger?" he said, right behind me. Now that he wasn't screaming, I recognized the voice. I turned around. Sure enough, it was the same cop that fucked with me, Quaid, and Twon that time we were on our way home from the basketball court. "Ohhhh, it's you!" He smirked. "Get your fucking ass against the gate!" He shoved me, and I tripped on the curb as I went for the gate. I reflexively held my hands out to regain my balance.

"Eyo, don't be fuckin roughing up my cousin!" said Charles.

"And what are you going to do about it? Huh?" He grabbed Charles from behind and slammed him to the ground. He hit the pavement hard, and me and Twon both whipped our heads around mad quick.

"Eyo, what the fuck! That's police brutality, nigga!" said Twon.

"Shut the fuck up before you get some too." The cop put his knee on Charles's back, trying to yank his arms together so he could cuff him. "Stop resisting!" he bellowed.

"Turn back around!" yelled the other officer.

"What are you arresting him before?" I said. "Cuz we played a stupid song?"

"Just shut up and face the gate."

"No, I have a right to know why you're arresting me," said Charles, trying to out from under the officer's knee.

"I said stop resisting!" said the officer. He pushed his knee harder into Charles's back.

"ARGH!" Charles grunted in pain. He tried to wrench out of the officer's grasp.

"STOP!" yelled the officer, hitting him in the back with his club.

"What the fuck, nigga!" said Charles.

"Charles, just stop moving."

"He's reaching!" said the other officer.

"No, he's not!" I said.

"Turn your ass back around! Reaching!"

"No, he's—"

POP! POP!

I heard the gun go off before I even saw it. "FUCK! CHARLES!" We stared in shock as blood soaked his shirt. I looked at the officer who shot him. "YOU FUCKING SHOT HIM! YOU FUCKING SHOT MY COUSIN!"

"HE WAS REACHING!" screamed the officer, getting in my face.

"NO THE FUCK HE WASN'T! I SAW THE WHOLE THING!"

Two other cop cars pulled up along with an ambulance. When I saw the EMTs, I damn near lost my mind.

"My fuckin cousin! My fuckin cousin...." I repeated over and over again as we were handcuffed and brought to the police station.

* * *

This was turning out to be the craziest, most fucked up night of my life. My mom, Rose, and Quaid's mom, Gina, put their money together to bail me and Twon out of jail since we didn't really have no serious charges like that. Twon's mom, Charlene, had hung up the phone on him when he tried to explain to her what happened. He tried to play that shit off, but I knew my nigga was hurting.

He kept telling our mothers that he would pay them back when he had the chance, but they told him he was good.

The only thing I could think about was Charles the whole time we was answering all the fucking questions. They sure had a whole lot of fuckin questions for us, but when they was dealing with Charles, they was on some 'shoot first, ask questions later' bullshit.

When we finally got the fuck out of there, we headed straight to the hospital. My mom had picked us up while Auntie Gina waited with my Auntie Shameka, Charles' mother, at the hospital. We found the family waiting room and settled in for a long night. Quaid was on his way up there with G-Ma. They had turned their phones off during their church service, so they didn't even know about anything that went down until after. Once they heard the news, they came straight to the hospital.

"What's up with Charles?" I said as soon as we walked through the door. They all jumped at the sound of my voice. I ain't mean to scare them, but I was all fucked up in the head due to the night's events.

"We don't know, baby," said Auntie Gina.

Auntie Shameka just sat there wiping her tears as they streamed down her face. Then she snapped. "What the FUCK did you do to my son, Hype?" She jumped up out of her seat and got up in my face.

I flinched. "What you mean, Auntie? I ain't do nothin'."

"Don't fuck with me! You probably caused this with your smart ass mouth. I told your fucking mother she should have beat your ass when you were younger."

"Wait, hold on!" My mom jumped in between me and her sister. "Don't be yelling all up in my son's face when YOUR son is the fucking drug dealer!" Shit was about to go down, so I jumped in between them as Auntie Shameka tried to swing on my mother. I held her arms down.

"GET THE FUCK OFF OF ME!" she screamed as she tried to wrench away from my grasp. "And I got something for your ass, bitch!" she yelled at my mother. "How dare you talk shit about my son while he's laying in a fucking hospital bed!" She went wild, trying her best to get out of my grasp. She put her head down and bit my arm, hard.

"Yo-o-o!" I exclaimed. My mother swung over my shoulder and punched her sister upside her head.

"GET YOUR FUCKING MOUTH OFF MY SON!"

Twon got into it as well, grabbing Auntie Shameka from behind. I grabbed my mother and pulled her off to a corner. I rubbed my arm where my aunt had bit it, though my heart hurt more from her accusations. I didn't show it on the outside because I was trying to be a man about the situation.

Auntie Shameka and my mother were still arguing.

"SOON AS HE LET ME GO, I'M-A LIGHT THAT ASS UP, BITCH!" Auntie Shameka screamed, trying to get away from Twon's grasp.

"You ain't gonna do shit!" yelled my mother.

Suddenly, the door flung open as Quaid and G-Ma walked in with G-Ma leading the way. "Both of y'all better simmer y'all asses down before we get kicked out of this got-damn hospital!" said G-Ma, as she strode into the middle of the room. She glared back and forth between her two daughters daring them to flinch at her. Neither of them moved.

Quaid softly closed the door behind him, his Bible in his hand. He looked tired and confused. "You alright, Hype?" I nodded, and then I realized I was still rubbing my arm. I quickly put my hands down by my sides and ignored the pain.

"Now, what's going on with my grandson?" said G-Ma, looking at Auntie Shameka.

"We don't know, Ma. The doctor won't tell us anything."

"What do you mean, they won't tell you anything?" It was G-Ma's turn to look upset.

"They won't let us see him. They won't tell me nothing about my baby," said Auntie Shameka, breaking down and sobbing.

"Come here, girl," said G-Ma. Twon let Auntie Shameka go, and she walked into G-Ma's arms sobbing uncontrollably. My mom was calm now too. G-Ma comforted my aunt and led her to her seat. She sat down next to her, rubbing her back. "Charles is going to be okay. You hear me? I said Charles is going to be okay."

Just then, we heard a soft knocking on the door, and the doctor walked in. He adjusted his glasses while holding his clipboard.

"Is this … are you the family of Charles Grier?"

G-Ma spoke up. "Yes, we are."

"Thank you." He paused.

"How is my grandson doing?" She stared straight into his eyes.

"Well, ma'am, we're doing all we can right now, but—"

"But what?" G-Ma's voice was sharp. We knew that tone. It meant *don't mess with me, boy.*

"His chances aren't good. With him being shot at such close range—"

"What are his chances for survival?" said Twon, looking scared.

"I don't really—"

"What is it?" Twon persisted, his voice laced with an edge of panic.

The doctor glanced around at all of us. "Less than five percent." Auntie Shameka let out a scream.

"Shhh," said G-Ma, the only one who seemed to be unfazed by the situation.

"That's all I have for right now, but I will be back later with another update." The doctor looked around at all of us, then he nodded his head. "Okay," he said, and exited the room.

"Momma, my baby! My baby!" My aunt was losing control. Everyone was crying. Quaid and Twon had tears in their eyes. I didn't even know how to feel right now. It was like one minute we was in the car, laughing and acting crazy, and the next minute we in the hospital with Charles fighting for his life.

G-Ma looked as if she had made a decision, and she stood up. "Hype, Quaid, come with me."

I snapped to attention. "Huh?"

"Come with me — outside." She put her arm around my shoulder as she walked toward the door. Quaid opened it. She turned back around. "Twon, I need you to keep an eye on these two." She pointed back and forth between my mom and Auntie Shameka. To Auntie Gina, she said, "Go to your sister." She went and sat with her sister, rubbing her back.

"Where we going, G-Ma?" I said as we walked toward the exit doors.

"Ain't no grandchild of mine about to die in this hospital. Not today!"

When we went outside, G-Ma stopped near the entrance to the building. She grabbed me and Quaid's hands.

"What are you doing?" I was so confused. I felt like I was about to break at any moment.

"We about to pray. My God is a healer."

"G-Ma, I don't know how—"

"Just say amen when I'm done. Bow your heads." Me and Quaid obeyed. "Father God, in the precious name of Jesus, we come before you right now, calling out to you for my grandson Charles. Now, Lord, you spoke to me and told me that this boy would live and not die, that he would breathe and not cease. Guide the doctors' hands, my God, and guide the nurses too. We know you put them here for this purpose, but we also know that you have all the power. Send your angels to encamp around him. Bring him through with a speedy recovery. All these things we ask in your mighty and precious name. In Jesus's name we pray, amen."

"Amen," said Quaid and me at the same time.

After the prayer, we went back to the family waiting room.

"Where did you go?" said Auntie Gina.

"We went to talk to Jesus," said G-Ma, then she sat down. Me and Quaid pulled up some chairs and sat down too. We waited for about thirty minutes, my heart beating uncontrollably as I silently prayed that G-Ma's prayer would work. I didn't even know God like that, but I sure needed Him to hear me now. Just as I finished my prayer and lifted my head, we heard a knock on the door again, and the doctor walked in. He stood there staring at all of us, then G-Ma spoke up.

"Well?"

"Well, uh … it seems that—"

"It seems that what?" said Twon, on the edge of his seat.

"He's going to be okay," said the doctor.

I let out a huge sigh of relief and glanced around at my family. They all looked shocked and happy except G-Ma. She looked totally peaceful, like she knew what the doctor was going to say before he even said it.

"Thank you, Jesus," she said.

"Well, yes, he definitely seems to have luck on his side," said the doctor. "Charles, I mean, not Jesus," he added, and everyone laughed to break the tension. "I'll be back with another update soon, but he's stabilizing pretty quickly. He may not even need to be here that long, maybe a few days, a week at the most, as long as he continues to improve. He's young and strong. I think he'll be fine."

"Yes, God!" said G-Ma, raising her hand in the air.

The doctor gave her a strange look then nodded his head once and left the room.

My mind was swirling with thoughts, but mainly I was thinking that maybe this God thing wasn't so bad after all.

Tierra

Twon has been really tense ever since what happened with Charles. He doesn't seem like he really wants to hang out or talk that much. I'm trying to be there for him and comfort him, but I don't think what I'm doing is working.

"Why don't we just watch a movie or something, Twon?" I said, rubbing his back. He tensed up at my words.

"I don't even think I can watch movies like that no more, Tierra."

At first, I was confused, but then I remembered that he, Charles, and Hype were on their way home from the movies when Charles got shot. "I forgot. I'm sorry," I said.

"It's alright." He was quiet for a moment. "I'm just really messed up on the inside, feel me?"

"Yes, I definitely understand. You went through a lot that night."

"I ain't never been arrested before, Tierra. Never even been handcuffed."

I turned to face him. He was finally opening up to me. "I know, and it wasn't even your fault."

"What if this messes up my life? What am I going to do? If those charges don't get dropped, that might mess up my chances of going to

162

college. They ain't gonna want nobody with a record. All my work will go down the drain!"

I could hear the pain in his voice and see it etched on his face.

"Baby, that's not going to happen. You didn't even do anything wrong—"

"Charles ain't do shit wrong either, and look what the fuck happened to him!"

I jumped at his words, but stayed silent. I wasn't sure what to say to that.

"I'm sorry, ma. I'm just really messed up in the head right now. I'm fuckin up on the job, I failed my last two tests, and my mother doesn't even give a fuck about me." He wiped a tear as it streamed down his face.

"Twon, that's not true," I said, my own eyes tearing up.

"Yes it is, Tierra. You know she hung up the phone on me that night."

I froze. "What do you mean?"

"She hung up the phone on me." He looked like he couldn't believe it himself. "I called her and told her that Charles got shot by the cops, and that me and Hype needed to get bailed out, and she hung up on me. Just hung up the fuckin phone in my face like I wasn't shit."

"She was probably just in shock or something." I said it, but I didn't really believe it.

"No, she wasn't in shock. I stayed at the hospital all night with Hype and them's family, and she never called me not once. Nothing. Then when I got home the next day, she barely even said anything to me. She just sent me to the store to get a fuckin pack of cigarettes."

"Wow." That was all I could say. I had no idea how to comfort him. "I'm sorry that happened to you, baby."

"I'll be alright," he said, trying to shrug it off, but I could tell he was deeply wounded by everything that had happened, especially the rejection from his mother. "Just gotta get my charges dropped. Get that shit off my record."

He had been researching like crazy on how to do this ever since that night. He and Hype were anxious about it. They had a court date coming up in a few weeks.

"Yes, you're going to be okay. And your mom is going to snap out of it. And you know I'm always here for you, Twon. Always."

He looked into my eyes, his bottom lashes still wet with tears. "I know, baby. Thank you."

* * *

Twon missed school the next day. He texted me and told me that he was feeling sick, but I know it had to be all those situations that were boggling his mind. I was trying to give him his space while letting him know that I was there for him, but it seemed like he was acting very hot and cold toward me. I don't know if it's the stress or what, but one minute, Twon opens up to me, and it seems like we're really connecting and getting closer, but in the next breath, he gets all tense and snaps at me.

I don't understand it. I hope that what I am doing is helping him, because I love Twon. I really do. It's just getting harder and harder to be there for him with the way he treats me. Then I wonder if I'm just being selfish, and if it's really that he's just going through a lot, but then I think about the fact that Twon had been acting this way before all that stuff went down with Charles.

I don't know what to do. I hope this all works itself out soon.

"Hey, girlie!" I looked up. It was Shaneece. She sat down across from me in the cafeteria. I was sitting by myself, lost in thought, when she came over to me.

"Hey," I said. "What have you been up to?"

"Oh, nothing. Just been hanging out with my man."

"Oh, really? Since when did you get a man, Miss Thang? And who is it?"

Shaneece and I had been sitting together at lunch quite frequently lately, and we had been passing notes back and forth in class since she got to the school. We were becoming pretty good friends, which was kind of unusual for me. I usually only hung out with guys, like Hype and Quaid, but Shaneece is the first girl that I feel like I can actually be friends with. She's so cool and so sweet. I feel totally comfortable opening up to her.

"Girl, I been had a man! It's been over a month now!"

"Okay, but you definitely never told me that."

"You definitely never asked!"

"Okay, well I'm asking now. Who is it?"

"Oh, you don't know him," she said, flipping her hand in the air. "He doesn't go to this school."

"Oh, okay. What's his name then, at least?"

"Markus."

"Word, what does he look like? I need some details, girl! Especially with my situation."

"He's tall and — wait. What situation? You and Twon are okay, right?" She looked very concerned all of a sudden.

"Not really," I admitted.

"What's going on?" She leaned forward eager to hear all about it.

"Well, we have been having a lot of problems lately. He's been going through a lot with his mom and with some situations he got into with his friends, and also some problems me and him been having personally."

"Wow," she said. "That's a lot. But I mean, he's okay, right?"

I nodded. "Yes, he'll be alright. But all of the situations are really putting a strain on our relationship, plus we got our own issues."

"Well, maybe if you guys are able to resolve your issues, the other stuff will be easier for him to deal with."

"But that's the thing," I said, my face reddening. "I don't think our situation can be resolved."

Shaneece looked confused. "Why not? What's going on?"

I leaned closer to her. "Well, the thing is, me and Twon have never had sex. He's been ready for a while, but I'm not."

"Whaaaaat?" She looked totally surprised as she sat back in her seat. "But ... why not though? You're not like, a virgin or anything, are you?"

I nodded my head. "Yeah, I am."

"Girrrrl, you crazy! How old are you?"

"Seventeen."

Her eyes widened at my words. "Seventeen? And you still haven't had sex yet? And how long have you and Twon been together?"

"Almost two years." I gulped. "Matter of fact, our anniversary is coming up soon."

"Wow," she said. "Y'all been together almost two years, and never had sex? That is crazy. I lost my virginity at fourteen."

"I know, a lot of people lose it pretty early, but I just never felt like it was the right time for me."

"I mean, do you trust him?"

"What do you mean?"

"Like, obviously if he's been with you over a year, he must really have feelings for you. Has he ever cheated?"

I looked at her like she was crazy. "Girl, hell no! Twon knows I would kill him if he ever did me like that. Shoot, he would probably kill me too if I ever did it to him."

"True. But if you trust him, why don't you just do it?"

"Because ... I just don't think I'm ready." I didn't want to tell her the real reason, which was because I had been going to church a lot more lately, and I was worried about my relationship with God. I'm pretty sure one of the requirements for salvation is probably to not have sex before marriage, so I don't want to do anything to get in the way of being saved.

"Girl, if I were you, I would let go of that fear and just give it to him. You guys have been together long enough. Nobody's going to look at you crazy."

"I don't know ... I'll think about it."

On the one hand, I did want to have sex with Twon, but on the other hand, I was deeply concerned about my standing with God.

* * *

Quaid and I were sitting at his kitchen table going over my homework. He was still tutoring me for my math class. I must admit, without his help, I don't know how I would have made it!

"Boy, you need to be a teacher with the way you be breaking these problems down!" I said with a chuckle.

"I do okay, but I don't think I'm that great of a teacher. I think you are just a good student." He smiled at me.

"Aw, thank you!" I said, gently nudging his shoulder.

He glanced at my hand then looked into my eyes. I removed it from his shoulder and leaned back in my seat.

"So ... now that we're done, are you hungry?" he asked.

"Boy, you know I am!" I said, getting excited. My stomach was definitely growling at me, and Quaid could cook!

"You sure your mom won't mind you being out too late?"

We both looked at the clock on the microwave. It was almost 9:00 p.m. "No, she won't mind. She knows I'm with you. Plus, she doesn't really care how long I'm out, as long as I come back home by 11:00 p.m."

"That's good. How about some spaghetti?" He got up from the table.

"Now you know that's my favorite food. Stop playing!" I was really excited now.

Quaid turned around in shock. "Really? Mine too! I never knew that."

"Well, it is." I watched him as he pulled the meat out of the fridge, turned on a pot of boiling water, then put the meat in the pan and seasoned it, humming all the time. Pretty soon, it was smelling so delicious in the kitchen that I wanted to push him out of the way and eat from the pan! My mouth watered. "That smells so good, Quaid. You should be a chef."

He turned around again. "Didn't you just say I should be a teacher?" He grinned. I could tell he was pleased with the compliment either way.

"I know, but that was before I remembered you could cook. Maybe you could do both!"

"Stop it!" he said. "I do okay, but I'm definitely no Chef Stanley." He was referring to a famous chef who had a reality show on TV.

"Shoot, right now, I bet your food taste better than Chef Stanley."

He chuckled. "You're just saying that because you're hungry."

"I'm serious!"

"Mmm hmm." He licked his lips and looked directly at me.

I suddenly felt a little nervous inside. Every now and then, Quaid would give me this look, like — I can't explain it, but it was like this strange look, almost like he wanted me or something. I knew that couldn't be it because he knows I'm with Twon, and they're like, best friends, but it does seem like that sometimes....

"Tierra?" he said, breaking me out of my reverie.

"Huh?"

"I said, does Twon ever cook for you?"

I snorted. "Boy, you know Twon can't even boil water! You might need to give him some lessons one day."

He shook his head. "Nah, I'm good."

"Why you say that?"

"Oh, nothing. It's just that I would feel weird teaching another man how to cook."

From the way he said it, it didn't seem like that's why he said he was good, but I wasn't going to press the issue.

"Do you want me to help fix the plates?" I said.

"Oh, no. You sit there and relax. You're in my kitchen now." He got out some plates and forks and quickly fixed our plates then brought them to the table. "What would you like to drink?" he said, handing me a napkin while he put his next to his plate.

"Um … what do you have?"

"Just the basics — soda, water, juice."

"You got any Kool-Aid?"

He laughed. "Just like a black woman!"

"Hey, everybody likes Kool-Aid!" I pretended to be offended by his statement. He went to the fridge and pulled out a big pitcher of Kool-Aid. I chuckled as he poured two large glasses. "Thank you," I said, as he handed me my glass before taking his seat.

We ate mostly in silence. I knew I was smacking like crazy, but at this point I did not care because I was starving, and this spaghetti was out of this world. Quaid stared at me as I finished my plate.

"Would you like a to-go plate?" he said with a grin.

"Um, sure. I think my mother would love some." I definitely was trying to play it off, but Quaid saw right through my greedy self.

"Yeah, okay." He said, getting up and fixing me some Tupperware. "Now, you know there are rules to this," he said as he put the Tupperware into a plastic bag and tied it.

"What rules?"

"Well, first of all, you have to return my Tupperware, and second of all, you can't return it without filling it up with something good."

"Okay," I said, ready to take the challenge. "What would you like to eat, Chef Quaid?"

"Oh, you definitely tried it with that one!" He laughed. "I don't care. Anything is fine with me, as long as it's good."

"Okay, I got you." I took the bag from him.

"Thank you," he said. "I'll be waiting. And you can't cheat either. Your mom can't do it for you."

"Really, Quaid? You trying to play me like I can't cook?" I set the plastic bag on the counter and took a step toward him with a little bit of swagger, I have to admit.

He shot me a sheepish grin. "Well, if I recall correctly, Twon did have some stories...." He tried to dodge me as I swatted his arm. I missed but then swung again, and he grabbed my arm. I swung with my other arm and he grabbed that one too, pulling me closer to him while simultaneously putting my arms behind my back.

"Cheater!" I panted, trying to wrestle out of his grasp. He looked down at me and smiled.

"Don't try to fight it. You are not getting out of this grip, girl."

I struggled against him, but it was to no avail, so I tried to head-butt his chest. This only caused him to burst out laughing.

"What was that supposed to do?" he said.

"I ..." I was about to answer him, but I suddenly became intoxicated by his scent. I don't know what in the world he was wearing, but that cologne was on point! I looked up into his eyes, and that's when I noticed that Quaid had some extremely long eyelashes. They were even longer than Twon's, and that was saying a lot. Something about the way it felt to be all pressed up against him like this made me uneasy. He must have sensed this, so he let me go. We stood there for a few minutes in awkward silence.

"I should get you home," he said.

"True."

He got his keys from the couch in the living room and we left his house. We were mostly silent on the way home.

"Thanks for the food, and for the ride home."

"Of course. Any time."

I walked into my house trying to process everything that had happened that night.

* * *

Hype and I were filling out scholarship applications at his house. We had each filled out at least twenty applications by now. I hope we get accepted to at least some of these colleges.

"This one doesn't look like it wants too much," I said, pushing a paper toward Hype.

He picked it up and examined it briefly. "Yeah, this one's cool — only five hundred words. That's way better than that other bullshit talking 'bout a thousand words."

"All this writing though!" I said. "They should just switch our English class, and have us use that time to do all this writing."

"True. That would be one way to kill two birds with one stone."

"How's Charles doing?" I asked all of a sudden.

"He a'ight."

"And how have you been doing since that night?"

"I don't know, Tierra. A lot went down that night. It was crazy."

"I know, Twon was telling me."

"Yeah, and his mother did him dirty, yo."

"I know, he told me."

"You know Charles almost died that night?"

A shiver went all throughout my body. "Really?"

"Yeah. The doctor said he only had like a five percent chance of survival."

"So how did he pull through so quickly?"

"Real talk?"

"Yeah, what happened?"

"G-Ma took me and Quaid outside, and she sent a prayer up. Next thing I know, the doctor walks back in the room talking 'bout Charles is gonna make it."

"Really? Wow!"

"Yeah!" It was crazy. I never seen nothing like that before. I don't really know God like that, but He definitely looked out that night, for real."

"True."

"Oh yeah, I forgot to tell you!"

"Tell me what?"

"I asked Quaid about that question you had."

"You mean when I was asking about being saved?"

"Yeah. He told me some real deep stuff."

"So ... what do you have to do?"

"I don't know, he was saying that you had to believe Jesus died for your sins or something like that. I'll have to ask him again to understand it better."

I rolled my eyes at him. "Really, Hype?"

"What?"

"That's all you remember?"

"Look, girl, I was trying to help you out with your scary self."

"Shut up. Ain't nobody scared."

"Okay, why you ain't ask G-Ma then, huh?"

I got quiet.

"Yeah, yeah. Don't try to play me."

"Whatever." I rolled my eyes in mock irritation. "Well, can you ask him soon, because I really need to know."

"I still don't see why you can't just ask him yourself, but okay. Don't he tutor you like every week or something?"

"Yes," I said, my heart fluttering slightly.

"So why don't you ask him then?"

"Cuz we be focused on homework."

"Psshhht. Bullshit! You know my mom and Quaid's mom be gossiping all the time. Quaid's mom said that homework ain't all you and Quaid been doing."

My face grew hot. "What do you mean?"

"She said Quaid been cooking you dinner and shit."

"Oh my gosh, Hype — you didn't tell Twon, did you?"

"Nah, I ain't no snitch. Besides, even if he does have a crush on you, I know Quaid wouldn't try anything. He's too much of a goody good."

I relaxed slightly. "Yeah," I said, though I couldn't fully meet his eyes.

"Wait…." Hype said, as if he sensed something. "Nothing's going on between y'all, right?"

"No, no!" I said quickly. "He just tutors me. That's all."

"Cuz you know that would really cause some shit to go down if it did, right?" He stared into my eyes like he really wanted me to understand what he was saying.

"Yes, I know, and I promise you that nothing has ever happened between me and Quaid, and nothing will."

"A'ight, cool," he said. "I just would hate to see the effects of some shit like that going down, nah mean?"

"Yes, I definitely understand."

* * *

Twon and I were laid up in my bedroom watching TV. He had his arm around me, and I was pressed up against him. "This show is so boring," I said, looking up into his eyes. He looked like he was deep in thought. He definitely hadn't been paying attention to the show; that much was obvious.

"What are you thinking about?" I said.

"Us." He didn't look down at me to meet my eyes.

"What about us?"

"Well, you know our anniversary is coming up, right?"

"Of course, boy! We have to make some plans." I leaned up on one elbow then sat cross-legged to face him.

"Well … I already kind of had some things in mind." He slid his beautiful eyes over to mine.

"Oh, really?" I scooched up close to him. "What were you thinking?"

"Well, I was thinking that we could go somewhere real nice for dinner first," he said. "Maybe do a little slow dancing or something. Then, later on that night, maybe we could get a hotel room."

My heart dropped.

"A hotel room?"

"Yeah," he said. "I figured that since it will be two years on that day, it would be a nice way to finish the night off."

"And what would we be doing in the hotel room?" I said, holding on to a glimmer of hope that he wasn't thinking what I thought he was thinking.

He stared at me like I was crazy. "What do you think, girl?"

"Twon—"

"Tierra, it's our two year anniversary. You mean to tell me you still ain't gonna be ready?"

"No, Twon. I won't."

He sucked his teeth and sat up in the bed too, with his legs hanging off the side. "That's some bullshit, Tierra, straight up. How the fuck you still not going to be ready after two whole years?"

"Twon, you don't understand—"

"Damn right, I don't understand. It's not like we just got together last week or some shit. We been together for two years! How much more time do you need? Do you know that this is way past the usual time for a couple to have sex? Are you trying to wait 'til marriage or something? Or is it just me that you don't want?"

He was really going in on me now. "Twon, I can't do this right now."

"You know what? I'm tired of this bullshit, for real, Tierra. We been doing things the way you want this whole relationship. I been way more than patient with your ass. But this has to stop, like ASAP. For real. I don't know what else you want from me."

"I don't know why you can't understand that I'm just not ready!"

"WELL HOW THE FUCK CAN YOU NOT BE READY AFTER TWO FUCKING YEARS?"

"DON'T YOU FUCKING RAISE YOUR VOICE AT ME!"

"You know what? Fuck this shit. I'm out." He snatched his wife-beater t-shirt off the back of my chair and roughly pulled it over his head. He put his shoes on as well.

"So you just going to do what you always do, huh?" I crossed my arms. "You just going to leave like you always do."

"Damn right I'm gonna leave. If my own girl don't wanna take care of my needs, then it sounds like I need to find...." He stopped himself.

"Find what?" My heart was beating fast now. I got off the bed and stepped closer to him. "Find what, Twon?"

"I was going to say it sounds like I need to find somebody else, Tierra."

My heart shattered at those words. "What do you mean, find somebody else, Twon?"

He walked to the front door.

"So you not going to answer me?" I felt so crazy, I wanted to grab him and turn him around, and make him talk to me. He opened the door then turned back to look at me.

"I just gotta go," he said, and then he left.

Twon

Damn, why did I say that to her? I really didn't know why I said that. I was just as surprised as Tierra was when the words came out of my mouth. I was deep in thought as I drove away. I didn't even know where I was going. I just knew I had to get out of there. My phone was buzzing like crazy with text messages. When I got to a red light, I quickly checked them. They were all from Tierra saying she wanted to talk. I turned my phone off. I didn't really have any words for her right now. I mean, I know we gotta talk about this shit sooner or later, but right now the shit was just too fresh.

I didn't really mean what I said about finding someone else. I would never cheat on Tierra. I love that girl with all my heart. It's just that life has been crazy lately.

I'm coming to grips with the fact that even though I live with my mother, I'm basically a fucking orphan. I can't get that shit out of my mind how she just hung up on me that night that Charles got shot. Even though he turned out okay, and we all got our charges dropped a couple days ago, it stuck in my mind how she did that to me.

Over the years, my mother has done some fucked up shit to me, straight up, but I never really felt like I had confirmation of her feelings toward me until that night. How could you be so heartless toward your own son?

I shook my head as I pulled up to Quaid's house. Both his and his mother's cars were outside. Hype didn't have a job, so if Quaid was home, nine times out of ten, Hype was there too. I didn't see Charles's car, so I wasn't sure about him. I walked up to the front door and knocked. Nobody answered, but I heard laughter coming from the inside, so I twisted the doorknob. The door was unlocked, which was pretty normal. Me and Hype and them were so close, we always showed up to each other's house unannounced, and none of our moms cared if any of us just walked in. My mother didn't care period, so I guess that didn't really count, but their moms wouldn't mind if I just walked in either. I entered the living room where Quaid, Charles, and Hype were watching a Kevin Hart standup show.

"What's up, y'all?" I said, giving everyone dap before I sat down.

"Nothing," said Hype. "Just watching these DVDs. Can you believe Charles never saw this one?" He gestured toward the TV.

"Man, you know Charles is always late."

"Forget y'all, man," said Charles, his eyes glued to the screen. "I'm trying to watch the show."

"How you feeling, man?" I said.

His face turned serious for a moment, but his eyes didn't leave the TV screen. "I'm good."

"Look at him, soaking it all up," said Quaid, who was drinking some Kool-Aid.

"Eyo, you got any more of that in the fridge?" He nodded. I hopped up and went to the kitchen where Quaid's mom and Hype's mom were sitting at the table talking.

"Oh, hey Twon!" said Quaid's mother.

"Hey, Auntie!"

"Boy, you a trip!" she said, laughing. I gave them both hugs.

"What, y'all know I'm family," I said.

"Yeah … I guess we can say that. You been coming around long enough eating up all my food. Matter of fact, do you want some of this chicken?" She got up and walking to the stove to dish some up for me.

"Now, Auntie, you know I want some chicken!"

"I know you do!" she said, chuckling again as she fixed me a plate. She piled it up just the way I liked it. My heart panged slightly as I realized that in this moment, she was showing me more love than my own mother ever showed me. In fact, she always did.

"Thank you." I swallowed back the lump in my throat as she handed me the plate.

"No problem. You want some Kool-Aid too?"

I nodded. "You know it!"

"I'm surprised y'all still got all that food left with the way Quaid been cooking for Tierra lately," said Hype's mother, sipping on some tea.

I almost dropped my plate, I turned to her so fast. "Huh? What do you mean?"

"She didn't mean anything, Twon. Relax," said Quaid's mom as she handed me a tall glass of Kool-Aid. "How have your classes been going?" I knew she was trying to change the subject, and Tierra wasn't really a discussion I wanted to have with her anyway, so I let it drop for now.

"They been alright. Just trying to get things caught up since … what happened."

"True."

"Hey, you didn't block us in, did you?" said Hype's mom. "We were about to go get our nails done."

"Oh, no, I parked on the street in front of the house. Y'all got room to back out."

"Thank you, baby." To Quaid's mom, she said, "Girl, let's get up out of here!" She downed the rest of her tea, and those two women were gone so fast I knew they couldn't wait to get away from us boys and all our noise.

They love us, though, and I was kind of glad they left when they did because this nigga Quaid definitely got some explaining to do.

I tried to remain calm as I ate my food, but the more I looked over at Quaid, and the more I saw him sitting there laughing like he didn't have a care in the world, the more pissed off I became.

I spoke up, finally. "Eyo, Charles, pause that shit, nigga." Everybody looked at me like *whatchu doin'?*

Charles paused the DVD. "What's up?" he said.

I ignored him and launched straight in on my target. "Quaid, what the fuck you got going on with Tierra?"

"Aw, shit. I knew you was in the kitchen with them women for too long," said Hype.

My head shot toward him. "Wait, fuck you mean? You knew about this shit too, nigga?"

"Knew about what shit? Nigga, nothing's going on for me to know about!" said Hype.

"Seem like some secrets going on around here. What's up, Quaid?" Quaid had sat there silent, like he was unsure what to say or something.

Quaid met my eyes, and I saw a challenge in his. "What are you talking about, Twon?"

"Don't act stupid, nigga. Fuck you doing cooking for my girl?"

"Wait, wait. You're getting all bent out of shape because I cooked *dinner* for your girl while we were *studying* I might add?"

"Yes, nigga. That's not your fuckin place!"

"Look, you can't control my interactions with Tierra, Antwon. We've been friends for as long as you two have been dating."

"The fuck I can, nigga. I better not hear about you cooking for my girl again or there's gonna be problems." I stood up. Hype, Charles, and Quaid stood up too.

"Yo," said Hype. "Chill. This don't need to even go down like this. We been boys since childhood. If Quaid says nothing's going on, I think you should believe him, Twon, and Quaid, if Twon don't want you cooking for his girl, don't cook for his girl. Simple as that."

"Real talk," said Charles. "This is really no reason to start no drama. This is light shit."

"Right," I said. "As long as he agrees."

We all looked at Quaid. "Fine. I won't cook for her anymore."

"Good." I sat back down to finish eating my chicken, and now it was cold. That pissed me off too.

We had reached an agreement, but something told me this would not be the last of this situation between him and Tierra — or me, for that matter.

* * *

I walked into the house after a twelve-hour shift at my job. I was exhausted like a mutha. My boss was riding me like crazy, especially since I had been fucking up lately due to the Charles incident. I was trying to stay in his good graces because I needed to work to save money and pay my phone bill, my car payment, and my car insurance, but if this nigga kept fuckin with me, I might have to show my ass and find another job.

"Hey, Ma," I said. My mother was sitting on the couch in the living room watching a reality show.

She didn't answer, so I went upstairs and took a nice, hot shower. After I was done, I was ready to hit the sheets, but then I remembered that I still needed to talk to Tierra. We hadn't really had a full conversation since our argument the other day, and I was still trying to figure out how we could proceed as a couple. I wanted to talk to her soon because I never liked to let too much time pass after an argument, but at this point I didn't know what to say.

I considered it then shook my head and decided against it. I was too tired to get into another argument right now, and I didn't want to mess around and say some crazy shit like I did last time, so Tierra would just have to wait 'til after I woke up.

I flicked my lights off, closed my room door, and laid down on my bed after turning off my phone and putting it on my nightstand. It was about to be lights out for me in T-minus ten seconds.

Just as I was succumbing to my heavy eyelids, my door banged open and my lights flicked on. My mother walked into my room.

"Twon, I need to talk to you."

"What's up, Ma?"

"Well, first I need you to go to the store for me and get me a pack of cigarettes. And second, I need you to start paying rent."

"Wait, what? I can't afford no rent, Ma! How much you talking?"

"I need two hundred dollars a week starting next week."

My eyes popped open wide. "Two hundred dollars a *week*? Ma, that's almost the whole rent!"

"Okay, well, you're forgetting about food, and toiletries, and everything else. I've been letting you live for free for long enough. It's time you took some responsibility."

"Ma, I don't have that kind of money. I only work on weekends as it is, and the factory don't even be paying me that much. If I give you two hundred dollars a week, that's basically my whole paycheck. Is there any way to reduce it?"

"No, there's not. I'm tired of scrounging and scraping for dollars while you out here sitting pretty. I need some money, and you need to pay me."

"Ma, can you change it to a hundred a week? That's still pushing it, but at least I'll be able to afford my phone and car—"

"Did you hear what I said? I need two hundred a week from you, boy, or you need to find a new place to live."

"Wow," I said, unable to fully comprehend what she was saying. "So you're saying that if I don't basically give you my whole paycheck, even though I can't afford it, you're going to kick me out?"

She stared at me like I was stupid while she nodded her head. "Yes, that's exactly what I'm saying. You have been freeloading around here long enough. Time for you to start paying something. Learn some responsibility."

"But, Ma, I am responsible. I been working since I could legally have a job. I bought my own car and pay my own bills. I do good in school, and I stay out of trouble."

She snorted at my last statement. "Stay out of trouble, huh? So you call getting locked up and calling my phone in the middle of the night to get bailed out staying out of trouble?"

That was a low blow. "Ma, you know that wasn't even my fault. None of us did nothing wrong."

"Y'all should have known better than to be fucking with those cops!"

"That's true, but—"

"But nothing. Look, I'm done with this conversation. My answer is final. I need two hundred a week or you can get out of my house. Now go to the store and get me a pack of cigarettes." With those words, she turned and walked back downstairs to the living room.

My mind was heavy with trying to think of a plan for how I could come up with the extra money because there was nowhere else I could stay besides with my mom, and if I got my own apartment, I might as well quit school because I would have to work full-time to afford it.

The only thing I could think of was picking up an extra shift or two at work, but I was already pushing it with working twelve-hour shifts every weekend. It was going to be very hard to keep up my grades if I had to work even more hours.
"Fuck it," I finally said to myself. "Just gotta do what I gotta do."

I went downstairs and left the house to go get my mom her cigarettes.

* * *

"Eyo, Hype, didn't you say that nigga Jamel is a manager up at Sports Locker?" Me and Hype were walking back to his house from playing basketball against two other guys. Charles was at home, and Quaid was studying for a test.

"Yeah, why?" He looked at me. "You about to quit your job or something?"

"Nah, nah. I gotta get some more hours, and my boss said he can't give me part-time hours during the week at the factory, so I gotta find a second job."

"What you need a second job for?"

"Cuz, man, my mom's trippin'. She busted up in my room the other day out of nowhere, talking about I gotta start paying rent."

"Word? How much she charging?"

"Two hundred dollars a week, nigga."

"Two hundred — that's crazy! Did you tell her you ain't really have it like that?"

"Yeah, but she don't care. She said if I don't pay her, she gonna kick me out."

"Yo, son, that's fucked up. Why is she doing this all of a sudden?"

"I don't know, bruh, but it seems like it's just one thing after another in my life."

"I know the feeling. Well, I'll talk to the nigga. He might still be hiring."

"A'ight, bet. Let me know what he says."

"I gotchu."

We parted ways when we got to his house.

On my way home, I contemplated finally calling Tierra to see what was up with her, but I still didn't know what to say.

"Fuck it," I said, taking my phone out. *Maybe I'll think of something when she answers.*

Just as I clicked on my contacts to type in Tierra's name, my phone rang with an incoming call from Shaneece. I answered it immediately.

"Hey, Shaneece, how's it goin'?"

"Hey, Twon." She sounded nervous.

"What's up?" I said, remembering our last conversation on the phone. It was mad weird. She had just called me out of the blue, asked me if we were friends, then hung up on me.

"Listen, I can't talk for long, but I just wanted to let you know that I'm sorry about what happened when I called you the other day. My dad actually made me call you and ask that."

"Really? Why?"

"Because him and my mother are always trying to control my life. He won't let me talk to any guys or have a boyfriend while I'm in high school. He saw that I had made some calls to you. They took my car, and now my father is monitoring my every move. That's why I haven't been answering any of your messages online or your text messages."

"But why doesn't your dad let you talk to *me*? What did I do?"

"Cuz you're a boy, that's why. He's just crazy. I can explain it better in person if you meet up with me."

"Um … cool, I guess, as long as that won't get you in more trouble with the old man. Where you want to meet up at?"

"Well, I'm working at the mall right now, so if you come up here, I can take a break and talk with you."

"Oh, word? What store you work at?"

"Sports Locker."

"Oh, word? I actually might be about to start working there myself."

"Really? That would be so great! The guys who work here are such lames."

I chuckled. "Girl, you crazy. Well I hope I do get it, but I'll head up there now so we can talk."

"Great. Call me when you get here. I'll come right out."

"No problem." We hung up the phone.

I thought about whether it would be a good idea to meet her at the mall, especially since me and Tierra were on the rocks right now. I definitely didn't think she would take too kindly to me hanging out with another girl.

I contemplated calling Shaneece to say never mind, but I ended up saying fuck it and went to meet her anyway. Tierra was letting Quaid's ass cook for her. She shouldn't have a problem with me talking to Shaneece.

* * *

On my drive home from the mall after talking with Shaneece, I started feeling mad guilty. I was truly fucking up. I don't know what it is, but I really feel drawn to her. She's mad cool to hang around with, there's no drama, and she's a real sweet girl.

Heck, if I wasn't with Tierra, I definitely would have hollered at Shaneece by now. I knew Hype said he was feeling her before, but Hype wasn't really no settle down with one chick nigga. That was me. He said he had a girlfriend now, but the nigga didn't even want to mention her name, so everybody knew that meant his little experiment wasn't going to last long. That's definitely not to down him, cuz me and Hype is basically like brothers, but that's just who he is when it comes to girls.

I definitely needed to talk to Tierra before the day was over, so I decided to drive by her house to see if she was home. I especially needed to go because I just spent like thirty minutes up at the mall laughing and joking it up with Shaneece, and I could not have that on my conscience.

I pulled up, got out the car, and was on my way up to Tieera's front porch when she walked outside holding a plastic bag in her hand with what looked like a Tupperware container inside.

"Twon!" she said, looking kind of nervous.

"What's up?" I said, staring at her suspiciously as I got closer. "Where you going?"

"Oh, Quaid was about to tutor me, so he's on his way to pick me up."

"What's in the bag?"

"Oh, nothing."

The back of my neck prickled up like a muthafucka. She was lying to me, and I knew it. "Well, it doesn't look like nothing to me."

"It's just some cookies, Twon."

"Cookies for who, Tierra?"

"Um…."

"Cookies for Quaid?"

I had this crazy ass feeling building up on the inside. I ain't never felt like this before, but I felt like some crazy ass shit was 'bout to go down based on whatever answer was about to come out of her mouth.

"Yes, Twon. Why are you so angry? It's just some cookies."

I grabbed the bag from her hand and flung it into the middle of the street. "WHAT THE FUCK YOU GOT GOING ON WITH THIS NIGGA? HUH?" I knew I was overreacting, but I didn't care.

"Twon, what are you doing?" She looked at me like she was scared of me.

"Are you fucking this nigga or something? Huh?" I stepped even closer to her, and she stepped back. "Is that the real reason why you don't want me?"

"I don't even know what you're talking about, Twon. I've been calling you and texting you for over a week, blowing up your phone, and you're talking about I don't want you." Her eyes filled with tears.

"Oh, don't start that crying shit now. I'm sure you wasn't crying when you was baking this nigga cookies and shit."

"What's going on here?" said a voice behind us. We both looked. It was Quaid. My anger built to the boiling point as I walked toward him.

"Twon, no!" said Tierra.

"Quaid, what the fuck did I tell you the other day? Huh, nigga?"

"What are you talking about, Antwon?" Quaid looked confused.

"You know what? Both of y'all muthafuckas is testing me. I told you I don't like that shit with you cooking for my girl. Then the next time I turn around, you got her baking you some fuckin cookies."

"Look, I never had the chance to talk to her about our conversation. She didn't know."

"Well, both of y'all know how I feel about it right now. I don't want y'all—" I cut myself off as another idea came to mind. "Matter of fact, this little tutoring shit y'all got going on, that's done as of tonight. Tierra, you gonna have to find another tutor. Quaid, I don't want you around my girl no more. Y'all getting too close for comfort."

Both of them looked at me like I was crazy. "You don't control me!" said Tierra. "You can't tell me who I can and can't hang out with!"

"I can if it's affecting our relationship." I was back to being heated again.

"And how's it affecting our relationship, Twon?" She leveled a steady gaze at me, like she was challenging me, and that did it.

"I'm-a put it to you like this: If I catch you with Quaid ever again, you and me are done."

"So you're giving out ultimatums now?" said Tierra. "Is that what we're doing?"

"Yes, Tierra. Like it or not, I don't trust you and this nigga together no more."

"And now Quaid has become 'this nigga'?" Her eyes narrowed at me.

"Yes, cuz some foul shit been going down behind my back."

"You know what? I've been dealing with your attitude long enough, but now you're just being paranoid, and that's too much for me."

A new feeling came over me as I realized what she was saying. I was mainly just blowing off steam when I threatened to break up with her if she kept talking to Quaid, but now it seemed like she was on some real shit.

"And what the fuck is that supposed to mean?" I said.

"It means that I'm not going to wait for you to break up with me over some stupid shit, Twon. I'm done. This was the last straw. We been dealing with issues for way too long now. I can't do this anymore. I wish you the best." With those words, she turned around and walked to her front door.

"Tierra." She ignored me. "Tierra!"

She didn't even turn around to look at me before she went into the house and closed the door. I turned to Quaid, still not fully processing what had just gone down.

"Look, Twon, I'm sorry," he said all sheepish and shit.

"Yeah, whatever mufucka." I stalked to my car, put the key in the ignition, and peeled out of there, not giving a fuck about speed limits or anything.

Shaneece

I was cheesing like crazy after Twon left. We hung out for my whole break. It was great. I thought he would be mad at me for hanging up on him that day, and on top of that, I was totally embarrassed by the way my father made me call him, but thank God, Twon was an understanding type of guy. I felt like I could vibe with him on a deeper level than any other guy I had met, including my ex-boyfriend back in my hometown. I felt like Twon truly understood me, especially since he had problems with his mother like I had problems with my mom and dad.

I felt a little bit guilty over basically playing Hype. I mean, he did get me a job, and he was always offering to be a shoulder for me to cry on, but to be quite honest, he just wasn't Twon. There was something about Twon that I needed, something that drew me to him that I couldn't explain.

And the way we connected whenever we did talk, I felt like he might be feeling the same way.

The next hour or two of my shift went by slowly. There were hardly any customers, so my coworker and I were taking turns leaving the store for 30 minutes at a time and chilling in the food court. My turn was next, so when he got back, I quickly made a beeline to the food area so I could sit down. As soon as I got there, my phone began buzzing in my pocket. I took it out and looked at it.

It was Tierra. What was she calling me for?

My hand flew to my mouth. She must have found out about me and Twon hanging out today! My heart was pounding as I contemplated whether I should answer. I quickly decided that I should, because if she asked about it, I could make something up to play it off, but if I didn't answer, she might think I was ignoring the phone out of guilt or something.

I decide to play it cool, keeping my voice lighthearted and casual. "Hey, what's up?"

"Oh, my gosh, Shaneece," Tierra said, sounding way off. "Tell me why me and Twon just broke up." She was sniffling on the other end, and it was clear that she was in the middle of a major crying jag.

My jaw dropped. *That quick?* My thoughts raced. "What do you mean, you broke up?" I said, trying to sound understanding.

"We got into an argument, and it was the last straw. I just couldn't do it anymore, so I broke up with him."

"You broke up with him?"

"Yeah, girl, and now I'm regretting it. I want to call him, but I don't know what to say."

Shit! She's asking me for advice, but I am definitely not helping them get back together.

I quickly tried to think of something to say. "Well, I think..." I began, but my phone started beeping. I looked at the caller ID. It was Twon! *Shit shit shit!* I had to answer his call. "Listen, Tierra, I have to call you when I get out of work. My break ended a couple of minutes ago, and my boss is already calling me wondering where I am. That's him beeping in. I'm so sorry, girl."

"Oh, that's okay," she said, sniffling. "Just call me when you get off."

"I will. Talk to you soon." I quickly hung up with her and switched to Twon before it stopped beeping.

"Hello?"

"Hey, Shaneece?" He sounded so hurt, it broke my heart.

"Hey, what's going on? Are you alright?" I said, feigning like I didn't know the situation.

"Nah, I'm really not. Do you have any more breaks at your job tonight? I really need to talk to somebody."

"Of course, no problem at all. I actually have another one coming up in about an hour. I can meet you up at the same place we were talking last time."

"Thanks. I'll be there."

"No problem."

We hung up. I went back to the store full of excitement about seeing Twon again. He needed to talk to someone, and he called me!

* * *

I tried my best to be a shoulder for Twon to cry on, but I'm not sure I did a good job. I just gave him some generic advice about "giving it time" and "letting Tierra have her space." I felt really bad for him because he looked so distraught, but at the same time, I was mainly hoping that he would get over her quickly so that I could drop Hype, and Twon could be with me....

I know it's probably kind of messed up for me to think that way, especially since me and Tierra have become such good friends, but I can't help how I feel about Twon. Ever since I first saw him, I felt like we had a special connection, and that only grew stronger when we shared with each other the stuff we were going through with our parents. I feel like he's good for me and I'm good for him, and we can help each other get through anything.

"SHANEECE! What the FUCK did I tell you?" My father's voice boomed as soon as I opened the front door, causing me to jump from being startled.

"What are you talking about, Dad?" I said, my heart racing from his sudden outburst. He walked over to me from the living room as I closed the door, my mother following closely behind him.

"You know what I'm talking about, Shaneece. I told you to stop talking to that boy, Twon, but you called his number today, and you spoke to him twice."

"What are you talking—?"

"Don't start that stupid shit, Shaneece. Give me your phone."

I reluctantly handed my phone to him. He quickly searched my call history then showed me Twon's number. "This," he said. "This is what I'm talking about. You tried to change his name to Maria, but the number is still the same. I told you before, I'm not stupid Shaneece. Now you can say goodbye to this phone."

"You're taking my phone?" My mouth dropped open in shock.

"Yes. You don't know how to follow directions, so I have to teach you a lesson."

"But, Dad, I need my phone. My boss calls me, and—"

"I don't care. You should have thought about that before you disobeyed me."

"But Dad—"

"No! That's final!"

"Honey," my mother said to my father when she saw the helpless look on my face. "What if there's an emergency? Why don't we just give her one more chance?"

"Baby, I'm trying to make sure she remains pure. We never had to deal with this with Shanelle."

My head popped up like *what?* Little did my father know, I had lost my virginity several years ago, and as for Shanelle, his little angel, she had slept with more guys than she could count before the tenth grade! I would never tell on her though, because I loved my sister, but my father was so blind that it was crazy.

"I know, I know," my mother was saying. "But I just don't think it's safe for us to take her phone when she may need it." I knew that my mother was only trying to defend me because she still felt bad about the mark my father left on my face, but at this point I didn't care. If it worked, I would be grateful, because without my phone, I would never be able to get with Twon.

"Okay." My father said, finally. "We will give her the phone in the morning when she leaves for school, and she will return it to us when she gets home each day."

My mother looked at me. "How does that sound, honey?" Her eyes pleaded with me to accept it.

"Okay." At least it was better than nothing.

* * *

"Damn girl, you really went in on me today!" said Hype. We were laying in his bed after our latest sex session.

"We always go in on each other."

"I know, but today was different. It was like it took on a whole new meaning or something."

That's because I was pretending you were Twon, I thought, but I would never say that out loud. "Boy, stop," I said, pushing his head.

"Eyo, I been thinking," he said, sitting up to face me.

"Thinking about what?" I said, turning to face him as well.

"I been thinking about your whole situation wit your pops, and I want to help you out."

My heart rate quickened. "What do you mean, you want to help out?" I said slowly.

"I think I should talk to him. Maybe if I explain to him that I have good intentions, he won't mind us being together."

"No, Hype. No way. My dad would never go for that."

"Come on, Shaneece. We have to at least try. We been together for over two months now, and I'm tired of hiding our relationship from everybody. Literally nobody knows about us. Doesn't that bother you?"

"Not really," I said bluntly.

His expression changed at the tone of my voice. "Fuck you mean, not really? Don't you want to breathe? Most girls want all their friends to know about their man. How can you be so okay with hiding this for so long?"

"I'm not like most girls."

He chuckled. "Shit, you right about that." He paused. "But for real, though, I think that as your man, I want to try to help you out. I want to say something to your father. If it doesn't work, then we can go back to the way it was, but if it does, then we can finally start being together freely. I'm really feeling you, girl."

I looked into his eyes. He looked very sincere. But there was no way in hell I was letting him talk to my father. Not just because I didn't want my father to know about us, but because of Twon. There was no way Twon would want me if he knew I was sleeping with one of his best friends. I had to end this thing with Hype before things went too far.

"Well, Hype, I don't know what else to tell you. I don't want you talking to my father. And if you are tired of hiding our situation, then you can break up with me."

He looked shocked. "So it's like that? You would break up with me that easily?"

"Yeah. I understand you not wanting to hide the situation."

"It's not a fucking situation, Shaneece. This is a fucking RELATIONSHIP. We been together for over two months. I ain't never done this shit with no other girl before."

I could see that he was getting agitated, but unbeknownst to him, that's exactly what I wanted.

"Well, it's not my fault that you got in your feelings and don't know how to handle it."

"Bitch, what?" He said, getting up out of the bed. "Who the fuck you think you talking to like that?" He was really getting heated.

"You're the only other person in the room, Hype."

"So you just gonna shit on me like that? Huh? You just gonna talk to me like I ain't shit?"

"I mean ... it's not like we're in love or anything."

"Yo, get the fuck up out of my house, yo, for real. You on some bullshit right now."

"If you want me to leave, that's fine with me."

"Damn right I want you to leave. Talking to me like I'm some lame ass nigga."

"So, are we done? Is it over?" I pulled my shirt down over my head and reached for my pants.

He shook his head at me like he couldn't understand what was going on. "Yeah, bitch. We done. Go live your miserable ass life and deal with your abusive ass pops by yourself. See if you find another nigga like me that actually cares about your fuckin snobby ass."

"Oh, trust me, honey, I already have." I reached for my shoes.

His eyes almost popped out of his head. "Fuck you mean, you already have? You fuckin another nigga? Who is it? One of them niggas at your job?"

"Don't worry about it. We're not together anymore, so it's not your concern."

"No, bitch, who the fuck is it?" He grabbed my arm as I attempted to walk out of his room.

"Get your hands off of me, Hype." I tried to snatch my arm away, but he wouldn't let go.

"I said who the fuck is it, Shaneece?" In his eyes I saw anger mixed with hurt and desperation. He really must have liked me, but at this point, I was just ready to be done.

"I'm not telling you, so leave me alone."

"BITCH, I'M THE ONE THAT GOT YOU THAT FUCKING JOB!"

"I DON'T GIVE A FUCK WHAT YOU GOT ME!" I was desperately trying to get his hands off of my arm, but he was way too strong. He was hurting me, and I bruise easily. I was trying to wrestle away from him because I didn't know how I would explain a bruise to my father. "GET THE FUCK OFF MY ARM!"

"No, you gonna fucking tell me who you been fuckin." He grabbed my other arm and held me tightly.

"Get off me, Hype!" I struggled to get free, but to no avail.

"No, I'm not letting you go 'til you tell me what I asked you."

"Get off of me or I'm calling the cops and pressing charges!"

He froze at my words. "Bitch, you would really put me in jail over some bullsh— You know what? Fuck this shit!" He flung me away from him, and before he could come at me again, I opened the door to his room and ran down the stairs to the front door.

"Yeah, get your THOT ass out my fuckin house!" he yelled, leaning over the banister to make sure I heard him. "And you lucky I don't hit no females."

I slammed the door and rushed to the bus stop so I could get to work on time.

* * *

The next day, Tierra and I snuck away from school during lunch so we could talk about what happened between her and Twon. I tried to get information out of her by passing notes during class, but she said it was "too much to write," and my father took my phone every day when I got home from school or work, so I didn't have the chance to call her about it.

We ducked into a booth at Bailey's, a fast food restaurant that sold burgers, fries, and pizzas.

"I sure hope we don't get caught out here," said Tierra. "Girl, my mother would be so mad at me!"

"Me either, girl," I said, taking a bite of my pizza. I shuddered at the thought of what my father would do to me if he knew how much skipping I had been doing lately.

"That pizza looks good!" she said.

"You want a slice?" I pushed my plate toward her.

She shook her head. "Oh, no. My greedy self needs to just stick with this burger."

"That burger is kind of big."

"I know, and they always make sure their fries are fresh. That's what I love about this place."

"I know that's right, but we didn't come here to talk about burgers and fries. Girl, you have to tell me what happened between you and Twon. On the phone the other day, you sounded so distraught. Girl, what's up???"

I hoped that I didn't sound too impatient with my words. I mean, of course I already knew what happened because Twon told me about it when he came to visit me that day, but I wanted to hear Tierra's side as well.

Tierra swallowed before she spoke. "Well, you know how I told you that we've been having problems lately, right?"

"Yes."

"Well, it just got to be too much for me. I was about to go over our friend Quaid's house so that he could tutor me, and—"

"He?" I said. "You're getting tutored by a guy?"

"Well, yeah, Quaid is friends with me and Twon. We've both known him a long time. He's been tutoring me all year."

"And Twon was okay with this?"

"Um ... yeah. It was Twon that actually told me to start getting tutored by Quaid."

That seemed strange to me, but I let her continue.

"So anyway, I was coming out of my house because Quaid said he was on his way. I had baked some cookies for him because—"

"Wait ... what? You baked him some cookies?" Now I was totally confused. If this Quaid guy was just a friend, why was she baking him cookies?

"Yes," Tierra said, looking like she was getting upset.

"Why were you baking him cookies if he's not your man?"

"Because, he had fixed me some spaghetti one night while he was tutoring me, and he let me have a to-go plate in a Tupperware container. He said that I had to return his Tupperware with something good in it, but that's not the point of the story. The point is—"

"Wait, Tierra. I don't mean to keep cutting you off, but it seems to me like that's exactly the point. That's probably why Twon was mad. You had some other guy tutoring you, cooking for you, picking you up in his car, and now you're baking cookies for him? Did you guys have something going on?"

"NO!" Tierra exclaimed, her face reddening. We looked around to see if anyone had heard her outburst, but no one seemed to be paying any attention to us. "No," she said more calmly. "Me and Quaid are just friends. I was not cheating on Twon with him."

"But you don't think that sounds a little suspect though? I mean, I'm just looking at it from Twon's perspective."

"Yeah, it seems to me like you *only* see Twon's perspective." Her voice was dripping with sarcasm.

"Look, I'm just trying to get the whole picture here."

"I understand that, but you're not even listening to me."

"Okay, I'm sorry. I won't cut you off anymore. Go ahead." I took a sip of my soda while she continued.

"So anyway, like I was trying to say, I was waiting outside with the cookies for Quaid. Twon just rolls up on me out of nowhere after I had been calling and texting him for a whole week. He snatches the cookies out of my hand and throws them in the middle of the street, then he threatens me and says that he doesn't want me and Quaid around each other anymore, and that he's going to break up with me if he sees us together again. So at that point, I just couldn't take it anymore. I told him I was done, and I just walked back into the house. Quaid was out there while we were arguing, and he tried to knock on the door and call my cell, but I didn't answer. It was just too much for me." A tear slid down her face.

"Wow," I said, taking in her words.

"What do you think I should do?"

"Well … first, let me ask you a question. Are you sure you still want to be with Twon? Like, are you really even feeling him like that?"

"Of course I am! We've been together for two years!"

"Yeah, I know, but from what you've been telling me about your relationship, you've been on the rocks for a while. It seems like you guys have more arguments than good times."

"But the arguments are only because he keeps pressuring me to have sex with him."

"Yeah, and why haven't you?"

"Why haven't I had sex with him?" She looked at me like I had lost my mind to even ask that question. This was weird. I needed to know more.

"Yeah, girl! Like you say, you've been together for two years. Why has it taken this long for you to give it to him?"

"I'm just not ready."

"But how are you not ready after *two* years?"

"It's complicated."

"What is it?"

"I don't really want to get into all of that, especially not here in a public place."

"Okay, but did you tell Twon why you weren't giving it up?"

"I told him I wasn't ready."

"But did you tell him the *reason* you weren't ready?"

"No. I kind of hinted at it, but I didn't come out and tell him the reason."

"Why not?"

"Because he wouldn't understand."

"So, you're telling me that you been with this guy for two years, and you don't think he understands you?"

"No, he just wants to have sex. He won't care what my reason is. He just wants to do it. And that's my main problem with him."

I sat back in my seat. "I think you need to really, really think about whether you even want Twon or not."

She put down her burger and leveled a steady gaze at me. "Why are you saying that?"

"Because from everything you're telling me, you guys have been done for a long time now. The other day was just a formality."

Tears filled her eyes. "I guess I never thought of it that way. I'm going to really have to think about this."

"You do that, and let me know what you come up with." As soon as I said that, I hoped she didn't figure out why I needed to know so badly.

"Okay," she said, her voice small.

"Alright. Now we have to get back to school before they realize we're gone."

Twon

My whole life seems like it's fucked up at this point. I lost my girl, I basically lost one of my boys, and I was about to lose my crib before I got this job up at Sports Locker. Maybe I just need to focus on school and work right now. I'm 'bout to graduate this year, so I don't need no more drama in my life. I'll just make sure these grades is up so I can get into college and get some scholarships. I'm good on everything else.

But for real though, a nigga been hurting. Me and Quaid was supposed to be boys. I've known him since childhood, and he's basically the reason I lost Tierra. That's some bullshit.

And my mom ... don't even get me started on that shit. She really wasn't playing about that $200 a week. She couldn't even give me a grace period or nothing 'til I got my first paycheck from Sports Locker. No, she said she wanted her money right now.

At this point in my life, the only thing going good is my friendship with Shaneece. She's the calm to my storms, for real. Matter of fact, I think we're scheduled to work together tonight....

"Hey Twon!" she said, flashing me a smile as I walked into the store.

My demeanor immediately lifted. "Hey girl," I said, giving her a hug.

208

"Mm, you smell good!"

"Thanks," I said, cheesing.

"So ... how's everything?" She looked concerned all of a sudden.

"Um ... I'll talk to you about it a little later." I eyed one of our coworkers who was about to leave because his shift was over.

"True," she said, getting my meaning. "We'll talk later." After a few minutes, Reggie clocked out and left the store.

"I can't believe we work together now!" said Shaneece. "This is SO cool!"

"I know, huh?" I was kind of happy about it myself.

"So ... what's up? How's everything?" She had that concerned look in her eyes again.

"Man, life's been crazy. I feel like I'm losing everything, honestly."

"Losing everything? Why do you feel that way?"

I opened my mouth to answer, but just then, a customer came into the store. "Y'all got them new Air Forces?"

"Of course," said Shaneece. "What size?"

I watched Shaneece as she dealt with the customer. It seemed so natural to her. She was so sweet and attentive. It turned out that the only pair we had in his size were on display, so she hooked him up with that pair. I watched their entire interaction, smiling at her as the customer left the store.

"So that's how you get it done, huh?" I said with a smirk.

"Boy, stop." She chuckled.

"I'm saying, though, I might need some extra training. With skills like that, you 'bout to take Jamel's job!"

"Stop it!" she said, nudging my arm. "Let me go to the back to get some shoes to put on display."

She was back there for quite a while, so I figured that she must have been having trouble finding them. I went to the back to help her out. I saw her trying to jump up higher and higher to reach some shoes that were on one of the top rows. I busted out laughing at the sight.

"Don't you laugh at me!" she said, her face a little red from exertion.

"Let me show you how it's done," I said, easily grabbing the shoes and handing them to her.

"What-ever," she said, rolling her eyes.

"Looks like you need a man in your life to handle some things."

She paused then looked up at me. "You're right about that, I do need a man in my life … to handle some things."

"You still ain't found nobody yet?" I was kind of shocked, but for some strange reason, kind of happy as well.

"Well, I sort of did, but we broke things off. He wasn't for me."

"Who was it?" I knew I shouldn't be asking, but I have to admit, I felt kind of jealous at the thought of her being with someone else, even if it was before I was available.

She brushed it off. "Oh, it was nobody. We weren't right for each other."

"Was it the dude you were talking about before? The one you were crushing on?"

"Nope. Not him. But he did become recently available though...." She stepped forward, a dreamy look in her eyes.

"Um ... Shaneece?" I said, nervous that we might get caught at work if things went further.

"What's up?" she said, licking her lips while staring at mine.

"Um ... I think we should get back out on the sales floor."

Her face fell at those words. "Okay."

Hype

Shaneece been on my mind heavy since we broke up. I can't believe this shit. I always told myself that I would never fall for no girl like that because I didn't believe in that relationship shit, but shorty got me falling heavy. I don't understand why she didn't even want me to ty to talk to her pops. I mean, the worst the nigga could say is no, right? And if he said yes, then we wouldn't have to deal with all this hiding and sneaking around stuff anymore. Isn't that usually what girls want if they in this type of predicament?

I been feeling bad for the way things ended, so I decided to text her during class to see if she wanted to meet up. *Yo, can we talk?*

She wrote back a few minutes later. *About what? I thought you were done with me.*

I know, but I don't like the way things ended between us. Can you meet me in the locker room during lunch? There shouldn't be nobody in there during that time.

Okay.

'A'ight. See you soon.'

I ain't going to lie, I was kind of nervous as lunch time got closer. I wasn't really sure what I was going to say to her. I just wanted us to at least be cordial again.

"Hey," she said when I entered the locker room.

"Dang girl, you here already?" I said, trying to break the ice.

"Well, you forget that my class before this is right next door. I just pretended to go to my locker until everyone left, then I snuck in here."

"True, true. You good with that slick shit." I chuckled.

"You're not so bad yourself," she said, stepping toward me and putting her arms around my neck. I put my arms around her waist and pulled her close.

"You think you can forgive me for what went down?" I murmured as I stared into her eyes.

"Of course, Boo. Already done."

"Shit, shorty, you're really one of a kind." What kind of girl would forgive that easily?

Before I knew it, I was kissing her. Not just any kiss, either. I was kissing her to let her know that I meant it, to let her know that I wanted her.

"Mm, Hype!" she moaned.

"Wassup, baby?"

"Let's go to one of the stalls."

"That's cool with me," I said with a smirk, feeling my heat rise. "You just make sure you keep that voice down so we don't get caught."

"I'll try," she said, staring at me seductively as she pulled me toward the stalls. "But I won't make any promises."

* * *

I walked over to Quaid's house after school that day to see what was up with him and if he wanted to play some one-on-one. When I walked into the living room, I saw him sitting on the couch with a Bible in his hand, looking like he was deep in thought.

I chuckled. "What, you 'bout to preach this Sunday or something, nigga?"

He looked up from his reading. "No, man. Not at all." He didn't sound like his usual upbeat self.

"You a'ight? What's going on?"

"You haven't heard?"

"Heard what?"

"What happened with me, Tierra, and Twon."

"You, Tierra, and Twon? What the … I though y'all squashed that when we was watching that Kevin Hart!"

"No, no, it was after that."

"So … what happened?" I took a seat across from him.

"Well, he and Tierra are broken up, and neither of them are speaking to me. Long story short, I went over to Tierra's house to pick her up for tutoring. I hadn't had a chance to speak to her about Twon's feelings toward us cooking for each other. I guess she had baked me some cookies. Twon got angry. They started arguing, and Twon threatened to break up with her if he saw us together again. Tierra broke up with him and went in the house. Twon drove off. I've been trying to contact both of them ever since, leaving text messages and voicemails, but neither one of them are answering."

"Damn." I sat back in the chair, taking it all in.

"I know," said Quaid. "I'm not sure what to do."

"I mean … Quaid. Be real with me. Was you trying to get at Tierra?"

"Not purposefully, no. But I do have feelings for her. I always have, from the moment I first saw her."

My mouth dropped open in shock. "From the moment you first saw her? What the fuck?"

Quaid held his hand up. "Hold on, man, let me explain. Two years ago, I was at the park with Twon and Charles, and we had just finished playing basketball when Tierra walked by. I already knew her and wanted to approach her, but I was too shy. I wanted to get her number, but Twon rushed and got it before I could, and he was the one that ended up with her."

"What the hell? So Twon low-key stole Tierra from *you*?" This shit was confusing as hell.

"Basically, yes." Quaid nodded.

"How come you never said anything? I definitely never knew about this."

"I tried to just let it go, but my feelings for her never went away. I know it's wrong, but I can't help how I feel."

"Damn," I said. "Well, I really don't know what to say. I mean, you my cousin, and Twon been my boy since way back. I don't even know how to advise you, cuz this shit is complicated."

"I know. I mean, I'm trying to do the right thing. I believe I owe both Twon and Tierra an apology for my actions, because at the end of the day, I should have had more respect for their relationship, but I would be a liar if I said that I'm not a little bit happy that they aren't together anymore."

"Damn. This is some shit."

"I know," said Quaid. "What do you even do in a situation like this?"

* * *

I walked into my English class the next day and went straight for Tierra. I kind of felt bad that I didn't even know about the situation between her and Twon. I had been so caught up in my own problems with the whole Shaneece situation lately that I hadn't been keeping in close touch with her or Twon.

"Hey," I said, sitting next to her.

At that moment, Shaneece walked in. I was sitting in her usual seat, but I didn't think about that until she walked into the room and saw me. She raised her eyebrows at me, but then she went to sit up near the front. I guess she didn't want to draw attention to us, so that's why she played it off.

"Hey," Tierra said. She was staring blankly into space.

"Yo, I heard what happened with you and Twon. You want to talk?"

She turned to me with tears in her eyes. "Not right now. Later."

"Oh, okay," I said. "Well I'm definitely here if—"

"Alright, everybody," said a voice at the front of the room. All of the students stopped their side conversations and looked at our English teacher, Mr. Richardson. Standing next to him at the front of the class was some black dude dressed in baggy jeans and a black t-shirt.

The fuck is this nigga? I thought. He was definitely not a student, judging from his looks.

"We have a special guest today," said Mr. Richardson, gesturing toward the black dude. "This is Dr. Chris Young. He is a Sociology professor at State University, and he is here to tell you guys a little bit about the life of a college student."

Doctor? I thought. That definitely wasn't the first thing I thought from looking at this dude. He looked like a regular guy to me. He wasn't dressed like no doctor, and he looked like he had some hood in him judging from the tattoo up his left arm. I sat up in my seat, intrigued.

"Good afternoon, everybody," said Dr. Young. "As your teacher said, I'm a professor at State University, and I wanted to share with you guys some information about what it's like to be a college student."

I stared at him. The dude looked completely comfortable standing up there in front of us. He had some swag about him, based on his demeanor, but at the same time, you could tell that he was highly educated by the way he carried himself.

"Before we begin, does anyone have any questions about college life, or what it's like to be a student?"

A couple of hands shot up around the room, and he answered all of their questions with ease. It seemed like he was a really cool guy. Even Tierra snapped out of her funk and asked a question. I wanted to ask him some things myself, but I was too scared. I didn't want to say anything stupid and fuck up his presentation, so I just kept my mouth shut. But low-key, I was taking in everything he said, and I even wrote some things down. At the end of class, I sat in my seat while everyone else got up to leave because I really wanted to say something to Dr. Young, but the more I sat there, the more confused I became. I didn't know what to say. After sitting there for a few more moments, I just decided to get up and leave. I had to get to my next class anyway.

As I made my way out the door, I heard him say, "Young man!"

I turned around.

"Hey," I said.

He reached his hand out and shook mine. "Did you have any questions back there?" He pointed to my seat in the back of the classroom.

He really caught me off guard with this one. "Uh, uh … no. No, I don't think so."

"Okay," he said. "Well, if you think of anything, here's my card." He handed me his card. I put it in my pocket. "My office phone and email address are on there. Feel free to contact me at any time. And if you want to go to State next year, we are always looking for new students in the Sociology department."

I was surprised at those last words. My eyebrows raised slightly. "Thanks, man," I said, blinking at him.

"What's your name?"

"Oh, my name is Hype."

"Hype, huh?"

"Yeah."

"Okay, Hype. I hope to hear from you. I won't hold you up from getting to your next class, but feel free to contact me if you have any questions about anything."

"Thanks. I will."

"Okay, sounds good. It was great to meet you, Hype." He shook my hand then walked away.

I stood against the wall thinking about his words. Why did he single me out to give me his card? I didn't see him hand one to anybody else. I never had a teacher really take to me before, so I didn't know how to handle the situation.

But for some reason, the dude seemed like he really wanted me to contact him, like he saw something in me or something. Even when he found out my name, he didn't trip. I've had teachers actually turn their noses up at my name before, and back in elementary school, I overheard two teachers talking shit about my mother because of it. As a result, I guess I never really thought I could be anything other than what I was: a regular nigga.

But now, after this presentation … I don't know. Maybe I could actually succeed out there in the college world. I don't know though. I'll have to think about it.

BRRRRRRIIIINNGG!

I flinched as the bell rang to start the next class. "Shit!"

I was definitely late.

* * *

Tierra and I walked back to my house after school to fill out some scholarship applications and talk about the situation with her and Twon. I could tell it was really eating her up because she barely said two words the entire walk there, and we usually be laughing and joking all the time.

"So, what happened?" I said as we entered the kitchen. Tierra sat down at the table while I went straight to the refrigerator. "You want some juice?" I said, poking my head up to look at her.

"Sure. Thank you."

"A'ight." I poured us both some juice and brought our glasses to the table. "So what happened with you and Twon?"

"I don't know what to think anymore, Hype. I broke up with Twon because we've been having so many issues lately, and I don't even know if I want him back or not."

"What kind of issues was y'all having?"

"Well, I'm sure you heard about the fact that he blew up over Quaid cooking for me, and me baking Quaid some cookies."

"Yeah, Quaid told me what went down that night. Was that it, or did you have other issues?"

"That was more like the tip of the iceberg. He's been hot and cold with me for a while. One minute, we're all lovey dovey and cool, and the next minute, he's blowing up at me because I won't have sex with him."

I almost spit my juice out in shock. "Y'all never had sex???"

She dropped her head slightly. "No. I'm a virgin, and I'm not ready to give it up."

"Oh, shit. I never knew that." I took a swig of juice to fill the awkward silence. "That explains why that nigga been so uptight lately." I chuckled.

"Hype." The look she gave me let me know she wasn't up for my jokes today.

"My bad, but why, though? You two been together a long time. I thought you was mad crazy in love with him."

A tear slid down her cheek. "Look, I know this probably won't make sense to you because the only thing guys seem to care about is sex, but I've been going to church a lot lately, and I really want to turn my life over to God, and I know that having sex outside of marriage is a sin. If I have sex with Twon, then that might mess up my chances of getting saved. I don't want to go to hell, Hype."

"Damn." I didn't know what to say. "Well, I'm not no expert on God or anything, but won't He forgive you if you do something wrong?"

"I don't know. But I don't want to do it and ruin my chances."

I sat there in stunned silence. This was some next level shit. "Damn," I repeated. "What I would usually say in a situation like this is that it's a question for Quaid or G-Ma, but Quaid is part of the problem, so the only other person I can think of that would know what to do in this situation is G-Ma."

"But I can't ask G-Ma about this, Hype!" Tierra looked terrified at the prospect.

"Ask me about what, and why not?" said G-Ma, entering the kitchen at that exact moment.

Both me and Tierra's heads whipped around. G-Ma was standing right in the kitchen doorway. Apparently, neither of us noticed her coming in the house.

"Ask me about what, Tierra?" G-Ma repeated. "And why you looking so scary, girl? Ain't nobody finna bite you!" She walked into the kitchen, set her purse down on the table, and clasped her hands in front of her.

I looked between Tierra and G-Ma. Tierra looked terrified while G-Ma looked cool, calm, and collected. I almost busted out laughing at the sight, but I didn't because I knew how serious the situation was. Tierra looked like she was too scared to talk, so I tried to change the subject.

"Oh, it wasn't nothing, G-Ma. Tierra just stressing about some school situations."

"Don't try to play me, Hype," said G-Ma. "Your light-skinned ass ain't never been a good liar."

This time I did burst out laughing. "That's messed up, G-Ma!"

Even Tierra let out a chuckle. I shrugged my shoulders at her as if to say, *I tried*.

"What you got to talk to me about, girl?" said G-Ma. "Don't be shy."

"Well … I'm kind of ashamed." Tierra's eyes filled with tears.

"Ashamed of what? Not having sex with Twon? Being a virgin?"

Tierra's mouth dropped open. "You heard us?" Her face reddened from embarrassment.

G-Ma chuckled. "Honey, it wasn't like y'all was whispering. I don't know how y'all didn't hear me walking through that front door. Matter of fact, Hype, where your Momma at?" she said, turning her attention to me. "I keep telling that girl to stop leaving that door open."

"G-Ma, we always leave the door unlocked. Ain't nobody gonna do nothing."

"Times is changing, honey."

"Let somebody try to break up in here," I said, feeling myself getting heated.

"Boy, stop," said G-Ma, pushing my head. "You can't fight a bullet with a fist, and you *better* not be packing." She shot me a stern look. "But anyway, back to Tierra. Why are you ashamed?"

"Basically, what you said. I'm probably the only girl at high school who's still a virgin…." Tierra sighed.

"Gir-r-r-rl, being a virgin ain't nothing to be ashamed about. And wanting to be saved is the best decision you could ever make in your life."

"So you don't think I'm wrong for not having sex with Twon?"

"Listen, I know you young people are having sex left and right these days, and because of that, it probably seems like everybody is doing it, but don't you believe that, honey. Everybody ain't doing it, and you don't have to be part of the crowd that is."

"But how can I show him I love him if I'm not doing it? And what if he doesn't want to be with me if I tell him that I want to get saved?"

"You can show him that you love him without having sex with him. Or, you all can go ahead and get married. That is one option."

"Get married?" said Tierra, like G-Ma was speaking a foreign language. "We're only in high school!"

"Well, you want to have sex, don't you? And you say that you love him, right? So are you telling me that you love him enough to have sex with him, but you don't love him enough to marry him?"

Tierra looked confused. Hell, at this point, even I was confused. G-Ma was spitting some higher level shit right now.

She had our attention now. "What I'm trying to say is this: Sex is a very serious commitment. You are giving your body to someone. You are opening yourself up to one of the most vulnerable situations that you can ever be in. You can get pregnant, you can get an STD, or even if neither of those things happen, you can get so caught up with a person that you fall even deeper for them, and then, if they decide they don't want to be with you anymore, that can be even more devastating because you've bonded with them on a physical level. Trust me, honey, I know."

"What do you mean?" said Tierra.

"I have three daughters: Hype's mother, Quaid's mother, and Charles's mother. Do you think they all have the same father? And do you think I am still with any of their fathers today?"

"Ew, G-Ma, I don't want to hear all that!"

"Boy, stop! You know where babies come from. Besides, you need to hear this too. It's not like these girls are out here having sex all by themselves, you know." She turned back to Tierra. "But anyway, honey, I am not trying to tell you to marry Twon. I am just trying to get you to see the serious commitment you are making if you do decide to have sex with him, and also, the possible outcomes of that commitment if things don't work out."

Me and Tierra sat there in silence taking it all in.

"That makes a lot of sense," she said, finally.

"She always right," I said, but I didn't mention anything about the guilt I was feeling about hooking up with Shaneece on the down-low now that G-Ma explained it like that.

Tierra

After that, I went home feeling kind of stressed. G-Ma really put things in perspective for me. What if I do have sex with Twon and then things don't work out, and we end up not together anymore? We *have* been having lots of issues lately. I still love Twon, and I want to be with him, but there are so many problems between us that I'm not sure how we can make this thing work.

I sat there on the couch deep in thought, until my mother's voice startled me.

"What's going on?"

I quickly looked up at her standing in the doorway. "Oh, nothing. I was just watching TV."

"Watching TV, huh?" she said. "Girl, that TV is watching you." She walked over to the other end of the couch and sat down with one knee under her and her body angled toward me. "What's up?"

"I'm just really worried, Ma."

"About what? You and Twon getting back together?" I had told my mom how Twon blew up at me over the cookies, but I didn't tell her the main reason we were having issues.

"Yes, and the fact that things might not be able to work out between us."

225

"It's more than the cookies, isn't it?"

I looked at her in shock. "How do you know?"

"Girl, I know you! I'm your mother. I gave birth to you, and I have been watching over you all of your life. What else is it? You can tell me anything."

"I don't know if I can talk to you about this." I wasn't sure how my mother would feel about me thinking of having sex with Twon. We had never really had "that talk" in my younger years. She mainly just told me to keep boys out of my pants and to focus on school.

"About what?"

"About ... stuff related to sex."

"Have you had sex with him?"

"No. I'm a virgin, but I was thinking about having sex with him."

"I see. Well, what's stopping you?"

My mouth dropped open in shock. "You think I should do it?"

"No, I'm not saying that. What I'm saying is, if there was no reason for you *not* to do it, you would have done it by now. What's the reason for you not doing it?"

"Oh ... well, you know how I've been going to church lately, right?"

"Mm hm. Quaid's church, right?"

"Yes. The one with him and his grandmother."

"How's she doing? That lady is a trip!"

"Yes, she is," I agreed. "But she's really cool when it comes to giving advice."

"You went to her for advice?"

My heart dropped. I hoped my mother wouldn't be mad at me for talking to G-Ma about the situation before I talked to her, but that situation kind of just … happened. "Well, kind of." I hesitated. "Well, not really. I was talking to Hype, and she overheard us."

"Oh, I see." My mother nodded. "Well, what did she say?"

"She basically … well, the whole thing was, I was afraid to have sex with Twon because of the fact that I have been going to church lately, and learning about being saved. I don't want to do it with him and then lose my chances with God."

My mother laughed at that last statement. "Lose your chances with God? Well, I'm not an expert on the Bible or anything, but I do know from when I was younger and went to church that you don't lose your chances with God for having sex. God can save you regardless of the situation you are in. Back when I was younger, there were a couple of prostitutes that came to our church, and God ended up saving both of them. One of them has her own Christian radio show now, and the other one is in the choir. Neither one lost their chance with God, and both of them are doing good now."

"So, do you think I should do it?"

"Have sex with Twon? Honestly, I would say no."

"Why not?"

"Because, Tierra, sex comes with a lot of responsibility, and it can end in a lot of heartache if not done with the right person."

"So you're saying that Twon is not right for me?"

"I'm not saying that. I'm just saying, look at my life. You never know how things will turn out. I've had sex with multiple men, including your father, and how many of them am I with today? None."

"Why do y'all automatically think that me and Twon are going to break up?" I felt myself getting frustrated.

"Wait, who is y'all?"

"You and G-Ma. Both of y'all are basically saying the same thing."

"Well, I don't know what perspective G-Ma was coming from, but I can tell you from my own experience that although you may feel like you are in love and that you and Twon are going to be together forever, sometimes it doesn't turn out that way. And to be perfectly honest with you, I wish I had waited until I was married to have sex."

"Married?!?" My mother was sounding just like G-Ma!

"Yes, married. I know that's not the popular view nowadays, but I wish I had waited. Maybe a lot of things would've turned out differently...."

"Well, what if you *had* waited until marriage to have sex, and things still didn't work out?"

"I don't know how to answer that. It's hard because you can't go back and do things differently, so you never know. But honestly, I still wish I had done it that way because even if it didn't work out, I still believe that would have been better."

"Well, I don't know if I can wait all the way to marriage for sex."

"Ultimately, it is your choice. I'm just telling you as your mother that I don't agree with that decision for you. I am telling you from personal experience, and that's probably what G-Ma was saying as well, that it's better to wait. You will spare yourself a lot of possible heartache in the end."

"Alright, Ma. Well, thank you."

"No problem. Now I am exhausted!" She stretched and yawned. "I am about to go upstairs and take me a nice bubble bath then go straight to sleep. I'll talk to you tomorrow, baby."

"Okay, good night, Ma."

"Good night. And don't worry about the situation. It will work itself out."

That last statement touched my heart and gave me the comfort that I needed. We hugged, and she went upstairs.

It seems like I have a lot of thinking to do.

* * *

After my mom went to sleep, I decided to take a walk to the corner store to get some snacks. I knew I probably shouldn't because it was getting dark outside, but I had a lot on my mind after the conversations with her and G-Ma. I made it to the store, got my snacks, and was on my way home when a car pulled up and slowed next to me.

"Tierra?"

I turned to look at the driver. It was Quaid.

"What are you doing out here walking? It's almost dark!" He looked concerned.

"I just went to get some snacks." I held up my bag.

"Get in," he said, unlocking his doors. "I'll give you a ride home."

"I'm not sure that's a good idea, Quaid." I mean, of course I wanted a ride, but I definitely did not want Twon seeing us. That would probably just ruin all chances of us getting back together.

"Look, I know a lot has been going on lately, but I'm not just going to let you walk home by yourself in the dark like this."

"Quaid, I'm good. The street lights literally just came on."

"I'm not leaving, Tierra." He looked dead serious.

"Well, I'm not getting in the car."

"Well, I will just follow you until you get there, then."

"You will not!" I started walking toward my house. I was tired of all these boys pressuring me one way or the other, even if it was because they cared, but Quaid doesn't give up easily.

"Oh, yes I will." He began slowly driving next to me.

"Quaid, stop! You can't drive that slowly down the street. You're going to get a ticket!"

"Well, if you don't want me getting in trouble with the law, then I suggest you get in this car."

"Fine!" I walked over to the car and got in. "You are so difficult," I said, putting my seatbelt on.

"Hey, you're the one who made things difficult by refusing to get in."

"Whatever." I rolled my eyes.

"So, how have you been?"

"Good," I said, glancing around to make sure Twon was nowhere in sight. I don't know why I was so paranoid, but I really did not want him to see me in Quaid's car.

"What are you looking for?" said Quaid, looking kind of hurt.

"Nothing."

"Have you talked to Twon since the incident?"

"No."

"Tierra," he began, "I'm really sorry about what happened."

"Quaid, do you like me?" I asked, catching him by surprise if his expression was any indication. I felt like this was another discussion that needed to be had.

"Huh? Of course I like you."

"No, I mean, do you *like me* like me?"

He pulled up in front of my house. "I'm really not sure how to answer that, Tierra. Do *you* like *me*?"

It was my turn to be speechless now. I had heard the saying before, 'Don't dish it out if you can't take it', but I had never actually been in a situation that applied to until now.

"What do you mean?" I said.

"The same thing you meant. Do you like me?"

"Quaid, I'm with Twon."

"That doesn't answer my question."

"Well, you didn't answer my question either." I felt uneasy about this conversation. I don't know why I started this whole thing with

Quaid. I opened the door to get out. "I have to go," I said, grabbing my grocery bag and purse.

"I'm sorry about what happened with you and Twon," he said.

"Me too."

"So where does that leave us?"

"What do you mean?"

"Well, you're the one who just asked if I like you. Are we still friends? Or no?"

"Quaid ... I just need some time to think."

He looked hurt. "Okay. Well, I'll see you later then." I looked down at the door as I closed it then looked up just in time to see Twon shaking his head at us. He was sitting in his car across the street. Our eyes connected, then he drove off.

"Shit!" I said. Now what am I going to do?

* * *

When I got in the house, I immediately called Twon. The phone rang, but it went to voicemail. I called him again and again, back to back. Each time it went to voicemail.

"Come on, Twon!" I said, desperate for him to pick up. I tried calling him again. This time, he picked up.

"What?" he said aggressively.

"Twon, it wasn't what it looked like—"

"Fuck out of here with all that, Tierra. I saw it with my own eyes. I went to your house to see if we could talk and work things out, but your mom said you probably went to the store. So I waited for you, and you come back with *this* nigga? I'm done. Fuck it. DONE."

"Twon, it wasn't even like that," I said, as a tear slipped down my cheek.

"Yeah, okay," he said, sarcasm evident in his tone. "I'm going to ask you one more time, Tierra. Are you fucking this nigga?"

"No! Twon, the only one I want is you!"

"It don't look like that to me. Where was y'all coming back from, huh? Did y'all have a date?"

"No, I walked to the store to get some snacks, and by the time I was walking home, it was almost dark. He saw me and offered me a ride."

"And you just hopped in, huh? Fuck out of here, Tierra."

"Twon, I'm telling the truth. I was walking home, and he gave me a ride. That was it."

"You haven't been answering my phone calls, but *this* nigga giving you rides home and shit."

"Twon, I keep trying to tell you. It wasn't like that. He just happened to come along when I was walking home."

"Whatever, Tierra. I'm done." *Click.*

I tried to call him back six more times after that, but each call went straight to voicemail.

I don't know how this situation is going to work out.

* * *

The next day, I went back to Hype's house to talk with him about all these situations that were going on.

"I don't know what to do, Hype!" I sat down at the kitchen table. Hype went to the refrigerator and grabbed us some juice. "Thanks," I said, taking the cup he handed me.

"No doubt." He took a swig of his juice. "To be honest, I think you fucked up by getting in the car with Quaid."

"I know that now, but at the time, I was just trying to get him to stop following me. He said he wasn't going to let me walk home by myself."

Hype sat back for a moment. "Quaid's sneaky ass." He finally said.

"I honestly don't think he was being sneaky, Hype. Regardless of what happened, I think he was just being a friend."

"Yeah, sure." Hype gave me a side-eye like he wasn't at all convinced. "I mean … I know that's my cousin and all, but if you really wanted to work things out with Twon, you should have sent that nigga on his way. And Quaid know better than that shit too. I'm-a have to have a conversation with him."

"No, don't say anything. It will only make things worse. Plus, it really wasn't wrong for me to get in the car. It *was* getting dark, and Quaid was just trying to look out for me."

"True, but … man, y'all niggas is stressing *me* out with this shit. I feel like I'm being pulled in three separate directions. Quaid is my cousin, Twon is my boy, and you my lil homie."

"Lil homie? Really, Hype?"

"You know what I mean, Tierra. I'm just hoping y'all all put y'all heads together to work this shit out soon, because this shit is really fucked up on every level."

"I know. I tried to call him, but he didn't answer. Even after I tried to explain, he wasn't trying to hear it."

"I mean, part of me can't blame him. Would you answer his call if you seen him riding with some other chick? Not to mention, the same chick who had something to do with you and him breaking up?"

"It wasn't even like that."

"You keep saying that, but you and Quaid ain't fooling nobody. Well, at least *you* ain't fooling nobody."

"What are you talking about?"

"You like that nigga."

"Who, Quaid? Who said I liked Quaid?"

"Tierra, it's obvious. Ain't no way you and Twon would have all these issues with Quaid if it wasn't for the fact that you like him."

"So you think I was cheating on Twon too, huh?" I was really getting upset now.

"Don't twist my words around. I'm just calling it like I see it. You like Quaid. That's what's causing the problem."

"I never said I liked Quaid."

"You don't have to say it. Actions speak louder than words."

"And what have I done by my actions to prove that I like Quaid?"

Hype sucked his teeth. "Females, yo … y'all are so smart until—" He stopped when he saw the look I gave him. "A'ight, I won't go there. But on some real, the fact that you was still fuckin with this nigga after the fact that he was the reason you and Twon broke up, that shows me, and the rest of the world, that you like Quaid. If you had no feelings for Quaid whatsoever, there is no way you would have got in that car. You would have either let that nigga keep driving down that street, or you would have said something to him to make him leave. But one thing I do know is, you wouldn't have got in that car."

I sat there trying to think of a comeback, but I just couldn't. I had too much on my mind right now.

"Whatever, Hype." I got up from my seat and grabbed my bag.

"Where you going?" he said, looking all offended.

"I got homework to do."

"What, so you mad at me now?"

"No, I just have to go home."

"Okay, Tierra."

"Bye."

"Bye."

As I was walking down the street, my cell phone buzzed with a text from Hype. *Charge it to the game, Baby Girl.* I sucked my teeth and rolled my eyes.

Shut up, Big Head, I texted back. I could never stay mad at Hype for too long.

Twon

I was straight furious after seeing Quaid with my girl. That nigga got an ass whooping coming. Believe that. The only reason I ain't hooked off on him yet is because I know that him and Hype is cousins, and I'm close with the family. But after what I just saw, Hype just going to have to be mad with me.

I slammed the front door as I entered the house after school the next day. The whole day, Tierra kept texting me, asking me to meet up with her to talk during lunch. I didn't answer any of her messages, and I ended up skipping lunch so I wouldn't have to see her.

"Don't be slamming my got-damn door!" my mother screamed at me from the couch.

"Sorry, Ma," I said, trying to control my agitation. "I didn't see you sitting there."

"Well, why don't you see yourself going to the store to get a pack of cigarettes for me."

"I can't, Ma. I'm pressed for time. I have to go to work." I made my way toward the stairs.

"Boy, did you not just hear me? I said, go to the store to get me a pack of cigarettes!"

I whipped around to face her. I could feel myself getting more and more agitated by the second. "Ma, I just said, I have to go to work!" I shouted.

"Who the fuck do you think you yelling at like that? Huh? Get your ass down to that store and get me a fucking pack of cigarettes!"

I stared at her for a long moment then stomped to the front door and wrenched it open, slamming it hard behind me. I started my car and screeched down the street, careening around the corner. I was driving so fast that I almost hit another car that turned down my street. The driver honked at me, and I almost lost it.

"WELL, GET THE FUCK OUT THE WAY, THEN!" I screamed out my window.

He just gave me the finger and kept driving.

I pulled up to the store, kept the car running, and grabbed the cigarettes.

When I got back to the house, I threw the cigarettes down on the table next to the couch. "Happy now?"

"I don't like your attitude, Twon. I'm going to need you to simmer your ass down."

"I told you that I had to go to work. You 'bout to make me late. If I get fired, I won't have enough money to pay the TWO HUNDRED DOLLARS a week that you charging me for rent."

"Oh yeah, about that: I'm going to need two-fifty starting next week."

I almost grabbed a chair and flipped it over in response. "Ma, did you hear what I just said?! I can barely afford the two hundred a week, and now you trying to raise it to two-fifty. I already work TWO JOBS. How many hours do you work?"

"That ain't none of your business, boy. I need the money. There's bills to pay around here."

"Ma, I'm already paying the rent. What else is there that you can't afford? What are you doing with your money?"

"I've about had enough of you disrespecting me, boy. What I do with my money is none of your damn business."

"Ma, I can't afford two-fifty a week."

"Well, it sounds like you need to pick up some hours then. Matter of fact, didn't you say you were running late? While you standing there talking, you could have been at work getting my money."

"You really don't care about me, do you?" I chuckled at the realization.

"Get out my face and take your ass to work!" she spat. "And you better have my two-fifty starting next week, or you can find a new place to live."

"You know what?" I said, trembling with rage. "Maybe I should find my father. See if I can work things out with that nigga. Go live with him."

"What did you just say?"

"You heard me. Things with him would have to be better than the bullshit you putting me through."

"So you want to find your father, huh?"

"Yeah," I said, crossing my arms.

"Well, good luck with that." She snatched the pack of cigarettes from the table and stalked out of the room, slamming her bedroom door behind her.

* * *

I pulled into the mall parking lot with only five minutes to spare. I drove recklessly the whole time there — thank God I didn't get pulled over by the cops. I hopped out my whip and rushed into the building. "I hope this nigga Reggie don't be trying to talk the whole day," I said to myself as I hurried up to the store. Reggie was one of those people who loved to talk nonstop, and I wasn't in the mood today.

I rushed over to the time clock and punched in with two minutes to spare. I breathed a sigh of relief.

"Dang, boy. I can't even get a 'Hi'?" said a female voice behind me. I spun around to see Shaneece standing there, her hands on her hips.

"Hey, Shaneece. What are you doing here today?"

She rolled her eyes. "Reggie called out. He said something about his daughter being sick, so he asked me to cover for him."

"Oh. Well hopefully she's alright."

"Yeah. So what's wrong with you?"

"What do you mean?"

"Why do you look so agitated? And why did you rush in here like you were running from the police?"

"I didn't want to be late. You know how Jamel is about being on time and shit." Jamel was Hype's boy. He was mad cool, but he didn't play around when it came to his business.

"True, true. But it seems like something else is wrong though." Her facial features softened as she made her way over to me.

"It's nothing — just got a lot going on at home."

"Your mom?"

"Yeah. She just raised the rent on me to two-fifty a week when I told her I could barely afford the two hundred she's already making me pay."

"Wow, Twon, I'm so sorry to hear that." She rubbed my back gently.

I felt myself heating up slightly, so I stepped away, feeling awkward.

"How's things with your parents?" I said, trying to change the subject.

She rolled her eyes again. "The same. They are always finding new ways to control my life. The latest was taking away my cell phone after school. I already told you how they took my car, right?"

"Oh yeah, you did tell me that. Dang. That's fucked up, ma. I feel for you."

"I know. Thanks. That's why I'm working here. I'm saving up for my own car. They can't take that away from me."

"True."

"I just know it's going to feel so good to be able to do whatever I want, whenever I want." She stepped up close to me again.

I glanced down at her lips. She was wearing some shiny pink lip-gloss, and it was turning me on. I tried to glance away, but I was drawn to her. Her eyes looked so seductive, and her lips were so inviting. I was captivated by the moment. I leaned in to do what I had been secretly dying to do for a while now, but then we heard a bell ringing up at the front of the store.

"Shit!" I said, snapping out of it. "I almost forgot we was at work!"

* * *

I feel like I'm treading on dangerous ground with the Shaneece situation. I was trying my best not to be attracted to her, but she wasn't making the shit easy. And the problems I was having with Tierra were only fueling the fire. After work, I headed over to Hype's house to see if he was up. I didn't feel like going home yet. It was only 11:00 p.m., so my mother was probably still up. I wasn't trying to walk into that house until she was knocked out, because I don't think I can take anymore of her shit today.

I pulled up to Hype's house. The living room and kitchen lights were on, a good sign. I walked up to the door and twisted the knob. It was locked, which I found strange. Hype's mom never locked her door. I knocked a few times. I heard the TV go silent then I heard footsteps toward the door. It opened, and Hype let me in.

"Wassup, nigga?" he said, dapping me up. "What you doing out this late? Ain't it past your bedtime?" He smirked.

"Fuck you, Hype. Why your door locked?"

"Oh, that was G-Ma. She was here earlier, and she always getting on my mom about not locking the door in this neighborhood."

"Oh, for real?"

"Yeah." We made our way to the living room.

"What was you doing?"

"Nothing, playing *Call of Duty*, busting Charles's ass. Matter of fact, hold on."

I waited as Hype called Charles and told him he was done playing for the night. They talked trash back and forth for a few moments about who was winning, then Hype hung up.

"So, what's up with you?" said Hype.

"Nothing, man. My moms is tripping again."

"What she do this time?"

"Nigga, she raised the rent to two-fifty a week!"

"Damn! That's crazy. Why she keep raising the rent?"

"I don't know. I don't even know where this is coming from all of a sudden."

"How's the situation with you and Tierra?"

I tensed up at those words. "Same bullshit."

"Something new happened?"

I shot him a quick glance. It seemed like Hype already knew what was up. "Who told you — Tierra?"

"Yeah. She said that you saw Quaid giving her a ride home from the store."

I sucked my teeth. "Look, nigga, I know Quaid's your cousin and all, but I'm hooking off on that nigga the next time I see him."

"I understand you mad and everything, Twon. But you know I can't just let y'all fight. I mean, he's family, and you basically family too. I wish there was a way to squash all this."

"I tried that when I told that nigga to stay away from my girl."

"True...." said Hype, and he went silent on me.

"What?" I said, finally.

"Damn!" he said. "Y'all niggas situation got *me* all fucked up."

"How does our situation have you fucked up?"

"Cuz, man, I got Tierra confiding in me about what's going on between y'all, I got Quaid doing the same, and then with you and your situation — y'all trying to turn me into a black ass Dr. Phil."

I chuckled at this. "Shut up, Hype. But what did Tierra tell you?"

"Why don't you answer her phone calls so she can tell you herself?"

I sucked my teeth. "I'm not even trying to be dealing with that girl right now."

"Why not? Y'all been together long enough to work this shit out."

"I'll talk to her when it's time."

Hype stared at me then sighed. "A'ight, Twon. If that's what you want to do."

* * *

I had been avoiding Tierra's phone calls and text messages and dodging her at school for about a week now. She was still trying nonstop, which I guess was a good sign, but I wasn't sure I was ready to talk to her again just yet. I looked down as my phone buzzed with yet another text message from her. I waited until I got to a red light, then I read the message.

Twon, I know you're mad at me right now, but I wanted to know if you were coming over for Thanksgiving this year. My mom asked about it the other day.

"Thanksgiving?!" I said to myself. "Wow, time is flying." I hadn't even realized that the holiday was next week, which meant we would get a short break from school. My heart dropped as I realized that our anniversary was actually the day after Thanksgiving this year. I sat there reminiscing until I heard horns honking behind me when the light turned green.

"Oh, shit!" I said, driving again. The whole ride home, I debated as to whether I should answer her back, and if I did, what I should say. I mean, my mother never cooked for Thanksgiving, so I always ended up over at Hype or Quaid or G-Ma's house. I went over Tierra's house last year.

Things would probably be kind of awkward if I went over Hype or G-Ma's house because of my beef with Quaid, but then again, things might be awkward at Tierra's house, with our situation going on.

I thought about my dad. I never met the nigga. The only thing I knew of him was what my mother told me. She said that he had taken one look at me and said that I was 'too damned light skinned to be a seed of his' before he left. From what she said, he never turned back.

I briefly considered Googling him to see if I could find him, or at least see if he had some family that I could start connecting with.

I pulled up to my house, lost in my thoughts. Just as I killed the ignition, my phone rang. It was Tierra. For some reason, seeing her name on the screen made me angry.

"Why you keep calling my phone!" I said, skipping right past hello.

"Twon, I need to talk to you."

"You wasn't worried about talking to me before. I was blowing up your phone left and right, just like you doing to me. But your ass ain't have time for nobody but Quaid."

"Twon, I keep trying to tell you. It wasn't even like—"

"Whatever, Tierra. Stop calling my fucking phone before I block you." *Click.* I hung up on her. Part of me felt like I was wrong, and being a bit childish, but I had too much going on to deal with her bullshit right now.

Shaneece

It seems like Twon is really going through a lot lately. The situation with his mom reminds me of my parents. They don't neglect or reject me, but they treat me badly. I was so glad when he finally opened up to me at work the other day.

And for a moment there, it seemed like he was going to kiss me! Oh, my gosh, I am SO ready for that moment.

Tierra can play around if she wants to, but to me, Twon is a good man, and he deserves to be treated as such. I'm willing to do all that she won't do and more. She keeps coming to me for advice about the situation, but I just want to tell her so badly to let him go. Honestly, I don't feel like she deserves him, and there's no way that she could ever relate to him the way I can.

"Shaneece!" Tierra said.

"Huh?" I snapped out of my funk.

"I said, do you think I should do it?"

"Do what?"

"You didn't hear anything I just said, did you?"

"Um … no. I'm sorry. What were you saying?" I shot her a fake apologetic smile.

"I said that I think I'm ready, and I'm just going to tell Twon that we can finally go ahead and do it on our anniversary."

"Do what? You mean have sex?" *NO-O-O-O-O-O!* There was no way I could let this happen — not when I was so close.

"Yes." She blushed shyly. "I think it's time."

Yeah right, girl. You wouldn't know what to do with it no matter what time it was. I almost rolled my eyes it was so ridiculous, but I didn't. "What makes you feel like you're ready?" I said with fake interest, hoping my expression didn't convey how I really felt.

"I just know. We've been going through so many issues lately, and I really think that just going ahead and doing it will solve our problems. Maybe once we start having sex, Twon won't be so mad at me all the time. Maybe it will be a stress reliever for him. Plus, I really want to show him how much I love him."

"Well," I said, trying to think of a way to steer her against this decision, "As a girl who has experience with all sorts of guys, I have to ask: Are you sure that's a good idea?"

"What do you mean?" She looked confused and a little embarrassed at my smug confidence. Good.

"Because, you said before that you weren't ready. If you just go ahead and give it to him now, he might think you're just trying to use sex to get back with him. If it doesn't come from the heart, he probably won't accept it. Trust me, I know. It doesn't always end so well." I sighed wearily for emphasis. I was pulling this argument out of my ass, but I hoped it worked.

"But it IS from the heart!" she exclaimed. "I love Twon. I just want him to see it."

"I mean ... are you even on birth control or anything? You don't want to get pregnant by him, because that could really mess up your relationship."

"Birth control?" She looked even more confused.

Now we're getting somewhere! "Yes, girl. You have to cover all of the bases before you make a decision like this."

"But, can't we just use a condom? Are you on birth control?"

"Girl, condoms break easily. And of course, I'm on birth control!" I lied. Hype and I barely ever used condoms, and I had never been on birth control. "We can't just bring other lives into this world irresponsibly."

She sat there for a moment. "Wow," she said, looking defeated. "I don't even know if I can get birth control pills in time before our anniversary. And don't they take a while to kick in?"

"Oh, yes, girl. They take at least six to eight weeks to start working. For some people, up to three months." I lied again. This was just too easy. She was so gullible, but I'm sure she knew how to Google stuff too. I was treading on dangerous ground here, but at this point, I was desperate.

Her eyes widened. "Three months?"

"Yes, girl. This is serious business."

"Wow." She was quiet again. "Well, it looks like I might need to think of something else then."

Although part of me felt bad for what I was doing, another part of me was relieved.

* * *

After school, I snuck over Hype's house to have sex. After we finished, I took a shower then headed home. When I got there, my parents weren't home yet, so I fixed myself a late lunch and went upstairs to do some homework. After a few hours, I was exhausted from the day's activities, so I fell asleep, only to be awakened an hour later by my father bursting in my door and flipping on my lights.

"SHANEECE!"

I jumped up in my bed, alarmed at the sudden sound. "Dad?" I said.

"You think you're slick, huh?"

"What are you talking about?" I racked my brains trying to think of what could be making him mad at me now. I hadn't called or texted Twon, and he didn't know about Hype, so I really didn't know what this was about.

"What is this?" He handed me some papers that were stapled together. It looked like he had printed out the document I had saved on my desktop with a list of cars I was searching for online.

"It's just some cars I was looking at, Dad."

"You think it's fucking cute to keep antagonizing me, huh?"

"What are you talking about?"

"First you keep talking to this Twon character, even after I tell you that I don't want you talking to boys, then you try to be slick and change his name in your phone, and now you're trying to buy your own car."

"You took the car I had."

"I took it for a *reason*, Shaneece!"

"You didn't have a real reason to take my car! You just wanted to make my life miserable!" I jumped up out of my bed to face him.

SMACK! My face burned from the impact. "Who the fuck you think you yelling at?"

"I told you not to put your hands on her!" My mother came out of nowhere and started raining blows on my father's head and back. He grabbed her arms.

"Honey, I'm just trying to discipline her," he said calmly.

"Well, you don't have to put your hands on her to do that!" she yelled.

"Calm down," he said, and then he turned to me. "I want you to go to that job tomorrow and put in your two weeks' notice."

"No!" I said, not believing what I just heard.

"Do it, or I'll do it for you!" he boomed.

"Let the girl work, damn it!" said my mother. "She needs something to do since we won't allow her to date."

I looked at my mother. Her face was full of guilt.

"You know she's trying to use the money from that job to buy a car, right?" said my father.

"So what?" said my mother. "If she keeps her grades up and saves money to buy her own car and afford her own insurance, she is learning responsibility."

My father thought about it for a moment then calmed down. "Okay," he said finally. "You can keep the job. But if your grades start slipping, you're putting in your two weeks' notice. You hear me?"

I swallowed a lump in my throat as the tears streamed down my face. "Yes."

"I'm sorry for hitting you."

"Okay."

He nodded and stood there a moment, not knowing what else to do, then he and my mother left my room.

* * *

That was the second time my father hit me this year. I'm getting sick of him putting his hands on me and constantly trying to control my life. How would he feel if someone did that to him?

I loved both of my parents, but sometimes I felt like I hated them too. They provided a roof over my head, clothes for me to wear, and food for me to eat, but everything else they did made my life a living hell.

BZZZZZZZ! BZZZZZZZ! BZZZZZZZ!

I looked at my phone and saw that I had a call from my sister Shanelle.

"Hey," I said.

"Hey!" said Shanelle. "What's wrong?"

Shanelle and I were very close, and she could always tell when I was upset. "It's our parents again," I said.

"What did he do now?"

"He hit me again."

She sucked her teeth. "Why?"

"Because he was searching my desktop, and he found out that I was looking up cars on the internet."

"I can't stand when he does stuff like that," said Shanelle. "It's a total invasion of privacy."

"Well, at least you don't have to deal with it anymore. Ever since you got away, they totally zeroed in on me."

"I know," she said, sounding guilty. "And believe me, I would have stayed, but I didn't think I could deal with him too much longer. I honestly feel like, with all of the stuff I was into, I would have ended up hurting myself if I didn't get away from Dad."

During her high school years, Shanelle sneaked out countless times without my parents knowing it. She went to parties, she smoked, she drank, she slept with all types of guys, but my parents never noticed because she was always a straight-A student. They probably never would suspect me either, if I got grades like that. I'm more of an A-B student.

"I don't blame you. I'm counting down the days to graduation myself."

"That's right," she said. "And also, you can come stay with me for your winter break after Christmas if you want. It's only a week, but at least it will help."

"Oh, God, thank you!" I was extremely grateful for my sister's offer. I would do anything to get out of this house, even if it was only for a week. "Shoot, I wish I could stay with you for Thanksgiving, but I know you're coming here. Right?"

"Of course, girl. You know I couldn't leave you alone with them on a holiday!"

"Thank you," I breathed.

"Listen, I have a call coming in, so I have to let you go, but keep your head up. After Christmas, only half a year left, then you're free!"

"I know. Thank you. I'll talk to you later."

"Love you."

"Love you too."

* * *

Twon and I were scheduled to work together again today. I loved it when we worked together. It gave me a chance to be alone with him and to talk to him. I got there ten minutes early for my shift. To my surprise and delight, Twon was already there!

"Hey!" I said, walking over to him to give him a hug. "When did you get here?"

"Damn, girl, you smell good. I got here a few minutes ago."

"Thank you. You're here mighty early. Couldn't wait to work with me, huh?" I shot him a flirtatious look.

He blushed. "I try to be here early every day."

"Mm hm," I said, smiling. "So how's everything at home?" I walked toward the back of the store to punch in at the time clock. Twon followed me.

"It's the same. My mother is always tripping."

"Are you spending Thanksgiving with her?"

"I pretty much have no choice. I got beef with Quaid, so that pretty much cancels out his whole family, and me and Tierra are still on the rocks, so I'm not going there either. So I guess I won't be having no Thanksgiving this year, cuz my mom never cooks." He looked so sad that I wanted to wrap him in my arms and hug him.

"And you don't know anyone from your father's family, huh?"

"Nope. I've been thinking of looking him up lately though. Maybe if he has family out here, I could start getting to know them."

"You should do it. It's always good to have someone to talk to."

"That's true. I'm grateful that I at least get to talk to you, though."

This time, it was my turn to blush. "Well, I'm glad to be here for you. Hey, maybe I can bring you a plate or something on Black Friday. You're working the day shift too, right?"

His eyes lit up. "Thanks! You're working the same time, right?"

"Yeah … maybe we could even hang out together afterwards."

"Yeah… you know, that day is actually me and Tierra's anniversary — or at least it was supposed to be."

"Oh," I said. "Well, maybe if we hang out together, that will help take your mind off of it."

He thought about it for a moment. "You know what? I just might take you up on that. Thanks for the offer."

"No problem. Anything you need, I got you. *Anything.*" I shot him the most seductive look possible, and he licked his lips and blushed.

Hype

Shaneece was taking a shower after we just finished getting it in. I wished she could stay longer so that we could spend more time together, but she had to go to work. I was kind of looking forward to graduation — maybe me and Shaneece could go to the same college, or at least go somewhere close to each other so that we wouldn't have to hide our relationship.

I was contemplating asking her again whether she wanted me to talk to her father. I wanted to bring it up but decided against it because the last time I tried to say something, she broke up with me. I don't want to go through all that again because I'm really feeling Shorty... I think I might even be in love....

"Whew!" she said, emerging from the bathroom dressed in her work uniform. "The water pressure in your shower is so good!"

"I wish we could have took that shower together," I said, staring at her with a whole lotta want in my eyes.

"Boy, stop. If we ever did that, I definitely would be late to work."

I chuckled. "You might be right about that."

"Well, I gotta go, so I'll see you later, okay?" She stood on her tiptoes to kiss me.

"Cool." I said. "You sure you don't want to come over for Thanksgiving?"

"You know I can't, Hype. My parents don't let me go anywhere on that day."

"What about the day after? You work in the morning, right?"

"They make it a whole weekend event. I have to go straight home after work on that day to spend more 'quality time with the family'," she said, emphasizing her words with air quotes.

"Damn. So I won't even be able to see you until after the whole weekend is over."

"Don't worry, baby," she said, kissing me again. "Momma will make time for you as soon as school starts back."

"You better," I said, chuckling again.

She left, and not ten minutes later, Quaid's car pulled up. "Damn, that was close!" I said. If Shaneece had left any later, Quaid definitely would have caught us. Not that I think he would have said anything, but Shaneece was terrified about her parents finding out about us, and if Quaid saw us together, he might casually mention it to the boys and them thinking nothing of it, and once something like that got out, there was no tellin' what might happen.

"What's up, cuz?" I said, dapping Quaid up.

"What's up?" he said.

"Nothing. Just got finished doing some homework."

"Mm hm." He looked distracted and worried. "Listen, I need to talk to you."

"About what?"

"About what I should do about Tierra."

"What do you mean, 'what you should do about Tierra?' You better leave that girl alone, Quaid. You know Twon already said he wants to hook off on you."

"Yeah, I know, but that's his problem." Quaid's eyes dared me to challenge his reasoning.

I stared at him in shock. "That's fucked up, Quaid."

"Wait, I didn't mean it like that. I just meant that he's overreacting, that's all. It's his problem to sort out, no one else's."

"How is he overreacting when you're low-key trying to get with his girl?"

"I'm not trying to get with her! I just want us to be friends again."

"Quaid, you need to leave Tierra alone," I repeated. "This is fucking up lifelong friendships. Do you even care about that?"

"Yes, I do," he said. "But I just want to be her friend. That's all we ever were. The rest of you are making a big deal out of it."

"Well, I don't think you should try to get in contact with her any time soon. If anything, you should at least wait until she patches things up with Twon."

"How do you even know if they're getting back together?"

"I'm serious, Quaid. I don't like being in the middle of all this bullshit and drama. This is female shit. This ain't no damn reality show!"

"Okay, I'll back off." He didn't sound convinced, like he was saying it just to shut me up.

"That's good," I said. "I hope you mean it."

* * *

Thanksgiving dinner was lit! After G-Ma said her long ass grace, everybody dug into the food. I must say, this year, the food was on point. Pretty much all my family came: Quaid and his mom, and Charles and his mom. I felt kind of bad that Twon couldn't come. I knew his mom wasn't cooking nothing. She never did. Twon had always spent Thanksgiving with us — well, except last year, when he was over Tierra's house.

"Wassup wassup!" said Charles, as he walked through the front door.

"Hey, cuz!" I said, dapping him up. He dapped up Quaid then turned back to me.

"Where's Twon? He in the bathroom or something?"

"Oh, nah. That nigga ain't coming."

"Why not?"

"Nothing, just him and Quaid got a little beef going on right now."

"Corduroy Quaid got beef?" He chuckled. "I got to hear this shit. Where G-Ma and them?"

"In the kitchen throwing shade back and forth at each other."

He rolled his eyes. "Oh, God. Here we go. Let me go get a plate. I'll be right back, depending on how long it takes me to work my way past all those women in the kitchen."

"I know that's right!" I said, and we laughed.

He came back five minutes later with a large cup of Kool-Aid and a plate piled high with food. "Eyo, Quaid, set up one of those TV table trays for me." He waited as Quaid set it up, then he put his plate and cup down and sat down next to him. He was about to dig into his food when he realized he didn't bring any eating utensils with him. "Shit!" he said. "I forgot a fork!"

"Watch your mouth, boy!" said Quaid's mom, as she brought him a fork and some napkins.

"Thanks, Auntie!" He wasted no time digging in, attacking the chicken and mashed potatoes first.

"You're welcome. Good to see you. Maybe y'all can have a talk about your future."

"What about my future?" said Charles through a mouthful of potatoes.

"Boy, don't talk through your food," she said.

"Auntie, you always throwing shade," I said, rolling my eyes.

"Hmmph," she said, rolling her eyes back at me before she went back to the kitchen.

"Always talking shit," said Charles. He took a bite out of his chicken leg.

"Hey, that's my Ma," said Quaid.

"You know what I mean, man."

"So what's been up with you, man?" I said, trying to change the subject.

"Ain't shit," he said, taking another bite. "Still on the block, getting this money, know what I mean…."

"You know that's dangerous, right?" said Quaid.

"Look, everybody ain't a good little church boy like you, Quaid." Charles glared at Quaid and took a long swig of his Kool-Aid then swallowed it with a loud gulp.

"Nobody said you had to be all that," said Quaid. "But you should start thinking about your future. What are your interests?"

"Getting money and bitches."

I burst out laughing at that one.

"Come on, Charles," said Quaid. "Be serious." Quaid glared at me.

"Nigga, you ain't my daddy! Mind your business. If you want to do that school shit, do you, and I'll do me."

I wanted to say something to Charles too, but I didn't know how to approach him. Me and Charles were too much alike. We both talked a lot of shit, and neither one of us liked to back down. I decided it was best to just leave the situation alone for now.

I started thinking about my own future. Dr. Young had given me his business card that day at school. Maybe I would apply to the Sociology program, see what that was all about.

* * *

I decided to call Tierra that night to see if Twon went over to her house for Thanksgiving. I tried to call Twon first, but his phone went straight to voicemail. I hope that nigga's alright. I can't imagine not having family to spend Thanksgiving with. Maybe I should bring him a plate or something.

"Hello?" said Tierra, sounding like she just woke up.

"Oh, my bad. You was sleep?"

"Yeah," she said, sounding kind of sad.

"How was your Thanksgiving? Your mom cook a lot?"

"Yeah, she always does. It was lit. My cousins and grandparents and everybody came down."

"Shit girl, I might need me a plate."

"Boy, stop." She giggled. "I know G-Ma and them probably threw down over there at your house."

"You right about that, but you can never have too much food."

"You're silly. But hey, did Twon go over your house for Thanksgiving?"

"No, I was actually calling to see if he went to your house."

"No, he didn't. I tried to invite him, but he cussed me out and told me to stop calling his phone or he would block me." Her voice trembled when she said that last part.

"Damn. Well, I guess you just gotta give him some time."

"I've been trying to do that, Hype, but nothing seems like it's working. Tomorrow is supposed to be our anniversary, and it basically seems like we're never getting back together!"

"Damn, that is tomorrow, huh? Want me to try to talk to him?"

"No ... well, I had a plan for tomorrow, but I don't know if it will work."

"What plan?"

"I was going to just...." She took a breath so deep, I could hear it through the phone. "I think I'm going to just show up at his house and see what happens."

"And...?"

"Come on, Hype. You know what I mean."

"No, I don't."

"I was going to just go ahead and give him what he's asking for."

"Um ... you sure that's a good idea?"

"Why does everybody keep saying that?"

"Who's everybody?" I pretended to be offended. "I thought I was your BFF!"

"Boy, stop!" she said, giggling again.

"Nah, but for real though ... I mean, I know you ain't done it yet, but that's not usually how it goes down. You don't just roll up and say, 'Hey, let's have sex now' like you're ordering fast food. It happens cuz you can't resist it, like a train going down the tracks with no brakes. You sure you're ready for all that?"

She took a long pause before she answered. "I hear what you're saying, Hype, but I'm willing to do whatever it takes. I just want us to be back together. This is the longest we've ever gone without speaking, and I'm not ready to lose him."

"Damn, that's real. Well, good luck, I guess."

"You guess? Fuck you, Hype!"

"Look, girl, I'm not trying to envision y'all getting it in. 'Ooh, Twon!'" I mocked.

"Bye, Hype. I'm done with you."

"Girl, you know you can't get enough of me."

"Whatever. I need to get back to my beauty rest."

"A'ight. I'll talk to you later."

"Okay, see you."

"See you."

* * *

It seemed like everybody's ass had to work on Black Friday — Twon, Quaid, everybody. I ain't have nobody to chill with. Charles was with one of his jumpoffs. I briefly considered hanging out with Tierra, but I definitely did not want to hear any more about her plans to get it in with Twon. Honestly, I'm not sure if that's a good look for her, but she's gonna do what she wants to do regardless of what I say, so ... hey.

I spent most of my morning playing *Call of Duty*, eating leftovers, and talking trash back and forth with G-Ma.

When it got to be about 3:00 p.m., I decided to give Shaneece a call. I figured she was just getting to the end of her shift. Maybe we could sneak and chill together before she had to go back to her parents' house. She could probably just tell them that her boss made her stay over.

"Hello?" She sounded kind of breathless.

"Hey, girl. What's up?"

"Nothing. Listen, I just got off work, so I'm about to head home now."

"That's actually why I was calling you. I was trying to see if you wanted to come through before you had to go to your parents' house."

"Sorry, I can't do that. I have prior obligations."

Prior obligations? What was this chick on? "What do you mean, prior obligations? Can't you just tell your parents that your boss made you stay over or something?"

"Sorry, Maria. I will have to meet you next week. I'm sure we'll finish the project in time. Talk to you later."

"*Maria?* Shaneece, what are you—?" *CLICK.*

I stared at the phone for a few moments, shocked and confused. Why the hell did she call me Maria? Did her dad come up to the store or something?

I didn't know what was going on, but I felt it in my heart that something was up. I called her again. The phone rang then went to voicemail. I tried again and again, and both times, it went to voicemail. I tried one last time, and it went straight to voicemail, like she turned had it off.

I started feeling guilty. "I hope I didn't just get her in trouble," I said to myself.

I decided that I probably should call Twon. He actually worked with her up at Sports Locker. Maybe he seen if her dad came in the store or something.

I called Twon's phone. His shit went to voicemail too. That was strange.

"Maybe he left it off at work," I said to myself.

I waited half an hour before I called Twon's number again. It went straight to voicemail.

"Why this nigga got his phone off?" Then I remembered that Tierra said she was going to show up at his crib today for their anniversary.

I calmed down after that, happy that Twon and Tierra were finally getting back together.

Tierra

I stood in front of my mirror looking at myself in the lingerie that I had purchased earlier that morning. I thought my body looked okay... hopefully Twon would think so too. I went and got my hair and nails done just the way he liked it, and I even put a little makeup on to make today even more special.

I know that everybody seems to think that this is not the best decision, but in my heart, I feel like I just want me and Twon to get back together. I prayed to God that I was making the right decision. I knew that having sex wouldn't ruin my chances of getting saved, but I still felt kind of guilty about what I was doing.

"I really hope this works," I murmured to my reflection in the mirror. "I really just hope I don't make a fool of myself."

I had been doing some searching on the internet about sex and what it was supposed to feel like and be like. I felt kind of pathetic doing that because I felt like I was already supposed to know a lot of the stuff I found. I just hoped I wasn't bad at it. I had briefly considered calling Shaneece to ask her about some tips for the bedroom, but she seemed so adamant against me giving it to Twon that I decided against it.

Even though during our last conversation, Shaneece had said that condoms break easily and that birth control took a while to kick in, I decided that I was just going to have to take my chances. I went to the store and purchased some condoms. I just hoped that they were the right fit for Twon. I would be so embarrassed if they were too big or too small.

"Oh, well, if they don't fit, he can buy some next time. At least he'll know I put some thought into it."

I lotioned my body once again then put on a cute dress I'd found on sale. I had bought some sexy new heels, too so I put those in my purse to wear after I got off the bus.

I touched up my makeup then decided it was time to leave. I prayed that Twon was home. He had no idea I was coming.

As soon as I got to my front door, my mother called my cell phone.

I sighed. "Hello?" I hoped she didn't hear the irritation in my voice. Why did she have to call right now?

"What's wrong with you? What are you doing?"

"Nothing, Ma. I was about to do my homework."

"Oh, well, I was just calling to let you know that I won't be home until late tonight. I'm going over Stacy's house after work." Stacy was my mother's best friend.

"Oh, okay. I'll see you when you get here."

"Are you sure you're okay?"

"Yeah, why?"

"Because you sounded kind of upset just now, when you answered the phone, and I know that today was you and Twon's anniversary. Do you want me to just come home after work instead of going over Stacy's? We could watch a movie and order a pizza or something. Have a girls' night."

"Oh, no, I'll be fine."

"You sure? I mean, I don't have to go. And you know I'm more than happy to be there with you."

"No, I'll be okay. Have fun with Stacy."

"Okay. I'll try not to stay out too late. And make sure you call me if you want me to come home, and I'll fly right over there."

I chuckled. "Okay, Ma."

"Alright, I love you."

"I love you too."

We hung up. I felt so guilty for lying to my mother when she was only trying to help, but I needed to at least try to do everything I could to get back with Twon.

I took a deep breath, let it out, said, "Let's do this," and headed to the bus stop.

* * *

Before the bus rolled to a stop, I switched my flats for the heels I'd stashed in my purse. I stepped off the bus taking care not to trip, and as soon as I got to Twon's house, I saw his car parked outside. That was a good sign. I walked up to the front door feeling butterflies on the inside. I sincerely hoped he wouldn't just slam the door in my face and tell me to leave. I took a deep breath and knocked on the door.

After a few moments, I heard footsteps, then the front door opened. It was Twon's mother!

"Hi!" I said, feeling even more nervous now. I hadn't expected his mother to be there. Maybe we could just get a hotel room. I definitely did not want to have sex with Twon knowing that his mother was right there in the same house.

"Oh, hey Tierra!" She gave me a fake smile like she always did, but this time she followed it up with a raised eyebrow and a quick glance at my outfit. "What are you doing here?"

"Oh, I just came to see Twon."

"Well, you look nice." There was that look again, this time zeroing in on my sexy high heels.

"Thank you," I said, stepping past her as she held the door open. "It's our anniversary today."

"Oh, your anniversary!" She gave me another fake smile, and her look said *so that's what this is all about.* "Well, congratulations! Twon is upstairs in his room."

"Oh, okay. Do you mind if I go up?"

"Not at all!" She shot me another fake smile before going to the living room.

That was strange. His mother always faked being nice to me when I came over the house, but today, it seemed like she was on some kind of extreme. I put it out of my head because there were other more important things demanding my attention.

As I climbed the stairs, I heard these weird creaking noises, and it definitely wasn't the steps creaking. They were coming from somewhere upstairs.

"What in the world is that?" I said to myself. I got to about the third to the last step when I heard a female voice moaning.

That sound took my breath away. I hunched over trying to regain my composure as I heard the creaking and moaning increase, then a louder moan, a deep male voice this time, and then the moaning subsided as the bed stopped creaking. I sat there on the stairs with tears streaming down my face. No one needed to tell me what was going on in that room. Twon had found someone else, just like he said he would.

My thoughts were a whirl of confusion. *Why did his mother let me come up here knowing Twon had another girl in his room? What is going on in this house right now?*

Feeling sick to my stomach, I sat there trying to figure out what to do. There was no way I could see him after this, and I for sure didn't want him to come out that room and see me sitting on his stairs like some sort of pathetic loser. I held the banister to pull myself up, and got down one step when I heard Twon speak.

"Damn, Shaneece," he said, his voice deep and low and full of passion.

Something clicked in me when I heard those words. My body trembled with fear and rage as I stomped the rest of the way up the stairs and down the hall, and flung open his bedroom door.

Absolutely nothing prepared me for what I saw next. Twon and Shaneece were completely naked on his bed, and Shaneece was in the middle of going down on him. My mouth dropped open in shock.

Both of them whipped their heads up to see me.

"How could you?" I said. "HOW COULD YOU!" I screamed.

"Tierra!" Twon looked totally stunned, and Shaneece's reaction was about the same. She tumbled off him, clutching the blanket to cover herself and not doing a good job of it. I saw more of that girl's body than I ever wanted to see.

"YOU BETTER NOT TELL ME YOU BEEN FUCKING IN MY HOUSE!" I jumped at the sound as Twon's mother came up behind me and pushed the door open wider, forcing herself into the room.

"Ma!" said Twon, scrambling for an edge of the blanket to cover himself up, and pulling it off Shaneece in the process. The whole scene was too ludicrous for words.

"YOU TOLD ME THAT YOU AND THIS LITTLE THOT ASS HEIFER WERE DOING HOMEWORK!" screamed his mother.

Twon and his mother began arguing, but I heard nothing they said as I ran back down the stairs. At the last stair, my heel got caught on something, and I tripped and fell forward. I quickly retrieved my purse, changed into my flats, and burst out the front door, practically running toward Hype's house.

* * *

I don't know how I made it to Hype's house. I could barely see from the tears flooding my eyes. Every time I wiped them, more came, so I just stopped wiping and kept walking. When I finally got there, I banged on the door. Hype answered looking shocked and confused.

"Hey, what's...?"

I collapsed into his arms.

"Hype!" I wailed.

"Tierra, what happened?" He was trying to hold me up, but I sank to the floor, and he sank down with me, breaking my fall. "What happened, girl?" he said, rubbing my back.

"Twon cheated...." I tried to catch my breath, but I was hyperventilating by now.

"Calm down, calm down," he said, trying to soothe me as he rubbed my back. "What makes you think he cheated? It was probably just a misunderstanding. I know for a fact that he never mentioned nobody to me, so I don't think he's cheating."

"I … s-saw them…." I forced the words out of my mouth.

"You saw them? Saw them where?"

"I went to his house like I told you. His mom answered the door and said he was upstairs. I heard … creaking … and moaning … THAT FUCKING BITCH!" I screamed, jumping up off the floor and onto my feet in one swift motion.

Hype looked at me in shock. "What the *fuck*? How did you…?"

"I'm going back over there to BEAT that bitch's ass!" My heart pounded quickly as my body shook with rage.

"Nah, nah, Tierra, you too mad right now. I can't let you go over there. You might mess around and kill a bitch. Then you'll be locked up."

"I don't give a fuck if he or that little bitch dies!" I spat. I ran to his kitchen.

"Where you goin'?"

Hype chased after me, and when he saw me pull out a butcher knife, he held his hands out toward me. "Yo, Tierra … calm down, yo." His eyes were wide, and he looked nervous.

"I'm 'bout to kill him and that bitch!" I stormed past Hype and headed to the front door.

"Tierra, chill! For real! I'm not letting you go over there like that!" He stood there blocking the doorway to the living room.

"Get out of my way!"

"No, I'm not going to—"

"MOVE!" I screamed.

"What y'all doing in here? Tierra, girl, what you doing with that knife?" G-Ma walked around Hype and stood right in front of me.

"G-Ma…" Feeling like I might collapse, I dropped the knife, ran into her arms, and crumpled against her as she hugged me. "G-Ma…" I wailed.

"Shhhh … shhhh … tell me what happened, baby."

"T-Twon cheated on me…." I stammered. "I caught him doing it!"

"Oh … baby, I'm so sorry to hear that," she said. "Hype, put that knife back for me please."

Hype did what she said without a word.

My heart felt like it was breaking into a million pieces. "How could he do this?" I wailed.

"It's going to be alright, Honey," said G-Ma, rubbing my back to soothe me. "Sometimes things happen that we don't understand, but we praise God anyhow."

We sat there for a few moments, with G-Ma rubbing my back and offering comforting words while Hype tried to lighten things up by telling jokes.

Soon, my tears went away, and my feelings of heartache were replaced with anger and bitterness. "He had me blowing up his phone every day!" I spat. "Calling him and calling him, trying to make sure he had a good Thanksgiving. And it turns out he didn't want anything to do with me because he was busy fucking Shaneece!"

Hype's eyes gew wide with a look of confusion then shock and rage. "What you just say?! Twon been busy fucking WHO?!"

Twon

I feel like the ultimate fuck-up. I messed around and fucked Shaneece, Tierra saw it, my mom saw it, and then she threatened to kick me out. I don't know what to do. I never meant to hurt Tierra, I promise. I know I talked a lot of shit, and I was mean to her, but I never meant for any of this to happen. I liked Shaneece, and I was attracted to her, but having sex with her was a huge mistake. I feel like I just got caught up with the whole situation. I wasn't thinking straight. I don't know if Tierra will ever take me back. I would do anything to turn back the hands of time, but I know I can't.

"I need to get the fuck up out of here," I said to myself, as I pulled open my laptop and went to the Google search engine. A tear slipped down my face as I had a flashback of Tierra's eyes when she saw me and Shaneece. I wiped my tear away and typed in my father's name.

I was praying internally that I could find an address or phone number or something. I hoped the nigga would at least let me come and stay with him for at least a week. I just needed to get out of here. I was prepared to beg, to pay him money, whatever.

I just need to get out of here before I go crazy, and he is my last resort. "Shit, it's the least he can do for abandoning me all these years."

True story, I have never even heard the man's voice, never seen a picture, never got a birthday card, nothing. I searched his name, and the first couple of pages showed nothing. I got to the fourth page of results, and my heart dropped at the first one listed.

It was a news story about a man with my father's name who had been killed in a hit-and-run accident in my hometown. I swallowed a lump in my throat as I clicked on the link. I prayed that this was just a coincidence, and that it wasn't him. The link opened up to the story, which was dated the year I was born. My heart leaped to my chest as I read the story about how my father was killed on the day I was born while rushing to the hospital to see me for the first time. He never made it.

My heart sank to a place I had never felt before. I clicked another link, which led to an obituary. I finally saw his face, and I blinked back tears as I looked into the eyes of the man who helped to create me.

I looked just like him.

* * *

I sat there on the floor sipping on my third bottle of Henny. I knew I was drinking way too much — hell, I wasn't even a drinker like that, but this shit was too much.

"That nigga is dead. I never even got to meet him, and now I never will!"

My mind was filled with depressing thoughts. All in the same day I found out that I basically killed my father and broke Tierra's heart. I was zoned out listening to "Slippin'" by DMX when my mother came into my room.

"And now you up here drinking!" she said, stepping over me and picking up my two empty bottles of Henny. "You must *want* to get kicked out, don't you?" She snatched the third bottle out of my hand and went to the bathroom to pour it down the sink drain. I heard her throw the bottles in the bathroom trash, then she came back into my room. "Did you hear what I said, Twon? I asked you if you wanted me to kick you out, because that's exactly where you're headed." She stood there in front of me with her hands on her hips.

"How come you never told me?" I said, looking up at her from where I sat on the floor slumped against my bed.

"Never told you what? And you better not say nothing crazy. I don't care if you drunk."

"You never told me … about my father."

She froze at those words but tried to play it off. "What *about* your father?" She was full of attitude.

"You never told me … he died."

"Who told you about your father?" She took a step closer to me. "Who told you?"

"I looked him up on Google." My mind was swimming. I felt like I was going to throw up as the blood rushed to my head.

"Well, nobody told your old nosy ass to go fishing on the internet anyway. It was none of your damn business."

"What do you mean, none of my business? He's my father!"

"It was your fucking fault he died!"

I looked at her with hurt eyes.

"Yeah, that's right, I said it!" Her eyes were full of malice and hatred. "It was your fucking fault! If he hadn't been busting his ass off a third shift trying to get to the hospital to see you, he would have been thinking more clearly. This never would have happened, and he would still be here today! But no, I had to lose a good man and get saddled with a kid to raise by myself all in one day."

Her words cut me to the core. "You told me he abandoned me ... why did you lie to me?"

"Well, if I had to hurt, you had to hurt. It would hurt you more to hear that he wanted nothing to do with your sorry ass than for you to know that he died."

"Is that why you hate me?"

"Boy, fuck you! Hate doesn't even begin to describe how I feel about you."

I jumped up off the floor and ran to the bathroom because I could feel my insides rushing up to get out. I bent over the toilet to vomit, and when I was finished, I passed out.

* * *

I woke up the next morning on the bathroom floor. My t-shirt was soaked in vomit. I must have thrown up again in my sleep.

My heart burned with the memories of everything that happened as I slowly got myself up and took a shower. After that, I looked at my phone and saw more than a hundred text messages from Shaneece. I didn't even read them. This situation was all the way fucked up.

"What the fuck is going on with my life, man?" I said, staring at myself in the mirror. This year just seemed like it was getting worse and worse every day. A nigga couldn't catch a break if he wanted to.

I think the worst feeling of all was that I felt I had nowhere to turn. I couldn't turn to my mother, because she despised my existence. I couldn't turn to Tierra, because I broke her heart. I couldn't turn to Quaid, because we had beef. I couldn't talk to Charles because he wasn't the sentimental type. And now, I couldn't even turn to my father, because I killed him the day I was born.

I sat there on my bed, trying to think of another option. I was supposed to go work at the factory today, but I was already three hours late, so I knew I would get written up.

I called my supervisor to let him know I wouldn't make it in because I was sick. He got sarcastic with me, threatened to fire me if it happened again, then hung up the phone.

I hoped he didn't end up firing me because I was definitely quitting that job at Sports Locker. There was no way I could continue to work with Shaneece after what just happened. I didn't even know what I was supposed to say to her. I mean, I would feel bad for rejecting her, but I never really wanted to be with her. Tierra was my girl.

I liked Shaneece, and I felt drawn to her, but I didn't really want Shaneece like that.

I sat there for a few more moments, then I realized that I had forgot one person I could turn to: Hype.

"Damn, I hope this nigga picks up," I breathed as I called his number and waited for him to answer.

"What?" He sounded angry.

"Yo, Hype, you home? I need to come through and talk to you, my nigga."

"Oh, there won't be no talking, nigga. When I see you, it's head-ups on sight!" *CLICK.*

I stared at the phone in confusion. What was this nigga mad at me for? I mean, I know he was close to Tierra, but Hype was my boy.

I called him back to see what was up.

"Yo!" I said when he answered.

"Nigga, did you hear what the fuck I just said to you? I told you there's no room for talking." His voice boomed through the phone.

"Hype, what the fuck?"

"You think you could fuck my girl and just get away with it, nigga?" said Hype. "Yeah, you could do that shit to Quaid, but you got me fucked up, nigga. You got me *fucked* up."

"Hype, I don't know what you're talking about—"

"*Shaneece*, nigga! What was it? You was mad at Quaid and Tierra, so you decided to take it out on me? Huh, nigga?"

Realization dawned as I finally put two and two together. "Yo, Hype, for real. I had no idea Shaneece was your girl—"

"Yeah, whatever nigga. Like I said, you better lay low or you better be ready, cuz it's head-ups on sight!"

"Hype, I didn't—"

"Nigga, tell that shit to some bitch!" *CLICK.* He hung up on me again.

Shaneece

I have been calling and texting Twon repeatedly since what happened, but he won't answer me. I mean, I know that he and Tierra have a lot of talking to do, but I don't think it's fair for him to just brush me off. What we shared together that day was amazing. It was literally the best I ever had. Twon was way better in the bedroom than Hype.

I need to see him. I have been feigning for him like crazy. I know that I'm being reckless by calling him and texting him with my father monitoring my every move, but I'm not going to let him just take me away from the love of my life.

Yes, I said it: I'm in love with Twon. I have never met a man that I have felt so attracted to or one that I could relate to on every level. I know that he has to see it the same way. I mean, especially after what we shared on Friday.

I know he probably needed a few days to deal with Tierra, but I'm not going to wait forever. I'm ready to finally drop Hype so that I can be with Twon. We need to make this thing official. What he had with Tierra might have been cute, but she had her chance. In all honesty, I don't think she and Twon are right for each other anyway. She's better off with that Quaid guy, whoever he is….

I was shaken out of my reverie by the buzzing of my cell phone. I eagerly reached for it, almost dropping it in the process. "Finally!" I breathed, as I quickly pressed Answer and put it to my ear, not even bothering to check who was calling. In my heart, I knew it was Twon.

"Hello?" I said, breathlessly. "Twon, how are you?"

"So you could just move on to the next nigga, just like that, huh?"

I stared at the phone in confusion, then realization dawned when I looked at the name on the caller ID. "Hype … what's up?"

"What's up? Yo, you got a lot of fucking nerve, Shaneece. You just going to fuck another nigga behind my back, my best friend to be exact, then just say 'What's up' like nothing happened? You really are a fucking bitch."

I rolled my eyes and sighed. I was really sick of dealing with Hype and his shit. He was always trying to be up under me like he actually cared about me. I knew all about his reputation around school. He was nowhere near a saint. This dude had probably slept with half the female population at the school, and rumors even stated that some of that number could be faculty. There was no way that I was about to sit there and entertain this. I tried to let him off easy. "Hype, I'm sorry if I hurt you, but—"

"Sorry if you hurt me? Bitch, you ain't sorry now, but you will be. Believe that."

Who did he think he was, threatening me? This boy had a lot of nerve! "What are you going to do, hit me? I will call the cops on you so fast—"

"You ain't got to call shit on me cuz I'm not going to put my hands on you. I got one better for you. Since you like to fuck niggas so much, I figured I would share it with the world."

"What are you talking about, Hype?" He was making me nervous now. What did he mean, share it with the world?

"Just what I said. Let's just say that I have a few recordings that your dad might find interesting if he happened to stumble across them on the internet."

Blood rushed to my head and I suddenly felt dizzy. "You recorded us?"

"Nah, baby girl. I recorded *you*. You were so good at what you did that I decided I wanted to keep it for good memories to look back on. But now, since we ain't together no more, and you like to fuck niggas' best friends behind they back, I'm about to make you a star, baby."

I started feeling nauseous. "Hype, no. You can't do that. If my father saw something like that, he would kill me!"

"You should have thought about that before you fucked my best friend!" *CLICK.*

"Hype? HYPE?!" I screamed frantically into the phone, but he was already gone.

I jumped up out of my bed, my mind swimming as I paced back and forth. How did I not pay attention to the fact that he recorded me? How did I not even notice?

I picked up my phone and tried calling Hype back. It was no use. He refused to answer his phone.

I sank to the floor, hugging my knees in shame. A few minutes ago, I was on cloud nine. Now it seemed like my whole world was about to end.

* * *

I skipped school the next day and just rode around on the city buses. I stopped in front of one restaurant to have breakfast, then caught a few more buses until it was time for lunch. I knew that was probably a stupid thing to do, but I could not go to school. There was no way I could go to that place and have all those people looking at me, especially after Hype released those videos.

I had been checking all of Hype's social media accounts all night, praying that he wouldn't upload them. So far, he hadn't, but there was no way that I wanted to be there if he decided to share them with people at school. I don't know how I'm ever going to go back.

My only source of comfort was knowing that I would see Twon at work. I couldn't wait. I had my uniform in my backpack, and I was counting down the hours.

When it was finally time to go to work, I took the bus to the mall, went to the bathroom to change into my uniform, and speedwalked to the store. I prayed that Twon would get there early today so we could talk without interruptions from customers.

As soon as I got to the store, my heart dropped. Through the display window I saw Twon handing his uniform to Jamel and shaking his hand. He was leaving the store just as I was coming through the entrance.

"Twon!" I said. "What are you doing?"

He looked sad. "I just came to turn in my uniform, Shaneece. I can't work here with you anymore."

I felt like I had been slapped in the face.

"What do you mean, you can't work with me anymore? I thought we—"

"And why didn't you tell me that you and Hype were in a relationship?" Anger flashed in his eyes. "The whole time we was talking and kicking it, you never told me."

"I'm sorry." My head dropped in shame, and it took some courage look at him again. "I promise you he meant nothing to me. I wasn't even feeling him like that!" I reached for his arm, but he dodged me, a disgusted look on his face.

"So you fucking played him?" he said under his breath as a customer walked past. "Why?"

"I just wanted to be with you!"

"And how the fuck was you supposed to do that, fucking with my best friend?"

"Look, Twon. I'm sorry. I promise I'll make it up to you." I glanced nervously at Jamel standing near the register at the back of the store eyeballing me like *are you planning to work today?* "Please just let me...." I reached for him again, but he dodged me.

"No, Shaneece, me and you is done. I done already fucked up enough by messing with you in the first place. I should have just worked things out with Tierra, but now after fucking with you, I lost my girl and my best friend. I'm done." He walked away.

"Twon!" I called after him. "Twon!"

Tears streamed down my face as I stood there, willing him to turn around and come back, but he just kept walking, shattering my heart with every step. My mind went crazy trying to think of what to say or do to get him back. The love of my life was literally walking away from me.

* * *

I skipped school again the next day. Now I was running from two situations: Hype possibly sharing those videos, and Twon. I didn't even think about Tierra and whatever revenge she might cook up.

It felt like my life was slowly spiraling out of control. I knew that after today, I would have to just face the music and go back to school, because they would probably end up calling my parents if I just stopped showing up, but I didn't know how I could possibly face all of those people after what happened.

I felt so stupid. Twon was right — how could I have expected to be with him after being with Hype? I never should have messed with him in the first place. If Twon was who I wanted, I should have just waited until he and Tierra broke up, then made my move.

But now everything was ruined.

* * *

When I got to the mall the next day, I went to the bathroom to change into my uniform then made my way to Sports Locker.

When I got there, two other employees were standing there talking — Reggie, and the guy from first shift.

"Hey guys," I said.

"Hey, Shaneece," Reggie said, licking his lips and looking like he literally wanted to eat me. The other guy just waved awkwardly.

I wrinkled my nose at Reggie in disgust then made my way to the back to punch in. As I crossed the threshold to the back room, Jamel walked out toward me.

"Shaneece. I need to talk to you." His expression and voice were serious.

"Okay," I said, and followed him to the back. We went to his office, a tiny room off to the side of the inventory space.

He sat down behind the desk, and I stood in front of it.

"What's going on?" I said, feeling nervous. He looked too serious for this to just be a regular meeting.

"Look, I'm just going to cut to the chase. Shaneece, I'm gonna have to let you go."

My mouth dropped open in shock. "What? Why?"

"You fucked up my inventory."

"What do you mean?"

"Yesterday, you let two pairs of Jordans go missing out of the store. I looked at the camera footage, and it was two separate customers. Both of them bought two pairs each, but you only rang up one pair for each person. Normally, I would file something with the courts for this, but I figured it was an honest mistake because we were busy. Unfortunately, however, I can't have you working here anymore since you lost me six hundred dollars."

My eyes widened in shock. "Jamel, I'm so sorry! I didn't even realize that happened."

"I know you didn't do it on purpose, but I'm sorry. I have to let you go."

"Can I just get one more chance? Please? I really need this job." My eyes filled with tears. "I'm saving for a car, and there's so much going on right now. Please, just give me one more chance." A tear slid down my face. I wiped it away.

"Look, Shaneece, I'm sorry that you are going through hard times, but I can't keep an employee who lost me six hundred dollars. I'm giving you a break by not filing anything with the courts, but I can't have you working for me anymore. If you need a reference for another job, give me a call, and I won't mention this incident, but that's the best I can do. Sorry."

He handed me a tissue. I took it and wiped my eyes. "Thank you."

"No problem."

I turned to walk away.

"Shaneece?"

I turned back around. "Yes?"

"I almost forgot. Can you please make sure you turn in your uniform? It doesn't have to be today, but at least by the end of the week."

My face reddened with embarrassment. "Okay."

I walked out of the store with my head down, avoiding the eyes of my coworkers.

Hype

I've been toying with the idea of uploading those videos ever since my conversation with Shaneece. She hasn't been in school the past couple of days. I figure that's probably why. I want to upload them so bad just to fuck her whole shit up, but a part of me is still in love with her and cares about her.

Jamel told me he fired her yesterday, and Twon quit the day before. He asked me a few questions about Shaneece and Twon. I think he was low-key trying to tell me something was up between them. I told him I appreciated him for holding shit down, but I already had the situation handled. I've only known Jamel for a couple of years, but I been knowing Twon's ass since elementary school, and it seemed like Jamel was showing me more loyalty than Twon. How's that for some bullshit?

I never took Twon to be a disloyal ass nigga. I'm still fucking that nigga up on sight, I promise. I haven't seen him in school, but then again, we don't have any classes together, and our school has a lot of students, so it's easy for us not to bump into each other.

One part of me doesn't even want to fight Twon because we been boys since kindergarten, but another part of me wants to fuck shit up because of the principle of the whole thing. If you my boy, how you gonna fuck my girl? Granted, I never told him I was with Shaneece, but Twon is a straight-A student. You can't tell me he never put two and two together, especially after I been told that nigga I was feeling her. He should have automatically known. I never would have done no fucked up shit like that to none of my boys.

And that's not even to mention what he did to Tierra. It hurts me to see her hurt like that. I mean, I know niggas cheat — I've done it myself. But if this nigga claimed to be so in love with Tierra, and he's wanting to get back with her, how did he end up with Shaneece?

Sneaky ass nigga, he never even mentioned that he was messing with her. That's how I know for sure that he had to know Shaneece was my girl. That nigga ain't slick, snake ass nigga. I got something for his ass.

"Yo, Hype, you ready?" said Charles. Him and Quaid were standing near the front door, waiting for me to get my basketball so we could play two-on-two. It was going to be me and Quaid against Charles and this dude named Tito who was meeting us there.

"Yeah, I'm ready," I said, walking out the door with them.

When we got to the basketball court, my blood immediately started to boil when I saw Twon there playing one-on-one with this nigga named Larnell from a few blocks over.

"You done fucked up now!" I said, full of rage as I stalked toward him.

"Shit!" said Charles, seeing what was up and following right behind me.

"Hype, don't!" said Quaid, running up to get between us, but it was too late. I had already got to Twon.

"Hype!" He looked surprised to see me. *Yeah, you better be.*

BLAM! I hooked off on him, just as I promised. He was a little dazed, then he shook his head as a look of hurt and anger flashed through his eyes.

"So that's how you wanna do it?" he said, squaring off.

"Yeah, nigga. I told you. No words." I squared off as well, and we immediately started fighting. Twon kept grabbing at my legs, trying to scoop me, but my footwork was too fast for him. We were really getting shit in, tagging each other with multiple blows, while Quaid and Charles tried to break us up. Quaid tried to grab Twon from behind, but once Twon realized who it was, he snapped and started swinging on him. I broke free from Charles's grip and went after Twon again. Me and Quaid was busting this nigga's ass while Charles tried to break it up. I accidentally busted his lip in the process, and he called for Tito and Larnell to help him break it up. Both of them niggas had been standing there watching, but they finally jumped into the action and pulled us all apart.

"Y'ALL WANNA JUMP A NIGGA? FUCK BOTH Y'ALL NIGGAS!" Twon shouted, looking heated.

"FUCK YOU TOO, NIGGA! YOU KNEW WHAT THIS SHIT WAS!" I yelled back.

"All y'all niggas need to calm down," said Charles. "We supposed to be boys."

"Fuck that nigga, Charles," I said, still heated. "He ain't my fuckin boy, disloyal ass nigga."

"Nigga, I told you I didn't know she was your girl!" said Twon.

"Yeah, fuckin right, Twon, sneaky ass nigga."

Me, Quaid, and Charles started walking back to my house, while Twon hopped in his whip and peeled off screeching his tires.

* * *

My body was kind of sore the next day from all that fighting. Twon may not be my boy no more, but that nigga is a fucking problem when it comes to throwing blows. He definitely had hands, and he was holding his own when me and Quaid was jumping him. I kind of felt bad about that cuz we was stomping that nigga and everything, but the shit happened in the heat of the moment, so fuck it. It was a fight — what you expect people to do?

I feel mad conflicted about the whole situation. I mean, I want to believe that Twon really didn't know that Shaneece was my girl, but I find that hard to believe. How could that nigga possibly not have known? Me not telling him who my girl was is no excuse. That nigga could have put two and two together. I told him I was feeling her before.

I heard a knock on my front door. I got up to answer it. There stood Tierra.

"Hey," I said, letting her in and giving her a hug. She looked so distraught.

"Hey." She followed me to the kitchen and sat down.

"You want some juice?"

"Sure. Thanks." Her voice was dull.

"No problem." I poured her a glass of Kool-Aid and handed it to her.

"Thanks." She waited 'til I sat down. "I heard you and Quaid jumped Twon yesterday."

I stared at her. "Where you hear that?"

"It's all around the school."

"Oh." I drank some of my juice to collect my thoughts. "Well, that nigga got what he deserved." I set my glass down on the table like I was slamming a gavel in a courtroom.

"You make me want to do the same to Shaneece. Every time I see that girl, I want to kick her face in."

"Believe me, I understand."

"How come you never told me that you and Shaneece were together?"

"She made up some bullshit about her dad not wanting her to date, so she convinced me to keep our relationship a secret."

"Fucking THOT ass bitch."

"Shit."

"So how do you feel about the situation? Finding out about Twon and Shaneece, I mean."

"I feel fucked up, honestly. Twon was supposed to be my boy since way back, and I really had feelings for Shaneece. I think I was in love with that girl, Tierra, straight up. And she fucked me over with my best friend."

"I kind of feel the same way. I was definitely in love with Twon, and me and Shaneece were like best friends. You know she lied to me about who her boyfriend was. She told me she was with some guy named Markus!"

"Markus?" I said in disgust. "Don't tell me she was fucking yet another nigga."

"Who knows?" said Tierra, looking disgusted too. "Since she's obviously a sneaky bitch, I wouldn't put it past her."

"Shit, at this point, Tierra, I wouldn't put nothing past nobody. And that's real."

* * *

I decided to stay home from school the next day. A nigga needed a break from all this drama, and I didn't feel like having people swarming around me asking if I had beef with Twon. I already had mad messages in my inbox with people trying to see what was up, but I never been a gossiping ass nigga, so I just ignored them.

I played *Call of Duty* 'til I got bored, then I hit Charles up to see what was going on with him. We spoke for an hour about the situation. He tried to suggest that me and Twon should have a conversation to squash the beef, but I wasn't trying to hear that shit. We almost got into an argument, but we just hung up instead. I'll talk to that nigga again later, but I'm not trying to hear nothing about making amends with Twon. The way I see it, if a nigga show you he a snake, he a snake. So he can slither his ass away from me.

"What you doing here at home and not at school?" said G-Ma. She had just walked into the house.

"I didn't feel like going today. I'm sick."

"Boy, what I tell you about all that damn lying? You ain't sick, so don't try to play me. Now, what's wrong?" She pulled up a chair and sat across from the couch where I was stretched out.

"I don't really want to talk about it, G-Ma."

"Well, sitting here moping ain't gonna do you no good either. So what's up?"

"I just didn't feel like answering nobody's questions about Twon."

"You're really mad at him, huh?"

"Yeah. He was messing with my girl."

"Your secret girlfriend that I saw sneaking out of here a few weeks ago?"

My head whipped toward G-Ma. "You saw her?"

"Boy, I see everything. Yeah, I saw her little fast ass leaving out of here one day. I figured that was your little girlfriend. I hope you was using protection with her."

"G-Ma!"

"I'm serious, Hype. You can't forget that dream you was having a couple of months ago. I believe that was a warning from God. I hope you was wrapping it up with that girl."

"I did, sometimes."

"Well, you better hope you don't catch nothing, sometimes."

I sat up in my seat, furious. "How you gonna wish something like that on me?"

"Who you think you getting loud with? Damn sure ain't me, cuz I'll take your ass out." G-Ma stared directly into my eyes. I calmed down.

"I'm not getting loud, G-Ma. But how you gonna say something like that?"

"I'm just telling the truth, Hype. It's bad enough you out here having sex with all these girls. It just makes it even worse when you don't wrap it up. Do you even think about your future?"

"It's not even that serious."

"Yes, it is that serious. There are all types of diseases going around these days. You never know what anybody has between their legs. God already warned you. I'm just repeating what you already know."

"Well, God don't have to warn me no more. I'm done with that girl."

"Did she break your heart?"

I felt myself getting tense again. "I don't want to talk about all that."

"I understand that you don't want to talk about it, Hype, but I can clearly see that you had strong feelings for that girl. And I know that you may not want to hear this right now, but sometimes in life, we get what we pay for."

"What do you mean, we get what we pay for?"

"How many girls' hearts have you broken at that school?"

I just sat there. I knew what G-Ma was saying, but I didn't like it. I tried to do the right thing with Shaneece, and she shitted on me with my best friend. I know people say that you reap what you sow, but this just seems like too much right now.

Tierra

I sat down at my kitchen table, depressed. I had dark circles under my eyes from lack of sleep. I keep having nightmares of Twon and Shaneece together with her mouth on him. No matter how hard I try, I can't shake it. People say that when you're in high school, you don't really know what love is, but I love Twon, and it breaks my heart to think that he could possibly have cheated on me. We would have been together two years on last Friday. How could he?

I don't know how I will ever get through this. I don't feel like there is anybody I know who I can talk to. Hype says he was in love with Shaneece, so he might be able to relate to a certain extent, but they weren't together for two whole years, so I don't think he would fully understand. My mom and G-Ma were too old — their views on dating are outdated by now. I don't have any other girl friends. Shaneece was the only girl I ever really trusted like that, and look what happened. There goes that idea....

"Okay, now I don't like this, Tierra. You're going to have to talk to me today."

I snapped out of my daze and looked up at my mother. She was standing over me with a concerned expression on her face.

"There's nothing to talk about, Ma," I said blankly, a tear rolling down my cheek. I wiped it away.

"If there's nothing to talk about, then why are you crying?"

I sniffled. "It's nothing." My vision became blurry as more tears filled my eyes.

She pulled up a chair and sat down beside me, rubbing my back.

"Come on, girl. Let it out. I'm your mother and I love you. You can talk to me."

"You wouldn't understand."

"Why do you think I won't understand? What happened?"

"I caught Twon cheating on me." I covered my face with my hands. She stopped rubbing my back.

"You caught him cheating when?"

"Black Friday."

"Your anniversary? How? When? I thought you stayed home to do homework that day."

I looked at her in shame and guilt. "I'm sorry, Ma." My nose burned as more tears fell. "I lied to you about what I was doing. I was — I was just trying to win his love and get back with him!"

My body shook as I broke down. I felt my mother's arms encircle me as she rocked me back and forth.

"It's going to be alright, girl. It's going to be alright. You hear me? I've been here before. It's going to be alright." She kept repeating.

Something about my mother's words comforted me, so I let loose and told her everything. I told her how I had planned to sleep with Twon, how I got all dressed up and put on lingerie and makeup and sexy high heels, and how I went over his house that day and caught him with Shaneece.

"Ma, I don't know what to do!"

"Well … first let me say that although I am disappointed that you lied to me and that you were going to sleep with him despite the fact that I told you I was against it, I still understand why you did it. You're young, and you were in love. I get that, and I understand it. As a parent, I want what's best for you, so I try to help you make the right decisions, but some things are best learned on your own. How have you been feeling since that day?"

"I can't sleep. I keep having these nightmares about the two of them together, and I haven't really eaten much since that day."

"Well, we got to get you eating, and we got to get you back to sleep as well."

"But I don't have any appetite, and every time I close my eyes, the nightmares come back."

"Well, I know a solution to that one."

"What?"

"We're going to pray."

"Pray?"

"Yes. I may not be in the church now, but I was when I was younger. They always taught us to pray when we were involved in a situation that was out of our control. They said that Jesus cares about us, and we can cast all of our cares on Him."

"I don't really know how to pray, Ma."

"There's nothing really special to it. You just tell God what's on your heart."

I felt kind of awkward trying to learn how to pray in front of my mother, but she sat there right beside me the whole time. I prayed and asked God to help me get my appetite back, and to help the nightmares go away, and my mother prayed that God would wipe away my tears, and that He would heal my broken heart and work this situation out for my good.

After the prayer was over, I felt a sense of peace that wasn't there before. I didn't know what that meant, but I felt like maybe God was going to answer my prayers.

Twon

I've been trying to call Tierra back to back, but she's not answering her phone. I know that what I did was wrong, and even though we technically weren't together at the time, we still weren't fully done with each other. I don't think I will ever forget the look on her face when she saw me with Shaneece.

Shaneece is still calling and texting me left and right. I'm surprised that her father hasn't taken her phone from her — if she was even telling the truth about all that. I sincerely thought that Shaneece was just a sweet girl who was easy to talk to, but now ... I don't know. That was messed up what she did to Hype, and now I'm caught up in the middle of that shit too. Real talk, that hurts my heart, because Hype is my oldest friend. He been holding me down since kindergarten. Both him and Quaid been like brothers to me ever since the day we first met, and now it seems like all those years are about to go down the drain.

It's funny how life turns out. Niggas you thought would be there forever all of a sudden just drop you like nothing. He didn't even give me a chance to explain. I been trying to tell him that I didn't know Shaneece was his girl, but he's not trying to hear me. And then him and Quaid *jumped* me? That was beyond fucked up, yo. We supposed to be like family, and y'all just gonna jump me like that? That shit was wack.

While I was in the middle of calling Tierra for the thousandth time, my phone buzzed with a call from Shaneece. I didn't want to answer her, but I was sick of her blowing up my phone, so I decided to just set her straight.

"Hello?" I said in an annoyed tone.

"Twon?" she said breathlessly. "I've been trying to get in contact with you for over a week."

"Look Shaneece, there's really nothing for us to say to each other. What we did was a mistake on my part."

"How can you say that? I know that you have feelings for me, Twon."

"It's true that I liked you, but Tierra was my girl. And Hype was supposed to be your man, even though you conveniently failed to mention that to me."

She sighed. "That was a mistake, Twon. I never should have been with him. It was you I wanted the whole time."

"But I had a girl, and you knew that — a girl that was supposed to be cool with you."

"But she didn't deserve you!"

I stared at my phone not believing my ears. "What?"

"She wasn't the right woman for you."

"How do you know whether Tierra is the right woman for me?"

"She wasn't willing to take care of your needs. I was."

I sighed. This girl was something else. "Look, Shaneece, every relationship has its problems. I should have worked out my issues with my girl instead of running to you. Now, because of one mistake, I lost two relationships. I'm not doing this anymore."

"But Twon—"

"I meant what I said, Shaneece. I think it's best if you just lose my number. Stop hitting me up, because this is the last time I'm gonna answer."

"Twon—"

"Bye, Shaneece." I hung up the phone, then added Shaneece's number to my blocked list.

Shaneece

I cried myself to sleep after Twon hung up on me. How could he just act like there was nothing real between us? I don't know how I'm going to get through to him. It seems like at this point, the only thing he cares about is Tierra, but that can't be true, because if he really wanted her so badly, he never would have ended up with me.

I have been laying low in school since what happened, especially since I share classes with Hype and Tierra. Hype still hasn't released those videos, thank goodness. Maybe he changed his mind. He doesn't even look at me during class. He just sits in the back with Tierra, and I sit in the front. Every time I look in their direction, Tierra looks like she wants to kill me. I wonder if there is a way I can change classes. Winter break is coming up. Maybe I can schedule an appointment with my guidance counselor before we leave for break....

"Okay, everyone, we're going to do something different today," said our English teacher. "I'm going to put you in pairs to work on short stories together. The short stories have to include the following themes."

He turned to the board and wrote the requirements for our assignment. My mind began to spin as the blood rushed to my head. Pairs? He was putting us in pairs? What if he put me with Hype? Or worse, what if he put me with Tierra? I raised my hand when he turned back around.

"Yes, Shaneece?"

"Um, I was wondering … would it be alright if we picked our own partner instead of you pairing us up?"

I heard a few people agree with me, and a few people sucked their teeth.

"Unfortunately, no," said the teacher. "I already used a system to pair you guys up with one another. I put people together based on complementary strengths with regard to your writing."

I felt my face grow hot. I just knew in my heart that all hell was about to break loose, especially if he did what I thought he was about to do.

He called out the names of the pairs, and people moved their desks around to work with each other. When he got to my name, of course he put me with Tierra. I glanced back at her. There were daggers in her eyes.

I raised my hand again.

"Yes, Shaneece?" the teacher said impatiently.

"Um … I think I need a new partner."

He opened his mouth to speak, but before he could, Tierra jumped into the conversation.

"Yeah, that's right. She does need a new partner, because ain't no way I'm working with a little THOT ass bitch like her!"

"OOOOOOOHHHHH!" said my classmates as my face reddened with embarrassment then anger. I turned around and glared at her.

"What did you just call me?"

"You heard what I said, bitch. I didn't hear myself stutter."

"OOOOOOOHHHHH!" said the class again, egging it on.

"Ladies…." said our English teacher. *Christmas break can't get here soon enough*, he thought with a weary sigh.

"See, this is why I wanted to pick my own partner!" I said.

"Nobody want to work with your THOT ASS no way," said Hype, jumping in.

"And you just shut your mouth, boy!" I spat at him. "I know you ain't calling me a THOT with all the girls at this school that you have slept with."

"Bitch, that's irrelevant," said Hype. "I may fuck a lot of hoes, but I never fucked with best friends."

"Listen!" The teacher banged on a table to get our attention. "Listen," he repeated. "I will switch the groups around, but we are NOT going to do this in here. This classroom will not turn into a zoo!"

"Yeah, that's right, change that shit," said Hype, then he looked at me. "And your ass is lucky, Shaneece. My girl Tierra was bout to fuck shit up."

Hype

Me, Charles, and Quaid were playing *Call of Duty* at my house after school. "Like I said, I had my money on Tierra," I said.

"You shouldn't have been egging it on like that, Hype," said Quaid. "Tierra could have gotten into a lot of trouble for fighting in school."

"Man, Shaneece wasn't 'bout to do shit!" I said. "She knew Tierra would have lit that ass up."

"I mean, she did fuck Tierra's man, Quaid," said Charles. "You can't expect everything to be all peaceful between them just cuz they was in school."

"I understand that, but there is a way to handle things, not to mention a time and a place."

Charles whipped his head around and glared at him. "You mean like jumping Twon two weeks ago at the basketball court? You mean like busting my fucking lip up cuz I'm trying to break up three grown ass men? Let's talk about it." He had been heated with me and Quaid ever since that fight because he felt like we put him in the middle of the situation. I felt bad for busting Charles's lip that day, but it was an accident.

I stepped in. "Look man, we already apologized for that."

"I don't want to hear that shit, Hype. I still owe you an ass whooping."

"Come on, nigga. You know it was an accident."

"Shit, man, I couldn't get no play for a whole week 'til my lip healed, nigga. I had niggas clowning me, thinking I got my ass kicked, all because of y'all."

"My bad, man."

"Dead ass, Hype," said Charles, looking more serious now. "I think you should at least talk to Twon about what happened. At least hear the man out."

I held my hand up. "I already told you, Charles. We already went through this. I ain't trying to hear nothing Twon's snake ass got to say. That nigga fucked my girl. End of story."

"So you mean to tell me that you really believe Twon was on some snake shit?" said Charles. "After everything we been through, after all these years without one incident, and all of a sudden now Twon is a snake?"

"All it takes is one time to show your true colors."

"Hype, I agree with Charles," said Quaid, jumping back in.

I looked at him in shock. "How are you agreeing, Quaid? Did you forget that he hooked off on you for trying to break us up?"

"It was a fight. Everyone's adrenaline was pumping, including mine. The way I see it, I can't get mad at him for swinging on me. In his eyes, I was part of the reason he and Tierra broke up, and you can't forget that we did jump him, Hype. I really feel bad about that."

"Man, fuck that soft shit." I couldn't believe this. "I don't care what nobody say. Me and Twon are no longer friends. We ain't boys, we ain't buddies, shit, we ain't even associates. I want nothing else to do with that nigga."

"All this over some sneaky bitch," said Charles, still trying to convince me, but it was no use. Ain't nobody changin' my mind.

Tierra

Since my prayer with my mother, I've been able to sleep a lot better. I've had a few more nightmares since that day, but they've been diminishing. I've prayed a few more times about the situation, and I'm generally feeling better now. Twon has been calling me nonstop, but I just can't answer him right now. The wounds are still too fresh. I've seen him a few times at school, and he looked at me like he wanted to talk to me, but I just kept on walking. I'm not ready to deal with him right now. We have been through too much, and I'm not sure at this point if we can ever get back together, even though in my heart, I want to.

And that bitch Shaneece got another thing coming if she thinks she can just talk to me any kind of way she wants to just because we're in class. She gonna try to raise her hand to ask the teacher to switch like she didn't want to work with me. No, bitch, it's the other way around! Nobody wants to work with your THOT ass.

"Why you looking like you about to blow up a building or something?" said my mother, who just walked into the kitchen.

"My English teacher tried to pair me up with that girl today."

"What girl? The one who messed with Twon?"

"Yes." I seethed.

"What happened?"

310

"We almost got into a fight."

"Tierra…." my mother began sternly.

"Ma, you can't expect me to just be nice to her. I want to kill her."

"Hey!" my mother snapped. "Don't you let nothing like that come out your mouth again. Yes, you are angry, and you have a right to be, but don't go so far as to talk about killing somebody, especially over some boy."

"Ma, Twon is not just some boy. He was my boyfriend for *two years*. And she was supposed to be my friend!"

"I understand that, but you don't need to be talking about killing nobody. Words become actions, and actions like that will get you locked up."

"Ma, ain't nobody really gonna kill her. You don't have to take everything I say so seriously."

"Just don't let nothing like that come out your mouth again."

"Okay. I don't want to kill her. But I do want to fight her though. Every time I see her I imagine stomping her to the ground. I can't shake the feeling, so I know it's going to happen sooner or later."

"I think you need to stay away from that girl."

"I can't stay away from her. We're in the same English class."

"Can't you switch?"

"No, I don't think so. It's almost the middle of the school year. We're probably too far along."

"Well, maybe you could set up a meeting with your guidance counselor and explain the situation. They should be able to work something out so that everyone remains safe."

I snickered. "Right. She might need a witness protection program with the things I want to do to her."

"Tierra, I'm not going to tell you again. Stop talking crazy or I'll pop you right in your mouth. You ain't too grown for an ass whooping."

"Ma, chill!" I said. "I'm just playing, gosh."

"Well, like I said before, don't play like that."

"Fine," I said, sucking my teeth.

Twon

I heard about the incident between Tierra and Shaneece during their English class. Now the whole school knows about the situation. People keep coming up to me and sending messages to my inbox, trying to get information about what happened between me and Tierra. I deactivated my accounts. I don't have time to deal with all those nosy ass people. I decided to just ignore people or tell them I don't want to talk about it. Shit was depressing.

I've been calling Tierra left and right. I wanted to try to talk to her in school, but I didn't feel like it would be a good idea, just in case things got too heated. I definitely didn't want everybody all up in our business either, so I just left her alone.

I decided to try to call her again, just to see if she would answer. To my surprise, she picked up.

"Hello?" she said, her voice calm.

"Tierra?"

"What do you want, Twon?" she said in a flat tone.

"I want to talk to you."

"That's obvious." So was her sarcasm. "You keep blowing up my phone."

"I just want us to find a way to squash this so we can get back together. I miss you, baby, and I love you."

She snorted. "Nigga, please. Love ain't got nothing to do with what you did to me."

"Tierra, just let me explain."

"There's nothing to explain, Twon. You fucked Shaneece, point blank. I was calling you and calling you, trying to get back with you, driving myself crazy, and then it was all for nothing because you found some other bitch to lay with."

"It really wasn't even like that. I only slept with her one time."

"One time, my ass, Twon! That's bullshit and you know it. Don't try to play me. You were ignoring me for weeks. There is no way you only slept with her one time."

"I swear on everything, Tierra. It was only one time!" I was desperate for her to believe me.

"You know what? I don't even know why I answered my phone. Goodbye, Twon."

"No, Tierra, don't hang up on me. Please."

"And why shouldn't I?"

I swallowed a lump in my throat. "Look, baby, I know I fucked up, big time. But you have to believe that I love you, and I never meant for this to happen."

"Never meant for this to happen? Or never meant to get caught?"

"You think I feel good about hurting you? You think I feel good about losing my best friend?"

"Let's not even talk about that situation. What you did to me was shady, but what you did to Hype was beyond fucked up."

"That wasn't even my fault, though...."

"So it wasn't your fault that you cheated on your girlfriend with your best friend's girlfriend? What are you going to tell me next? That y'all slipped and fell into bed together?"

"Tierra, please listen...."

"Fuck you, Twon. Bye." *CLICK.*

I stared at my phone then threw it on my nightstand.

I would just have to accept the fact that me and Tierra were over.

Shaneece

Next week is winter break, and I still haven't been able to talk to Twon. He avoids me in school, and he refuses to answer my phone calls or text messages. He even blocked me on all of his social media pages. He probably blocked me on his cell phone too. Most people would tell me to just leave him alone, but I can't do that. I'm in love with Twon, and I can't shake how I feel. I feel like I'm going crazy over him. I just need him to speak to me, to give me another chance.

I purposefully sat behind him in our Physics class so that I could stare at him the entire time. I'm always so focused on Twon that I don't know how I'm still passing.

After class, I felt like I could not take it anymore, so I walked up to him at his locker.

"Twon!" I said, feeling nervous. This was the first time I had approached him in school, and I didn't know how he was going to take it.

"What, Shaneece." His tone didn't sound too friendly.

"Have you been getting my phone calls and text messages?"

"No." His voice was flat. "I blocked you."

"Why?"

"I told you to delete my number, Shaneece. I don't know why we have to keep going through this."

"Why can't you just talk to me? Why can't you just give me a chance?"

"Because I don't want you! I don't know how many times or how many ways I have to say it. Do you not speak fucking English? I keep trying to tell your ass that I never wanted you. I only want Tierra, but you can't seem to get that shit through your thick fucking skull. I. Don't. Want. You. Now leave me alone." He pushed past me and strode down the hall.

"Twon!" I cried out after him. "Twon!" I chased behind him. He turned around, his eyes full of fury.

"This is going to be the last fucking time I tell you this shit, bitch!" he said through clenched teeth. "You fucked up my life, you fucked up my friendship, and you fucked up my relationship. Even if I didn't want Tierra, I wouldn't have wanted to be with your sneaky THOT ass. You was trying to fuck me and my best friend at the same time. How the fuck you think that makes me feel? Huh? And what the fuck would I look like running after you after you been with my man's? I don't fucking want you, so leave me alone. You stressing me."

With those words, he stalked off. I stared after him, tears streaming down my face.

"Damn girl, he told you!" said a girl who was standing near us. I looked around. An entire crowd had formed, and I hadn't even noticed. My head was swimming. I felt like I was going to be sick.

"Hey," said a male voice behind me. I whirled around. It was a guy from my math class. "Hey, Shaneece. I know you and Twon ain't messing no more, but my door is wide open, baby." He smiled at me lustfully and licked his lips.

I wrinkled my nose at him in disgust, and in that moment, felt the vomit rush up to my throat. I quickly ran into the bathroom, barely making it to the stall before I released my insides in the toilet.

Twon

I ain't want to do shit but go home and go to sleep. My life is entirely fucked up. It seems like everything is happening to me all at once, and I don't know how much more I can take. I swear, if one more thing happens ... there's no telling what I will do. I got home and saw my mother's car in the parking lot. Damn. She must have stayed home today. I hoped she wouldn't say anything to me.

I quietly made my way into the house.

"Twon!" she said, as soon as I closed the front door.

"Yes," I said, my tone flat and uninterested, but she didn't get the hint.

"Come here."

I made my way to the living room where she was sitting on the couch. "What?" I said.

"Don't you 'what' me. I need you to go to the store and get me a pack of cigarettes."

"Ma, I'm tired, and I don't feel like going anywhere today. I just want to go upstairs to my room and go to sleep."

"I didn't ask you what the hell you wanted to do. I told you I needed you to go to the store to get me a pack of cigarettes. Now go."

I felt my body tremble as a wave of anger rose up inside of me. "Where's the money?" I said, trying to remain calm.

"I'm not trying to break a twenty, so you can just buy it."

"Well, I don't have it, so you're going to have to break a twenty today."

"Boy, I don't know who the fuck you think you been getting smart with lately! Get your fucking ass to the store and get me a pack of cigarettes."

"Ma, I told you, I don't have the money—"

"Well, you better got-damn find it!" she spat.

"FUCK THIS SHIT! I'M OUT!" I walked straight out of the house, slamming the door behind me. I didn't know where I was going, but I was getting the fuck up out of there. I swear, I can't take no more shit. I'm done.

Shaneece

When I go home from school, I had barely opened the door when my father practically yanked me into the house. "WHAT THE HELL DID I TELL YOU, SHANEECE?"

I started to feel nauseous.

"Dad, I—"

"Give me your fucking phone."

I turned to my mother with tears in my eyes. At that moment, I noticed that my sister Shanelle was there. "Mom," I said.

"I said, give me your fucking phone, Shaneece," my father repeated.

"Give it to him," said my mother.

I reluctantly handed him the phone and he violently threw it to the floor and stomped on it, breaking it into pieces.

"DAD!" My sister and I both screamed at once.

"That oughtta solve that problem," he said.

"How could you break my phone?" I said, tears streaming down my face.

"I told you to stop contacting that Twon character. Do I need to show you your phone records to see why I did what I did?"

"Dad, you don't understand...!"

"No, you don't understand. I told you more than once to leave that boy alone. But you disobeyed me, over and over again. Your mother and I gave you chance after chance, and you repeatedly defied us right behind our backs. You can't be trusted, Shaneece. You act like a sneaky little child that needs to be watched, so now we're going to treat you as such. You will not have a cell phone from this day forward. You will also not have a job. I don't give a damn how bad you want a car, you can take the bus. You're lucky your job ended up firing you, because otherwise I would have had to go up there in person and tell your boss that you no longer work there. Do I make myself clear? Do you understand this time, or do I need to repeat myself?"

"This isn't fair!" I exclaimed. "You're ruining my life!"

"No, I'm not ruining your life. I'm trying to stop you from ruining what's left of it."

I darted past my parents and my sister, and ran upstairs to my room.

Twon

I was driving so fast that I didn't even know where I was going. My head was clearly not in the game. I truly didn't give a fuck anymore. I had nothing left. It seemed like my life was never going to get better, so I decided that it was best to just let it go.

I'm sorry I couldn't be a better friend. I'm sorry I couldn't be a better boyfriend. I'm sorry I couldn't be a better son, but I did the best I could.

A tractor-trailer was coming swiftly toward me from the opposite direction on the bridge. I saw an opportunity, so I seized it.

I quickly swerved in front of him at the last possible moment and took a deep breath.

All I heard next was the sound of his horn then a loud crash and the smashing of metal, and I felt myself flying through the air.

Shaneece

I stared at the pregnancy test. There was no way I was seeing what I thought I was seeing — my eyes had to be playing tricks on me.

"Shaneece?" Shanelle knocked on the door.

"What?" I sniffled.

"What does it say?"

I was at her house for the rest of the week. My parents surprisingly let me go because they trusted my sister more than they trusted me. I told Shanelle that I had been feeling sick and throwing up lately, so she immediately took me to the store to get a pregnancy test. I stared at the result until my eyes turned blurry.

"Shaneece?"

I slowly got up and opened the door to face her. "My life is over," I said blankly, and handed her the test stick.

She looked shocked, but then her training as a nurse took over, and her expression turned calm. She looked at me.

"It's going to be okay, Shaneece."

"No, it's not! Dad is going to kill me!"

"No, he won't. He'll have to get through me first, and I won't let him!" She smiled to ease the tension, and I gave a nervous little laugh. "We will get through this together, Shaneece. We just have to get you set up with doctor's appointments, a proper eating plan, and some prenatal vitamins, and then we have to start planning the future. Are you still with the father?"

I hung my head in shame. "I don't know who the father is," I mumbled.

"What?"

"I don't know who the father is, Shanelle!" I snapped.

She looked disappointed, but her expression turned calm again. "Well, do you at least have an idea?"

I swallowed slowly. "It's between two guys. They're best friends."

Shanelle sighed. "Oh, Shaneece … well, do you want to try to call them? Or do you want to wait until later?"

"No, I might as well get it over with now." I wasn't thinking clearly. I grabbed my new cell phone that she bought me and dialed Twon's number first, praying that he would pick up. Of course, he didn't. But then I remembered that he had blocked my number, so he had no idea I was calling.

Next I called Hype. He answered on the third ring. "What?" he said.

"Hype, I need to talk to you."

"We got nothing to talk about, Shaneece."

"Actually, yes, we do. Look, this is important. I know you're mad at me now, but I have something to tell you."

"What the fuck you got to tell me, Shaneece?"

"I'm pregnant."

He was silent for a few moments.

"Hype?" I said, wondering if the connection was lost.

"I don't know why you telling *me* that shit. It ain't mine."

"Hype, stop playing games. We need to figure out how to handle this."

"No, *we* don't need to figure out shit! You fucked me and you fucked that nigga too. Sounds like a personal problem." *CLICK.*

I stared at the phone, wondering where I could possibly go from here.

A Note to My Readers

If you enjoyed reading *When Things Go Left*, please sign up for my email newsletter. One of the many benefits of joining the email list is that you get exclusive access to updates, excerpts from future novels, and information about book signing events that may be coming to a city near you! It's easy to join – just shoot me a quick email at tanishastewart.author@gmail.com. I love hearing from my readers!

Also, if you enjoyed this novel, please feel free to leave a review on Amazon. Not sure what to write? You can simply comment on your favorite character and your overall perception of the book (no spoilers, please ☺).

If you would like to connect with me on social media, here's where you can find me:

Facebook: *Tanisha Stewart, Author*
Instagram: *tanishastewart_author*
Twitter: *TStewart_Author*

I hope you enjoyed *When Things Go Left*. To learn what happens to Twon, Tierra, Quaid, Hype, and Shaneece, check out the next installment in the series, *When Things Get Real*.

See you next time!

Tanisha Stewart

Tanisha Stewart's Books

Even Me Series
Even Me
Even Me, The Sequel
Even Me, Full Circle

When Things Go Series
When Things Go Left
When Things Get Real
When Things Go Right

For My Good Series
For My Good: The Prequel
For My Good: My Baby Daddy Ain't Ish
For My Good: I Waited, He Cheated
For My Good: Torn Between The Two
For My Good: You Broke My Trust
For My Good: Better or Worse
For My Good: Love and Respect

Betrayed Series
Betrayed By My So-Called Friend
Betrayed By My So-Called Friend, Part 2
Betrayed 3: Camaiyah's Redemption
Betrayed Series: Special Edition

Phate Series
Phate: An Enemies to Lovers Romance
Phate 2: An Enemies to Lovers Romance

The Real Ones Series
Find You A Real One: A Friends to Lovers Romance
Find You A Real One 2: A Friends to Lovers Romance

Standalones
A Husband, A Boyfriend, & a Side Dude
In Love With My Uber Driver
You Left Me At The Altar
Where. Is. Haseem?! A Romantic-Suspense Comedy
Caught Up With The 'Rona: An Urban Sci-Fi Thriller
#DOLO: An Awkward, Non-Romantic Journey Through Singlehood